ROUGH CUT

Owen Carey Jones

First published 2011 by New Generation Publishing

Matador
Troubador Publishing Ltd
9 Priory Business Park
Wistow Road
Kibworth Beauchamp
Leicester LE8 0RX, UK
Tel: 0116 279 2299
Email: books@troubador.co.uk
Web: www.troubador.co.uk/matador

ISBN 978 1 78088 197 3

A CIP catalogue record for this book is available from the British Library

Matador is an imprint of Troubador Publishing Ltd
Printed in the UK by TJ International, Padstow, Cornwall

This book is dedicated to Jill, the love of my life, without whose support and encouragement over many years, it would never have been written.

Chapter 1

From the air, Ambergris Caye, off the coast of Belize, looks like most people's idea of paradise with the blue sea of the Caribbean turning green as it washes over the reef towards the beaches and the rich green foliage of the island.

Carter Jefferson's house on this idyllic island was not large but it sat on the edge of the beach, surrounded by palm trees, with a French window which opened directly onto the beach, something he had never failed to appreciate.

Carter was a tall good-looking black man in his late forties. He was a Belizean by birth and enjoyed few things more than relaxing on a lounger on the beach outside his house. On this occasion, while he was sitting there, he was reading a sheaf of papers which he had printed out from his computer. As he read each page, he put it on the pile of pages he had already read which were lying face down on the sand next to him.

Suddenly, Carter's eyes narrowed and a frown appeared on his face. He focused hard on what he was reading and then sat up and stared at the page in front of him. After a few moments he got up from the lounger and went into the house, taking the file with him. He went into his study and picked up his phone before tapping a number into it.

In New York, at the diamond testing station of the Gemological Institute of America where he spent most of his days, John Sprague heard his phone ring and plucked it from his pocket.

John was a diamond specialist based in New York and employed by The Federation of International Diamond Traders, an organisation which protects the interests of those whose business involves the buying and selling of one of the most valuable commodities on the planet. Carter had worked for the FIDT for many years before ceasing full time employment in order to give more time to his writing but he continued to work for them on an ad hoc basis, and a couple of days earlier, John had called him about an assignment. Although Carter was keen to focus on his new book, the FIDT was his main source of income and he knew he couldn't afford to lose their goodwill.

Carter stared out at the sea as he waited for his call to be answered. When it was, John's voice was cheerful and upbeat.

"Hi Carter, how's it going? Have you read the file yet?"

"Yeah, I've just been going through it." Carter paused for a moment before continuing. "John, can I ask you something?"

"Sure, go for it."

"How certain are you that the parcel of stones came from that particular mine in Guinea?"

"Well, that's what the trace showed. But you know the system as well as I do. The synthetics could have got into the distribution chain undetected at a few points along the way. As long as everyone further up the chain was in on it, so that all the numbers added up."

"Well, I'm just about done with the file," said Carter, "And I'm due to be in New York day after tomorrow to give a lecture at the Institute in the morning so maybe we can meet up after that?"

"Hey, yeah, that would be great. Say around two o'clock?"

"Two will be fine. I should be done by then. See you in a couple of days."

Carter put the phone down and a smile crossed his face. He looked at a framed photograph of a young woman which was on his desk and spoke to it. "It's been a long time, Nikki," he said, "Maybe it's time you and I had a get together. What do you think?"

Carter reached down and opened one of his desk drawers. He took out a small, rather battered address book and flicked through the pages before finding the one he wanted. Then he picked up his phone again and entered a number from the address book into it. A broad smile covered his face as he put the phone to his ear and waited. He was nervous, but he was excited too.

"*Nicole!*" Carter almost shouted her name when she answered and then relaxed a little before continuing. "Hi! Guess who?"

At the other end of the line, Nicole, all dressed up and ready to leave for a party, paused for a moment before responding. "No idea. Give me a clue." She absent-mindedly opened the diary that was on the table next to the telephone and leafed through its pages as she waited.

Carter wasn't too sure what to make of Nicole's response. Given what they had once been to each other, could she really not have recognised his voice? He decided to play along. "Oxford, 1985, a warm summer's night down by the river?"

Although he was at the other end of the line, thousands of miles away from her, Carter felt Nicole freeze.

"Carter?" she queried, not sure what to believe. "No way! It can't be you, not after all this time. Is it really you?"

"Oui, c'est moi," responded Carter, pleased that she had picked up on the hint. And now he could sense a smile on her face as she listened to his broken French.

"Well, your French hasn't improved any with the years," she said and Carter chuckled before gathering himself to speak again, an affectionate tone to his voice now.

"How are you, Nicole?" he asked.

"Not too bad. How about you?"

"Good. I'm good thanks. How's Andrew?"

After he had said this, Carter could hear the silence that reached out to him from Nicole and the smile disappeared from his face. He braced himself and spoke again.

"Nicole? You still there?

"Yes, sorry," she said, clearly conveying that there was something that Carter did not know, but about which he was soon to be enlightened. "Andrew died about three years ago. An accident on the motorway."

Carter's heart sank on hearing the news. Andrew had won Nicole's hand after his own attempts to secure her for himself had failed and he knew that Andrew's death would have been crushing for her. His heart went out to her but he also felt a sense of elation that Andrew was no longer on the scene. He controlled the less praise-worthy of the emotions he was feeling before responding to the news.

"Oh, Nikki, I am so sorry. I didn't know." Carter meant it too. He might be glad that Andrew was no longer around but his love for Nicole had always been sincere, it had never left him, and now he shared her pain. When she spoke, it was clear to Carter that she was putting on a brave face.

"Yeah, well, that's life, isn't it. Kicks you in the stomach every now and then. But enough of that!" Carter winced as he listened, he could feel her distress despite her attempt to be upbeat. He heard her sniff before she continued. "So! Tell me Carter, why the phone call, after all these years?"

"Oh, no reason really," he lied, and then thought better of it. "Actually, that's not true. I'm going to be in England soon, and... I was wondering if you would like to meet up? Maybe for a coffee... or... something?"

Carter had no idea what reaction he was going to get to his suggestion, especially given what he had just been told, and there was an extended pause as Nicole thought about it. Carter waited patiently and eventually she made up her mind.

"Yeah, OK, why not? Yeah, that would be nice. I'd like that."

Carter smiled but it was a smile tinged with the sadness he felt when he considered how devastated Nicole must have been when Andrew had died. Why had she never contacted him? He would have been there in a moment if she had.

"That's great," he said, "I'll give you a call when I get to London and let's try and arrange something, OK?"

"I look forward to it," replied Nicole.

"Me too." Carter rang off and put his phone back on his desk. He was delighted that he would soon be seeing Nicole again but in the circumstances, he was also a little apprehensive about how it would go.

In the lounge of her home at Darrington Hall, on the outskirts of the quiet village of Welburn in North Yorkshire, Nicole replaced the telephone receiver and closed the diary before heading for the door to the hall.

The hall was dominated by a large curving staircase with thick oak balustrades leading to the bedrooms above and the highly polished parquet floor was sparsely covered with a couple of rugs, allowing it to shine as the light hit it.

Nicole came into the hall and stood at the foot of the stairs looking up towards the landing at the top.

"Rob! Eloise! Come on, it's time to go," she shouted and almost immediately, Eloise, a slim attractive girl of twenty-one with long blonde hair, came down the stairs. She too was dressed for a party with her short tight skirt revealing her shapely legs.

"*Rob!*" Nicole shouted again, louder this time, and Rob, Eloise's nineteen year old brother, appeared at the top of the stairs. He was wearing jeans and a tee-shirt and his hair was ruffled. He leaned over the banister to speak.

"I'm not going. I've got a headache," he said as he turned away and headed back to his room. Nicole sighed and looked at Eloise.

"Come on, we'd better get going," she said, clearly not impressed by Rob's last minute decision to stay at home and not accompany them to the party.

A couple of hours later, the sun had set and it was dark outside. Now alone in the house, Rob had ordered himself a pepperoni pizza and was in the kitchen finishing off the job of cutting it into manageable pieces. As he opened the kitchen door on his way back to his bedroom, a shaft of light from the kitchen pierced the gloom of the hall, forcing its way through ahead of him. Once in the hall, he turned to climb the gently curving staircase to the floor above. Slowly, the hall returned to its sombre state of semi-darkness as the kitchen door closed, pressed shut by a creaky spring, and blocked out the light from the fluorescent lamps in the kitchen which Rob had typically left on.

Half an hour later, Rob was upstairs in his bedroom when the door from the study to the hall opened and two dark-clad figures, one wearing black combat trousers and the other a pair of black tailored trousers, crept silently into the hall. One of them scoured the hall carefully while the other looked into each of the rooms leading from it. Having convinced themselves that they were alone in the house, they stood to one side of the hall, beside a small table.

"It's probably upstairs in his bedroom," whispered one of them and they started to walk noiselessly towards the stairs.

Suddenly, they heard a door close upstairs. The two figures glanced at each other and froze.

"I thought you said no one would be in," said the shorter, stockier of the two, the one wearing the combats.

The two intruders looked towards the sound of Rob on the landing and tracked him with their eyes as he sauntered down the stairs, an empty plate in his hand. Rob first saw them as he reached the turn in the staircase, they were standing motionless, gawping at him, like a couple of barn owls unexpectedly caught in the blinding beam of a torch. The plate fell from Rob's hand, bouncing down the stairs and rattling as it settled on the parquet floor, the harsh sound echoing off the walls. Rob turned away quickly and was about to run back up the stairs and call the police when he stopped himself. Slowly, he turned back to face the intruders, one of whom he thought he recognised.

"Hello," he said, taking a couple of steps towards the one he had recognised. "What on earth are *you* doing here?" There was more enquiry than fear in his tone. "Shouldn't you be at the party? Mum said everyone was going to be there."

The taller figure, the one Rob had recognised, did not respond and Rob's suspicions grew. His expression changed as he challenged them.

"What's going on?" he said, "Why are you here? I don't understand." As Rob spoke, the shorter, stockier of the two intruders moved quickly to place himself between his accomplice and Rob. He stared up at Rob intimidatingly but Rob, who was six inches taller, swept him aside with a single movement of his arm and looked at the taller one again. Not to be outdone, the shorter one angrily squeezed himself between them again and started to push Rob backwards, hitting him repeatedly in the chest with the palms of his hands. Rob brushed his arms away dismissively as he spoke.

"Bog off, will you!" he sneered, "I'm not talking to you."

The two of them stared at each other, each defying the other, as the one Rob had recognised whispered urgently between clenched teeth, "Carl! Just back off will you!"

For all that he was shorter than his accomplice, Carl was powerfully built and his eyes were cold and brutal; he was not the sort of person to back away from a confrontation and Rob gasped as suddenly he felt a sharp pain sear through his chest. He looked down and saw Carl's hand gripping the handle of a hunting knife. The blade was plunged deep inside him and when he opened his mouth to scream, the only sound that escaped was a dull, deep groan. Carl's eyes stared up at him; they held no sign of any emotion, no guilt, no remorse, not even any pleasure. Carl pushed again with the knife, this time twisting it hard as he did. Rob gasped with the renewed sharpness and intensity of the pain and bent forward as the blade reached up behind his ribs. The seconds ticked by as Rob stared at Carl and Carl stared back at him, daring him to live. After a few moments, Carl wrenched the blade of the knife free and blood began to pump from the wound in Rob's chest. Rob watched, almost detached, as it splattered onto the patterned rug beneath him, some of it hitting Carl's trousers.

"What the hell have you done!" shouted the one Rob had recognised as Rob collapsed onto to the floor.

"Well what did you expect me to do? He saw us! And he recognised *you*." The amazement in Carl's voice emphasised the enormous gulf than existed between their differing moralities. "I had no choice. I had to do it."

Rob lay slumped on the floor, his hands clasped over his chest where the knife had pierced his solar plexus.

"What are we going to do now?" There was panic in the taller figure's voice but Carl remained calm.

"We're going to do what we came here to do."

"But what about him? What about Rob?"

"In a few minutes, he'll be dead."

"But we can't just leave him here to die! He needs a doctor."

Carl's patience snapped. "Are you thick or what? We're not going to call a doctor. Or an ambulance. In fact, we're not going to do anything that might get us caught. OK? There is no way I'm going back inside again."

As Carl stared defiantly at his accomplice, Rob's eyes slowly closed for the last time.

Nicole and Eloise were chatting happily as they drove home from the party along the dark, unlit lanes. It was a warm and humid summer's evening and Nicole had opened her window to let some air into the car. In the distance, she could hear the rumble of thunder and the trees beside the road rustled with the first stirrings of a wind.

As Nicole drove up to Darrington Hall, Eloise suddenly stopped in mid-sentence and stared at the front of the house. Her tone changed and became tense.

"Mum," she said, touching her mother's arm, "The front door's wide open."

Nicole stopped the car and looked at the pool of light spilling out of the doorway onto the gravel drive. She didn't say a word but got out of the car hurriedly and walked quickly towards the house, with Eloise following a few paces behind her. As soon as she entered the hall, Nicole saw Rob lying on the rug. She stopped and looked at him; he wasn't moving. Her hand went to her mouth as she stood motionless, unable to comprehend what she was seeing but fearing the worst.

Then, as the inescapable reality of what she saw forced itself upon her, she screamed Rob's name and her whole body started shaking uncontrollably.

Eloise heard Nicole's scream as she came into the hall behind her. When she saw what had so shocked her mother, she gasped. She looked at Rob, then at her mother, and then back at Rob. With Nicole still unable to move, Eloise approached her brother slowly. She saw the pool of blood that had seeped from the wound in his chest and knelt down beside him. Despite finding it difficult to breathe, Eloise forced herself to take Rob's wrist in her hand. She felt for a pulse but there was nothing, just the cold clamminess of death. Slowly, she got back to her feet and returned to her mother before gently guiding her across the hall and sitting her down in the seat next to the telephone table.

Heavy driving rain was spattering against the hall windows as Eloise picked up the telephone and dialled 999.

The day after Rob Darrington's murder was officially announced, Eloise decided to go back to work to try to take her mind off what had happened. She had been reluctant to leave her mother on her own but Nicole had insisted that she would be fine.

That day, the *Yorkshire Post* carried the story of Rob's death on the front page. A colour photograph had been provided at the request of the reporter, whose insistence on having it had brought him close to having the door slammed in his face.

The telephone kept ringing as people read the story and called to extend their sympathy. There were also several calls from other newspapers wanting to pick up on the story and Nicole's friend, Anna Baines, had come over early to see if she could do anything to help. Nicole had tried to answer the first few calls herself but she kept finding that she was unable to speak and had then asked Anna to deal with them.

The doctor had given Nicole some strong sedatives, the effects of which had left her feeling a bit groggy. In the kitchen, she made herself a mug of coffee before going into the living room and sitting down on the sofa, her mind a jumble of thoughts and memories of Rob. Next to the sofa, was the box of mementos from which she had selected the picture of Rob for the paper. She took a small bundle of photographs from the box and started looking through them. Tears spilled down her cheeks as she looked at one of Rob and Eloise taken on holiday only a few weeks earlier. They had been playing beach tennis and Eloise had fallen on top of her brother; they looked so happy. There was also one of Rob proudly holding his new toy, an iPad; it had been a present from her, given to him only ten days before his death, on his nineteenth birthday. Through her tears she could see again how pleased he had been with it and she recalled the evening of the day following his birthday.

She and Eloise had been entertaining Anna and her husband Jeremy. A couple of months earlier, it had been Jeremy who had offered Eloise a good job with his company, before she had even finished her course, not that there had been the slightest doubt about her passing her final exams and graduating.

As the evening had drawn to a close and Jeremy and Anna had left, Eloise and Nicole had been clearing up in the lounge when Rob had come into the room, excitedly holding the iPad in his hands. They had both looked towards him as he had entered but it was Eloise who spoke to him, voicing the thoughts both she and her mother were having.

"Nice of you to honour us with your presence," she said sarcastically.

"Hey, come on, Sis, admit it. If you'd just got an iPad, you'd be wanting to get it all set up too."

Rob looked up from his iPad, not really understanding why Eloise was annoyed with him.

"Yeah, yeah, whatever," she said in a bored tone before pushing past her brother and starting to collect the empty glasses. As she gathered them and put them on a tray, Rob continued walking round the room playing with his new toy.

Then, suddenly, he stopped and stared intently at the iPad before exclaiming, "What the fuck!" Eloise looked round and smiled but his mother was less amused by his language. She frowned as Eloise walked towards Rob, a mischievous smile lighting up her face.

"Ah, what's the matter, little brother? Is it broken already?" she teased as she wandered round behind him.

"This is weird," said Rob, continuing to stare at the screen of his iPad, oblivious to the fact that Eloise was now peering over his shoulder trying to see what all the fuss was about. Unable to see anything, she gave up and came round to Rob's side before reaching out and snatching the iPad out of his hands.

"Here, let's see," she said as she drew it towards herself and looked at it, noting that the screen of the iPad was covered with row after row of numbers in groups of six.

"Looks like spam to me," she said.

"That's because it's in code," said Rob, holding out his hand expectantly and waiting for Eloise to return the iPad to him.

Instead, she just rolled her eyes before responding, as many an older sister would, in a way that emphasised how stupid she considered her little brother to be.

"Oh yeah, course it is," she said, as she laughed at him mockingly, "How silly of me not to realise."

Rob angrily snatched the iPad back from Eloise and she turned away from him. Still smiling to herself, she picked up the tray of glasses and left the room as he gave her a drop dead look.

Reluctantly, Nicole put the picture back with the others, each of which recalled other happy times, and replaced the bundle in the box beside her. She was wiping her eyes with a handkerchief when Anna glided silently into the room. Anna was tall for a woman and slim and she carried herself with a natural ease and poise learned from many hours of walking up and down with a large book balanced on her head. Her hair was always carefully coiffed and her make-up perfect. She was every inch the society wife and had been married to Jeremy for more than twelve years.

Although Anna was considerably younger than Nicole, she was one of Nicole's best friends and the two had got to know each other quite well over the years. Nicole's husband's printing business, which was still functioning despite his demise three years earlier, did a lot of work for Jeremy's company and Nicole had been grateful to Jeremy for his support following Andrew's death. She was also grateful to him for giving Eloise a job, one which Eloise had told her she was enjoying very much.

"Would you like some more coffee?" asked Anna.

"No, I've still got some, thanks," said Nicole, picking up the mug from the coffee table and smiling weakly.

Anna sat on the sofa, close to Nicole, and looked at her sympathetically. "Are you all right?" she asked.

"I was just looking at some photographs of Rob. They made me start crying again."

Anna took her hand. "I am so sorry this has happened," she said, "He was such a lovely young man, so full of life, and fun. I still can't quite believe it." Anna paused. She looked at Nicole and then looked away. "I do wish sometimes that we could, you know, just go back in time and change what happens, don't you?"

Nicole looked at Anna uncomprehendingly and the two women sat in silence for a while, neither knowing what to say to the other. Although they had become good friends, always ready to help each other out, they were quite different. Nicole had never reached the point where she could honestly say that she understood Anna and their friendship had always operated on a slightly detached level. Theirs was not the closeness of bosom buddies who could empathise with each other and share their innermost secrets but Nicole valued their friendship for what it was, a source of unquestioning practical support whenever it was needed.

"Have the police any idea what happened?" asked Anna, breaking the silence.

"Not really. They seem to be completely baffled by the whole business. Apart from Rob's iPad, nothing was stolen. The only explanation they can come up with is that Rob surprised a burglar before he had a chance to take anything else and that the burglar fled in panic after he..." Nicole choked, unable to bring herself to say the words as she relived the moment when she and Eloise had found Rob's body slumped, lifeless, in the hall.

The next morning, as he walked along Madison Avenue in New York, Carter was blissfully unaware of the devastating events which had taken place in Yorkshire a couple of nights before.

At number 270 on that famous street stands the Education Center of the Gemological Institute of America and on that cloudless day in June, the sun shone brightly as Carter approached the building and went inside.

Twenty minutes later, Carter, dressed in a dark suit, white shirt and a rather flamboyant red and green tie, was preparing to deliver a lecture to a room full of students. Although he was not a natural public speaker, he was fairly relaxed about the task in front of him, having fulfilled the role quite successfully on a number of previous occasions.

"Good morning, students," he began, and slowly the room grew silent as the class stopped chattering.

"My name is Carter Jefferson, and I graduated from Oxford University with a masters degree in Geology in..." Carter paused to allow his little joke to mature, "...well it was a while back, long before any of you even existed." A few of the students managed a polite chuckle at this before Carter continued.

"After that, I took an interest in diamonds and ended up working for the Federation of International Diamond Traders here in New York, something I still do, but only occasionally, on a freelance basis now."

Carter looked up at the back row of the lecture theatre as one of the students, a young man dressed in jeans and a tee-shirt raised his hand and shouted out.

"I thought you were a hot shot author! That's what it says in your online bio." The other students laughed loudly at the interruption as Carter smiled and looked down at his feet, wondering how to respond. He was used to students attempting to unsettle him but this was a new tactic. After a few moments, he looked up at the student.

"Good to see you've been doing some research," he said, "I'm impressed."

Several of the students turned to each other and started talking about the revelation that their lecturer was an author. Carter watched them, considering how best to proceed before finally deciding to give them what they wanted.

"OK. Just so we can get this out of the way and move on to what we're here for today, it is true that I have written some books, including a novel based on one of my more interesting experiences." Carter paused as the room went quiet again, reflecting the students' new found interest in this man's background. "And, while I'm waiting for that to hit the best-seller lists and make me my fortune, now and again I get to tell guys like you everything I know about diamonds."

The room remained hushed and Carter smiled as he surveyed the students, most of whom were now sitting attentively waiting for him to continue.

"OK," he began, "So who can tell me? What *is* a synthetic diamond?"

Later that day, on the seventh floor of the Gemological Institute building, the floor which was occupied by the FIDT, Carter entered a meeting room and shook hands with John Sprague. The two men had become friends over the years and the handshake was followed by a brief hug.

As John lifted his briefcase onto the table and Carter sat down, John gave him a knowing look and smiled. He reached into his briefcase and removed a jeweller's eye-glass, a 10x loupe, and a pair of long tweezers, both of which he put on the table in front of Carter. Then he pulled out a piece of soft black velvet cloth and spread it out on the table. Finally, he reached into his briefcase again and extracted a pouch made of similar black velvet material. He loosened the cord of the pouch and emptied the contents, about twenty sparkling gem quality diamonds, onto the black cloth.

Carter picked up one of the diamonds with the tweezers and examined it with the loupe. As he turned the diamond over, examining it carefully, John spoke.

"They're all synthetic," he said, "but incredibly good quality, the best I've ever seen."

"It was bound to happen sooner or later," replied Carter, not taking his eye from the loupe.

John's response came in a resigned tone. "I know. We've always known it was just a matter of time. The fact that someone is making gem quality synthetics of this size and clarity isn't the problem. It's what they're doing with them that concerns us."

Carter replaced the diamond on the cloth. Then he put down the tweezers and the loupe and leaned back in his chair.

"OK, John, I'll take the assignment," he said, looking John in the eye as he spoke. "We can't have all the world's lovebirds thinking they're buying something that's been in the ground since… since forever, when what they're actually getting is something that was made in a factory last week!" Carter managed a faint smile before his expression turned more serious. "This case is of particular interest to me," he said, "because the mine in Guinea where the diamonds appear to have come from, is owned by Philippe Lacoste." Carter paused, waiting for a response from John.

"Yeah, and…" prompted John obligingly, a blank look on his face as he waited for Carter to continue.

"Well, the thing is, I know Philippe Lacoste. At least, I have met him. A long time ago, when I was at university in England, I had a girlfriend, a fellow student. She was his daughter and, hard though it might be to believe, he didn't like me." Carter smiled as John looked at him wondering where this information was leading. "But that's a story for another day. Where I'm getting to is that Monsieur Lacoste lives in the South of France, so that's probably where I should start my investigation, assuming you still want me on the case?"

"Definitely," said John, nodding emphatically.

"Well, I'm due to fly to Europe next week anyway. . ." said Carter, smiling as he anticipated what he would say next, ". . . for the UK launch of my last literary masterpiece."

John returned the smile. "Of course," he said and patted Carter on the shoulder, "I'd forgotten about that."

"So, if it's OK with you, I'll get onto this straight after that."

John nodded his agreement to Carter's proposal. "That's settled then," he said. "And you can have Conrad to help you as usual. I'll have him join you in England."

With that, John rose from the table and held out his hand. "Carter," he said, "Until we meet again."

The two men shook hands before Carter turned and headed for the door as John gathered up the synthetic diamonds and returned them to his briefcase.

Chapter 2

Rob's funeral was a quiet affair. Behind the hearse carrying the coffin, the black Rolls Royce in which Nicole and Eloise were travelling drove the few miles from the church to the cemetery.

Eloise sat stony faced, staring straight ahead and trying to work out why anyone would want to kill her brother. She couldn't believe that it was simply because he had caught a burglar in the house. Nicole cried quietly throughout the short journey.

In the black Daimler limousine behind them were Jeremy and Anna with Nicole's father, Philippe Lacoste, who had flown in from Nice the night before. Philippe knew the Baineses quite well, both through Nicole and also as a result of renting boats to them on their frequent visits to the South of France. Several other cars followed on behind.

Watery sunshine broke through the clouds for the first time that day as the cortege passed through the bleak, wrought iron cemetery gates and wound down the narrow road to the bottom of the hill. When all the cars had rolled to a halt, the funeral director led his men to the back of the hearse where, slowly and reverently, they removed the coffin and placed it on their shoulders. Led by Nicole and Eloise, the mourners followed on behind, their footsteps silent on the freshly cut grass. At the grave side the minister from their local church delivered the final words.

"Ashes to ashes, dust to dust… in sure and certain hope…"

Eloise squinted up at the sun and felt the warm rays on the soft skin of her face as she did. Her brother was dead and yet, somehow, she felt strangely peaceful in that place. She could hear the birds singing in the nearby trees and the scent of flowers from the many bouquets drifted past her.

And then it was over and the coffin was lowered into the grave. First Nicole and then Eloise tossed a small scoop of earth onto the coffin and left to return to the cars. Eloise sighed a deep sigh and turned to her mother.

"They will catch whoever did this, won't they?" She looked up at her mother's face and saw the tears welling up in her eyes.

"Of course they will, sweetheart. Of course they will."

But Eloise knew that in the week since Rob's death the police had made virtually no progress with the case. The post mortem had told them nothing new and their effort had been reduced to two men, for whom the case would just be one of many.

Back at Darrington Hall, the mourners wandered between the sitting room and the dining room where the food which Anna had prepared was laid out. On each visit they piled their small plates high with a selection from the lavish spread.

Eloise watched her mother smile painfully at the people who went over to convey their sympathy. She knew how difficult she was finding it and she was glad that mostly people were leaving her alone. She felt for her mother having to deal with this without her father and recalled what her mother had told her about how they had met. They had both been students at Oxford University at the time and they had met a few months after Nicole had experienced a difficult break up with her previous boyfriend. A whirlwind romance had followed and Nicole had never looked back. Eloise sighed and hoped that one day she would meet someone about whom she would feel that strongly. As she was lost deep in thought, she suddenly felt a tap on her shoulder.

"Hello, you," said a sympathetic voice; Jeremy Baines had crept up behind her.

"Oh, hi Jeremy." Eloise's voice lacked any real conviction that she was pleased to see him but her smile was warm.

When, a month earlier, Jeremy had offered her the job with his company, she had been happy to accept it. The offer had been an attractive one, good pay and interesting work organising and managing the company's promotional events throughout Europe.

As her mind wandered back to the scene before her, Jeremy continued to try to engage her in conversation.

"How are you liking the job?" he asked, "Have you settled in all right with us?"

"Hmm? Oh, yes. Fine, thanks," replied Eloise, reluctantly dragging herself back into Jeremy's presence and giving him her full attention.

"I hear good things about your organisation of our conference in Sainte Maxime next week."

"Good, I'm glad." Eloise paused for a few moments before continuing, "I was really looking forward to it, but now, after this…"; she waved her hand in front of her.

"Yes, I can imagine. But it'll do you good, I'm sure. The boat trip to Monaco, especially." Eloise smiled weakly as Jeremy continued. "Did I tell you Anna's decided to come with us? Says she'll need a few days somewhere warm after Moscow this weekend."

Eloise laughed politely. "Me too!" she said

"Are you all packed and ready? It's an early flight you know."

"Yup! Woolly hat and winter coat already in the case," joked Eloise.

"Good! And don't forget your gloves. You'll need them too," said Jeremy, playing along.

"You'd never guess it was the middle of summer would you?" added Eloise and Jeremy laughed.

"We'll pick you up at seven tomorrow morning, as planned, OK?"

Eloise nodded and smiled as Jeremy wandered off. When he had gone, her thoughts returned to the reality of the occasion, her brother's funeral. She stood alone, lost in her thoughts for a few minutes before Anna approached her. She reached out her hand and touched Eloise's shoulder, giving her a sympathetic look as she did.

"Lovely spread," said Eloise as Anna let her hand drop to her side, "It was very kind of you to go to so much trouble. I don't know how Mum would have coped without you these last few days."

"Glad to be able to do something to help," said Anna and she smiled warmly at Eloise. "It was the least I could do at such a difficult time."

"Are you still as busy as ever with all your charities?" asked Eloise, trying to make polite conversation. She knew very well that Anna was tireless in her devotion to those organisations which had won her support. Anna smiled slightly, happy for the topic of conversation to move on to something other than Rob's untimely demise and its consequences.

"Oh, yes. Still keeping busy winkling money out of people who have more than they should."

They both laughed dutifully and then there was a few moments of awkward silence before Anna saw

Philippe approaching. She put her hand on Eloise's shoulder again as she spoke.

"Oh, please excuse me, Eloise. I must just speak to Peter Brearly over there. He's promised to organise a fundraiser for me. I'll see you in the morning."

Anna glanced at Philippe as he approached and his eyes followed her as she darted off leaving Eloise on her own.

Eloise's grandfather was French, very French, and he had a commanding presence. A successful businessman in his seventies with fingers in many pies, he was tall for someone of his age and his face wore a tough, almost gaunt look although this was softened somewhat by a large grey moustache. Eloise smiled as he came up to her and they kissed each other on the cheek.

"Hello, Grandpa," she said.

"Eloise," he responded rather formally, "How are you doing?"

"OK, I suppose, in the circumstances." Eloise's answer was non-committal.

"This is a bad business," broached Philippe. "Whoever did this will pay for what he has done."

"The police don't seem to be making much progress," offered Eloise.

"Don't worry, Cherie, justice will be done. Of this I am sure."

Although Philippe was her maternal grandfather, Eloise hardly knew him and found it difficult to carry on a conversation with him. She could count on the fingers of one hand the number of times they had met and she had always been a little frightened of him. Eloise knew from what her mother had told her that he was a hard man to please. He had taken it badly when his daughter had announced her intention to marry an Englishman and this had resulted in a degree of estrangement between them. But he did care about his daughter and had been sorry when Andrew had died, leaving her to bring up his grandchildren on her own.

"This is a sad time," said Philippe, breaking the silence, "You will miss Rob very much, I am sure." Eloise nodded as Philippe paused before continuing with a change of subject. "I hear you will be coming to my part of the world soon," he said, trying to move her on to less depressing thoughts.

"Yes, next week, after Moscow. I should be looking forward to it but I'm not. I thought of asking Jeremy if I could give it a miss."

"No. You should come. It will help to take your mind off this... this tragedy. For a little while at least." Eloise nodded and there was an awkward pause before Philippe continued. "And make sure you come and see me while you are there, yes?" Philippe smiled. "Or I will be very cross with you." He wagged his finger at her and Eloise smiled back weakly.

Philippe gave Eloise another kiss on the cheek before drawing himself up to his full height and returning to circulating politely amongst the guests. When he had gone, Eloise leaned back against the wall and surveyed the scene; people standing around eating, drinking and making small talk while her brother lay cold and dead in his coffin.

Philippe Lacoste's part of the world was the French Riviera. He lived in Port Grimaud, a small town in the bay of St Tropez, about fifty miles south west of Nice. The town had been built on a swamp in the early nineteen-seventies and from Le Lac Interieur, a small lake at the heart of the town which is fed by the sea, a network of canals branch out allowing every house in the town to have its own quayside.

The town has the appearance of an old-established Provençale village with each house differing from its neighbours in some small detail of its outward appearance and each being painted in one of a wide variety of the typical pastel colours of the region. After it had been completed, Port Grimaud had quickly become a thriving commercial hub catering to an army of visiting tourists and boating enthusiasts.

Philippe's house was the most prestigious in the town and stood at the end of the Rue des Deux-Iles, one of the strips of land between the canals. It was here, in the living room of the house, that Philippe, having returned from Rob's funeral in Yorkshire, was awaiting the arrival of Gilles Renard, one of his employees, whom he had summoned to a meeting.

Gilles was a tough looking, muscular man who had grown up in a poor family and who, as a teenager, had followed a path of petty crime. Although this had landed him in trouble with the police on several occasions, Philippe had seen in him something of himself at that age and had wanted to help the young man.

Having built up an impressive portfolio of businesses which ensured that he never had to worry about money, Philippe was in a position to help Gilles and he had employed him to run one of his businesses, a yacht charter agency, something Gilles still did on a part time basis. Gilles would always be grateful to Philippe for that. It was the financial security afforded by that job which had enabled Gilles to follow Philippe's example and establish and build up a number of businesses himself, amongst which was a diamond cutting business based in Nice. As with Gilles' other businesses, Philippe's support had been critical. Through his diamond mine in Guinea, Philippe had built up a range of contacts in the diamond industry and had been able to introduce Gilles to the right people.

Over the years, Philippe had learned that he could trust Gilles completely and Gilles had become his closest confidant in matters of business, though not in matters of the heart, an area of his life which Philippe kept very much to himself.

As Philippe waited, Gilles walked along the road towards the house and when he reached it, he knocked on the door. Shortly afterwards, the door opened and he went in.

Inside the house, Gilles followed Philippe through the kitchen and into the living room. He stood still in the middle of the room as Philippe walked to the French windows and looked out across Le Lac. After a few moments had passed, he turned to face Gilles and when he spoke, it was clear that there was something on his mind.

"We need to make this right," he began, "Rob was my only grandson and from what I have been told about their investigations, we cannot rely on the British police." Philippe looked intently at Gilles, demanding a response and Gilles dropped his eyes before speaking.

"I will take care of it," he said, his tone both confident and matter of fact.

"How?" demanded Philippe, raising his arms in frustration, "How will you take care of it? What can be done?"

Gilles raised his eyes and looked straight into Philippe's eyes. "There are ways," he said, "Just leave it to me."

Philippe paused at this and thought about it for a few moments before nodding and turning back to look out of the French windows again, clasping his hands behind his back.

After a few moments had passed in silence, Gilles spoke. "Philippe, I know you have other things on your mind right now but I still need more diamonds."

Philippe continued to stare out of the window across the lake towards the sea as he spoke. "I have already told you, that is all they can produce," he said.

"Well it's not enough!" retorted Gilles, unable to conceal his frustration, "I have buyers wanting more. And I don't want them going somewhere else because I can't give them what they want."

Philippe turned quickly on his heel and locked eyes with Gilles.

"Gilles! It is a diamond mine, not a chocolate factory! If the stones are not there in the ground, we cannot dig them up."

Philippe turned away as he finished speaking and looked again across Le Lac towards the Capitainerie. "You will just have to find another supplier."

Gilles sighed before responding in a more gentle tone, "What about getting some more from… you know…"

Philippe turned from the French window and stared at Gilles for several seconds before speaking.

"You can ask me that? After what has happened?" Philippe relented a little and his tone changed to one of resignation, "You will have to wait until the next shipment. That will be in two weeks."

Gilles sighed and nodded his acceptance of something he couldn't change.

After Gilles had left, Philippe went into his study, a room off the living room. Slowly, he opened his laptop computer and pressed the start button. As it was firing up, he recalled what had happened a week earlier.

The sun had been shining brightly and he had been on board his boat which was moored at the Capitainerie, across Le Lac from his house.

It is from the Capitainerie that the harbour of Port Grimaud is administered and here, too, can be found the helipad, used by the rich and famous arriving from the airport in Nice. Beyond the Capitainerie, a curving breakwater protects the town from the sea and rising up from the breakwater, two dozen flagpoles bear the flags of the main sea-faring nations of the world.

Moored stern on between two similar sized boats, with its gangway reaching from the rear deck out over the quayside, Philippe's boat, the Fleur de Grimaud, was a sixty-five foot Johnson motor yacht. It was one of a number of luxury yachts which Philippe owned, and for which Gilles arranged charters, and it was the one he was currently using for his own purposes.

That morning, Philippe had been sitting in the saloon of the boat with his laptop on the table in front of him, ready to send an email. Beside him had been a hard backed book and a sheet of paper.

He had folded the sheet of paper and put it inside the book before looking at the screen of his laptop and starting to type some letters into the email address line. As he was doing so, and before he had entered more than a few characters, his phone started to ring. He stopped typing and looked across at the phone which was lying on the worktop in the galley. After a moment's hesitation, he decided not to answer the call and returned his attention to the laptop where two email addresses had appeared in a little window below the address line with the first of these being highlighted.

Philippe's phone continued to ring. He looked at it again in frustration before looking back at his laptop and quickly hitting the enter button, selecting the highlighted address. As he got up to answer the phone, he used the mouse to click on the send button.

Philippe then strode across the saloon to the galley, intending to answer the phone, but by the time he got there, it had stopped ringing. Now even more irritated, he returned to the saloon. He picked up the book and leant over his laptop to check that his email had been sent and as he did so, his expression changed to one of consternation. His head moved closer to the screen and he stared at it intently, unable to believe what he had done.

"Merde!" he exclaimed as he straightened up and looked out of the window. After a few moments, he managed to compose himself and absent-mindedly put the book, which was still in his hand, on the bookshelf. Then he returned his attention to his laptop and sat down in front of it. He checked the message again and sighed deeply before closing the laptop and rising to his feet.

Slowly, and still deep in thought, Philippe went up the steps to the galley. He picked up his phone and selected a number before pressing the call button and putting the phone to his ear. When the person he was calling answered, he spoke quietly, a tone of resignation in his voice.

"We have a problem."

Philippe was brought back to the present as the desktop picture on his laptop appeared. He looked out through the window of his study from where he could see the Capitainerie and, beyond it, the sea.

Opposite the Capitainerie in Port Grimaud, on the other side of the channel which leads from Le Lac to the bay of St Tropez and thence to the open sea, is the marine fuelling station. It is there that small boats and large motor yachts alike top up their fuel tanks before venturing out to sea and for almost three years, the fuelling station had been the workplace of Jacques Armand, a handsome, well toned young Frenchman.

As Jacques busied himself cleaning the pumps, a large motor yacht pulled in to the jetty and the owner shouted at him from the fly bridge.

"Eh, Jacques, faites le plein, eh?"

Jacques nodded and started to fill the boat's fuel tank with diesel, looking enviously along the lines of the boat. The owner of the boat watched him, smiling.

"C'est un bateau magnifique, n'est-ce pas?" Jacques ignored him and the boat owner continued. "Comment va ta tres belle mere? Elle est bonne?" Again, Jacques did not respond and the boat owner smiled an even broader smile. "Et ton pere? Comment va-t-il?" At this, Jacques gave the boat owner a withering stare, he didn't appreciate people mentioning his father. He pulled the nozzle from the tank before replacing it in the holder on the pump and approaching the boat owner. He held out his hand, palm upwards, as he spoke.

"Trente-deux euros."

"Sur mon compte." The disdainful response from the boat owner did nothing to make Jacques feel more relaxed in his attitude towards him and Jacques' hand dropped to his side as he looked away. The boat owner's laugh rang loudly in Jacques' ears as he pushed the throttles forward and the boat pulled away from the jetty. Jacques turned on his heel and stormed away from the petrol station as his boss watched from the office and shook his head.

A few minutes later, Jacques entered the Place du Marché, a large square at the centre of Port Grimaud, where a market is held twice a week and which is connected via a bridge over one of the canals to the

Place des Artisans. The Place d'Eglise, a third, smaller square just off the other end of the Place du Marché, faces onto Le Lac Interieur and houses the Roman Catholic church, the yacht club and the town hall as well as providing public mooring for visiting boats.

The market was filled with people wandering round the stalls as Jacques strode across the Place du Marché, his face clearly showing that he was very upset. He left the Place and walked along a canal and past the chandlery before going up the open stone steps which led from the canal side to his mother's apartment on the first floor. When he reached the top of the steps, he yanked the door open and went in, slamming the door shut behind him.

Claudine Armand, Jacques' mother, was an attractive woman with a winning smile. She heard the door open and slam shut and smiled to herself as she left the kitchen and came into the living room to greet Jacques. When she saw how upset he was, the smile quickly disappeared and was replaced by a look of concern.

"Jacques! What's the matter?" she asked.

Jacques gave her a foul look as he answered. "You need to ask?" he questioned as he disappeared into his bedroom.

A few moments later, he reappeared with his car keys in his hand. Claudine watched as he walked silently past her towards the door.

"Jacques!" she pleaded, "Where are you going?"

"Out!"

"Out where?"

"Just out."

The door of the apartment opened and as Jacques went through it, in the background, a concerned Claudine called out to him.

"But, Jacques! We've been through all this before!"

Jacques responded by slamming the door shut behind him and as he left the apartment, he took the stone steps three or four at a time before shooting out onto the canal side.

Suddenly finding himself amongst a mass of people, mostly holiday makers enjoying the balmy atmosphere, Jacques calmed himself and ran a hand through his untidy black hair before walking quickly up the steps to the bridge which joins the Place du Marché to the Place des Artisans. He fought his way through the people crowding the archway and strode across the Place, leaving the town behind him.

As he ran across the road which separates the town of Port Grimaud from the residents' car park, Jacques' unbuttoned white shirt flowed out behind him leaving his tanned and well defined torso largely uncovered. A passing motorist, surprised by his sudden appearance, sounded his horn and Jacques turned to look at him. He gave the driver a withering stare before walking on towards the car park where the little ice-blue Peugeot that had been his eighteenth birthday present from his absent father was parked.

Jacques had decided to go where he always went when he was upset, to see his half-sister, Yvonne, to whom he was very close. She lived in a fortified village nearly two thousand feet up into the Maures mountains, which rise up behind the bay of St Tropez. Like Port Grimaud, the village of St Pierre des Maures is a regular stopping place for tourists and in the summer it is packed with visitors from morning till night.

Jacques covered the ten kilometres from Port Grimaud to St Pierre in little more than ten minutes. He knew the road well and threw the car into the numerous sharp bends with considerable skill. Occasionally he misjudged a corner and left the tarmac, throwing up clouds of dry choking dust as he wrestled the car back onto the road again.

When he reached the picturesque little village, he parked, illegally, near the main gate. He called 'Hello' to the old men playing boules on the court near the gate and they waved to him. Jacques knew that he was popular with them, that they envied his good looks and devil-may-care approach to life. Once through the main gate, he pushed his way past the crowds milling around in the narrow streets until he came to the Gallerie St Pierre and went inside.

The gallery was just one of many in St Pierre and was on two floors with a small apartment above. The ancient three storey building which housed it, and several other shops, ran the length of the narrow cobbled street. The thick walls of the building insulated the interior, keeping it cool in the summer, and the gallery was always filled with people escaping from the heat of the day and pretending to examine the merchandise.

"Hi, Jacques."

Jacques recognised the voice coming from behind a little clump of middle aged women dressed in either flowery summer dresses or loud trousers, both of which were generally too tight and outlined rolls of unsightly flab. He pushed his way past them rudely and provoked a flurry of muttering about 'ill-mannered locals'. When he reached Yvonne, he grabbed her hand.

"Come on, I'll buy you a cup of coffee," he said.

"Jacques, I'm working!" she said as she pulled her hand back.

"Françoise can manage without you for ten minutes, can't she? I'll tell her."

Yvonne's assistant, Françoise, who worked part-time with Yvonne in the shop, saw Jacques marching purposefully towards her.

"Hello, Jacques. How about a kiss?" she said, puckering her voluptuous lips and closing her vast eyes. Everything about Françoise was larger than life, especially her appetites.

He skirted round to give her a peck on the cheek. "Look after the shop for a few minutes, will you? I'm taking Yvonne for a coffee."

Ten minutes later, Jacques was sitting with Yvonne outside a café, sipping a cappuccino. The hot afternoon sun shone into the little courtyard and lit up the ancient fountain at its centre. Yvonne picked up her coffee cup and drank from it as Jacques spoke.

"Did you sell anything today?" he asked.

"One picture and a couple of vases. That's all."

"Maybe you should get another job. You hardly earn anything from running the gallery and you have to spend every day there in the summer."

"True, but I do get the apartment above the shop as well. And I can always get Françoise to cover for me if I want some time off." Yvonne lifted her cup and smiled, "That's the advantage of being the manager."

As they chatted and drank their coffee, the anger that Jacques had felt towards his mother turned to remorse. She deserved better than that from him and he wanted to go home and make it up with her.

"I must go and make friends with Maman again," he said as he reached into his pocket and put some coins on the table to pay for the coffee.

"Oh, Jacques!" responded Yvonne, frowning as he got up from the table, "You haven't been upsetting her again, have you?

"It's her own fault. She still won't tell me who he is."

"Well, she must have her reasons."

"That's easy for you to say, you know who your father is."

"Not that it has made much difference to my life given that he disappeared without a trace before I was born!"

Jacques got up and turned to look at her. "I just want to know who he is, that's all. You can understand that, can't you?"

Yvonne nodded and smiled as Jacques gave her a peck on the cheek before disappearing down the nearby street, leaving her to finish her coffee alone.

Chapter 3

The centre of Moscow was bathed in the early afternoon sunshine as Jeremy, Anna and Eloise stood in Red Square and looked towards the Kremlin, a spectacular, if rather forbidding edifice.

Jeremy's company, Baines Automotive Ltd, manufactured parts for cars and had grown from virtually nothing when, at the age of twenty-four, he had bought it from the receivers. Now it was a major supplier to the motor industry, exporting to most European countries including France and Germany.

Across from the Kremlin, the GUM shopping centre dominated one whole side of Red Square. All of the world's most prestigious retailers occupied space in this building. It consisted of three floors, of which the uppermost housed the Demonstration Hall, a popular centre for exhibitions and conferences.

During this particular weekend in June, the World Automotive Parts Exhibition and Conference was taking place in Moscow. As usual, the event was split between the spacious Expocentre, about half a mile from Red Square, and the GUM Demonstration Hall where, each day, the main speakers addressed appreciative audiences packed tightly into the space.

The area around the entrance to the shopping centre was dotted with little groups of people talking and laughing as they waited for the start of the next conference session.

In one of these little groups, Jeremy was studying the conference programme, Eloise was checking the contents of her large carrier bag and Anna was surveying the picturesque scene when they were joined by Dimitri Surkov, who was also attending the conference. Jeremy and Anna had met Dimitri several years before when they had all been attending this same event and they had agreed to meet up at the conference every year since then. Dimitri greeted Anna and Jeremy warmly with a kiss on both cheeks before Jeremy introduced Eloise.

"This young lady is Eloise Darrington," he said, "She is taking over responsibility for organising our annual conference in Sainte Maxime and our presence at exhibitions such as this one."

"Welcome to Moscow," said Dimitri as he smiled at Eloise and indicated the city with a sweep of his hand.

"Are you also in the car parts business?" asked Eloise.

Dimitri smiled. "Not really. I work for Scientific Institute in Siberia where we do research into many things."

"So why are you here?"

Anna looked at Eloise in surprise at her directness.

"Dimitri's unit at the Institute specialises in research into the applications of graphite," she said. "Which, as I'm sure you know, is used in the manufacture of brake linings."

Jeremy looked at his watch. "It's almost two," he said looking up at Anna and Dimitri, "I'd better get in there. Are you coming, Dimitri?"

Dimitri smiled and held up his hands. "No, no, this session is too technical for me. I am just simple administrator."

"OK," responded Jeremy as he leaned forward and kissed Anna on the cheek, "I guess I'm on my own for this one." He turned to go. "See you later, darling. Have fun."

Jeremy walked towards the entrance to the shopping centre as the others watched him go.

"I must go too," said Eloise. "I need to get over to the Expocentre and check that our stand is fully supplied with literature after the lunch time rush."

Anna and Dimitri watched as Eloise walked along the road, past the Kremlin and round the corner. When she had disappeared, Dimitri turned to Anna and smiled.

"I buy you good Russian coffee, yes?" The invitation was issued without any expectation that Anna's response would be other than in the affirmative. He smiled as she nodded and they headed off together.

At about the same time as Anna and Dimitri were heading off to find a café in Moscow, Jacques and Yvonne were sitting at the dining table in Claudine's apartment as Claudine brought a bottle of wine and three glasses from the kitchen. She poured the wine into the glasses and passed one each to Jacques and Yvonne before sitting down. Then, in a very ceremonious manner, she raised her glass and smiled.

"Happy birthday, Cherie," she said and Jacques and Yvonne both raised their glasses in Claudine's direction before drinking from them.

Moments later, Claudine was still wearing a broad smile and Jacques and Yvonne looked at her questioningly, waiting for her to speak. Instead, she said nothing, she just continued smiling and pretended not to know why they were looking at her in that way.

"What?!" she said eventually, enjoying every moment and pretending not to be aware that she was behaving in an unusual manner.

Yvonne sighed as if to say 'you know very well what' but then she gave in and voiced what she and Jacques were both thinking.

"Why the big smile?" she asked, cocking her head on one side to emphasise the question.

"Well, today is Jacques' twenty-first birthday. Annnnnd, that means…" Claudine paused as she got up from the table and went to the sideboard, her gait almost a dance. When she reached the sideboard, she opened a drawer and extracted an envelope from it before returning to the table. "That means that you get this."

Claudine handed the envelope to her son, her smile now bigger than ever, if indeed that were possible. Jacques took the envelope, his face showing that he really had no idea what all the fuss was about.

"What is it?" he asked.

"Well, when you were born, your father put some money into an account for you which was to be given to you on your twenty-first birthday. And that's today!"

Jacques looked at his mother for a few moments before opening the envelope. Slowly, he extracted a piece of paper from it and unfolded it. As he looked at the piece of paper, his eyes widened. He looked at his mother and then back at the piece of paper before speaking in a dull mechanical tone.

"It says here that there is eight hundred and thirty-two thousand euros in the account." Jacques looked at his mother before continuing, his expression hovering between excitement and anger. "Is this some kind of joke?" he asked.

"No joke, Cherie," responded Claudine, "the money is yours, to do with as you wish."

Jacques stared at the piece of paper as the reality of the news sank in. Both Claudine and Yvonne were grinning from ear to ear as they watched him. Then he put piece of paper back into the envelope and laid it carefully on the table in front of him before fixing his mother with a stare.

"Who is he, Maman?" he asked and Claudine's smile vanished.

"You know I can't tell you, Jacques," she said, "I made a promise, a solemn promise that I never would."

Claudine watched Jacques, waiting for a response. It didn't come so she decided to continue. Although her voice was now flat, and conveyed her disappointment at his reaction, she managed a forced smile as she spoke.

"What will you do with the money?" she asked.

Jacques' expression changed as he realised the impact the money would have on his life and, slowly, a smile spread across his face. As it did, he looked at his mother.

"Do you really need to ask me that?"

At this, Yvonne, keen to keep the moment upbeat, jumped to her feet and raised her glass.

"To your father, Jacques, whoever he is!"

Jacques and Claudine looked at each other. Neither was quite sure how to react to Yvonne's interruption, so they followed her lead, getting to their feet and echoing the toast before their formal posture crumbled and they all started laughing hysterically.

At London's Heathrow airport, Carter's plane landed at eleven fifteen in the morning and taxied along the runway. Half an hour later, Carter was in the baggage collection area waiting for the bags from his flight to appear. He had his phone in his hand and looked at the screen as he waited for it to initialise. When it had, he pressed a few buttons and put it to his ear, a smile on his face. More than a week had passed since his call to Nicole and he was looking forward to speaking to her again.

"Nicole! Hi, it's Carter," he began. "I've just landed at Heathrow."

Carter listened and as he did, his expression changed, the smile fading to be replaced by a look of dismay.

"I don't know what to say," he said before looking round the room wondering how to continue the conversation.

All his hopes for his visit to Nicole, the love of his life, went out of the window when she told him what had happened to her son. Eventually, he decided what to say although he was very reluctant to say it.

"Do you want to cancel?" he began and then quickly continued, "Totally understand if you do, given what's happened."

Carter listened as Nicole told him that she still wanted to see him and the sooner the better as far as she was concerned. His head lifted on hearing this, no smile, it wasn't going to be easy, but at least he would see her.

"I've got a few things to do here today," he said, "But I'll be there late tonight. How about we meet up for lunch at my hotel tomorrow? Say, twelve o'clock, in the bar?"

At last the hint of a smile from Carter as he spoke. "Yeah, sure. See you soon." Carter rang off and stared at his phone as the bags started to arrive on the conveyor belt.

A little later that day, inside a bookshop on Oxford Street in the centre of London, Carter was sitting at a table signing copies of his book as people queued, waiting for their copy to be signed. Carter managed to smile at every proud owner of his literary masterpiece but his thoughts were two hundred miles away in

Yorkshire, with Nicole. He couldn't wait to be on the train to York but before that, there was something else he wanted to do.

The book signing over, Carter made his way to New Scotland Yard. He looked up at the building before making up his mind and walking purposefully towards the entrance.

An hour or so later, Carter was in a small office inside New Scotland Yard sitting at one side of a desk. Opposite him, Detective Chief Superintendent Lamont, a man of average height and build dressed in a suit, was sitting behind his desk looking at Carter's ID wallet. After carefully examining the contents of the wallet, Lamont returned it to Carter.

"What can I do to help?" he asked, raising his hands, palm upwards to emphasise his enquiry.

"I'd like to talk to the officer in charge of the investigation into the death of Rob Darrington in Yorkshire. There may be a link to my case."

Minutes later, Carter emerged from New Scotland Yard, clutching a piece of paper in his hand on which Lamont had written a name and a phone number. Once outside the building, Carter extracted his phone from his pocket. He punched in the number written on the piece of paper and waited for his call to be answered. When it was, he wasted no time.

"Detective Inspector Harris, please." Carter waited a few moments to be put through. "Hello, Carter Jefferson here. Chief Superintendent Lamont at Scotland Yard suggested I call you. It's about Rob Darrington…"

Chapter 4

About a mile from the centre of York, quite close to the racecourse, is the headquarters of the North Yorkshire Police. The building housing the offices is built of red brick, four storeys high and has a flat roof.

At nine-thirty on the morning after the day he had arrived in London, and having taken a late evening train from London to York, Carter drove up to the building and parked the car he had hired that morning in the public area of the car park.

Once inside the building, Carter, smartly dressed in a suit, approached the reception desk and told the receptionist that he had an appointment with Detective Inspector Harris. As he waited in the reception area, a policewoman approached him.

"Mr Jefferson?" she asked and Carter got to his feet. "Please come with me."

A few minutes later, Carter and Harris were sitting at opposite sides of the desk in Harris's office on the third floor of the building and Carter was filling Harris in about the case he was investigating. As he was doing so, Harris received a telephone call and he and Carter were soon on their way to a remote spot in the countryside where a dead body had been found.

During the twenty minute drive to the scene, Carter continued to brief Harris about his investigation and when they arrived, Harris parked his car behind a police van. From there, a policeman in uniform escorted them across a field and down a steep slope into a disused railway cutting.

Under the road bridge which spanned the cutting, two men in white overalls were bending over a body on the ground. Harris asked Carter to wait as he approached one of the men and spoke to him. Carter waited patiently, out of earshot, as the man explained to Harris what had happened and a few minutes later, Harris returned to Carter.

"Nasty one, this," he said.

"How long do they think the body's been there?" Carter enquired as they watched the men in white overalls continue to go about the business of examining the scene in minute detail.

"A couple of days, more or less," replied Harris.

"What happened?" asked Carter.

"Single shot to the forehead. Point blank range. Looks like an execution to me. Very professional. His hands were tied behind his back."

"Did you find the bullet?"

"It was in the grass behind where he fell, along with most of the back of his skull." Harris looked at the men working the crime scene and then back at Carter. "Come on, let's get back to headquarters."

The two men struggled up the steep bank and started walking across the field towards where they had parked.

"Do you know who he was?" asked Carter.

"Oh yes," said Harris, "He's well known to us. Been in and out of trouble since he could walk. But not for anything that would explain this."

"Got a name?"

"Spicer, Carl Spicer. He's been living in a hostel since his last spell inside. Assault with a deadly weapon we got him for that time, I think. Quite handy with a knife as I recall."

Carter and Harris left the field and got back into their car. As they drove back to police headquarters, and a couple of minutes had passed with nothing being said by either of them, Carter broke the silence.

"Tell me, Inspector, how many murders do you normally get on your patch in, say, a year?" he asked.

"Not many. Mine is a quiet beat. Last year we had three."

"And how many of them were executions like this one?" continued Carter.

"I haven't seen anything like this since I left the Met."

"So two murders in a week is a bit unusual?"

"I don't know what you're getting at but yes, yes it is."

"Well, what I'm wondering, is whether these two deaths could be linked? What do you think?"

"At this stage, I really have no idea."

Carter thought that there was a strong possibility that the two murders were connected; it was too much of a coincidence that two people should be killed so close together in terms of both geography and time. Maybe in some localities that wouldn't be particularly unusual but in a country backwater like Welburn in North Yorkshire, it was. Whether or not the two deaths had anything to do with his case was yet to be determined but he thought it entirely possible that Rob Darrington's murder had something to do with it, and if it did, then the second one, the execution, might also have some bearing on it.

As they continued on their way, Harris looked across at Carter. "Do you think these killings might have something to do with your case?"

"Yeah, I think maybe they do," answered Carter carefully. "It's too soon to say for sure but I'm meeting with someone later today who might be able to throw some light on what's going on here."

"I don't suppose you'd care to tell me who?"

"I'd rather not. For now, anyway. It's someone I was up at Oxford with."

"You went to Oxford University?" The Inspector cast a glance at Carter, an expression of disbelief on his face.

"Sure I did. Why so surprised, Inspector? Don't you think a black man from Belize should be allowed to attend one of your oldest and best seats of learning?"

"No, no, I didn't mean anything like that," protested Harris; he was not easily embarrassed but Carter's directness had caught him by surprise. "But if you don't mind me saying so, you don't sound very Belizean."

"That's because I lived in New York for fifteen years before moving back to Belize." Carter was enjoying Harris's discomfort but thought it was time he returned to the matter in hand. "About my meeting," he said, "As soon as it looks like there may be a connection, you'll be the first to hear about it. OK?"

"Yes, that would be very helpful," said Harris, "I'd like to be kept up to date with your progress. You certainly seem to have a very unusual and challenging case to crack. To be honest, if Scotland Yard hadn't briefed us, if Chief Superintendent Lamont who, incidentally, I was at Hendon with, if he hadn't personally vouched for you, I would have found it all just a little bit difficult to believe."

"Then I'm glad he did," said Carter, "Because it's all true and I'll most likely need your help before it's over."

"Do you get as much co-operation from the police in other countries as you do here?" asked Harris, changing the subject.

"Oh, yeah, sure we do. Couldn't do the job without it. Most of our cases spread across several countries. If national police forces weren't willing to help us, we wouldn't stand a chance."

When they arrived back at police headquarters, Harris parked the car and the two men got out and approached each other.

"Thanks for your time, Inspector," said Carter.

"No problem," responded Harris, "Please keep me posted and if I can be of any further help, let me know."

The two men shook hands before Harris gave Carter a friendly wave as he turned and walked off towards the entrance to the building. Carter waved back, pleased to have made contact with Harris; the man seemed personable and more than usually helpful.

As he drove back to his hotel, Carter wondered how this, his latest case, was going to turn out. He enjoyed working on complex problems, probably a spin-off of his time at Oxford, and although he had been keen to carry on working on his latest book, once he had discovered the connection to Nicole, someone who he hadn't seen for more than twenty-five years, someone who at one time he had thought might be his life-long companion, there was never the slightest chance of him refusing the case. Now that he was finally about to meet her again, he was excited but he was also apprehensive, even a little bit scared of how it would go. He had no idea what to expect after so many years and his thoughts took him back to his time in Oxford.

When he had met Nicole, she had been in the final year of her French Literature degree and he had been studying for a Masters in Geology. He had been older than her but only by a couple of years. They had met at an Oxford Union party and he smiled as he recalled that night. She had been impressed by his natural rhythm as he danced to the music and had told him so from the security of a group of girls with whom she was dancing.

"It comes with being from the Caribbean," he had said donning his best smile as she split off from dancing with her friends to dance with him.

"Where in the Caribbean?" she had asked as she gyrated to the music, clearly interested in him.

"Belize."

"Belize! Where the hell is Belize?"

"Just below Mexico."

They danced on for a couple of songs before Carter concluded that he was making progress with this girl and wanted to know more about her.

"What's your name," he asked.

"Nicole. Nikki to my friends."

"So, can I call you Nikki?"

"What? Are you asking for my phone number already?"

They both laughed at Nicole's joke and continued dancing until the music stopped as the DJ changed.

"Can I get you a drink?" asked Carter.

"Sure, I'll come to the bar with you."

"I was thinking we could maybe go somewhere a bit quieter?" he ventured and waited for Nicole to respond. She just smiled shyly so he pressed on. "I'd like to get to know you a bit better." Nicole nodded her agreement to the change of venue and, emboldened by this, Carter took her hand and led her out of the room as the music started up again.

They went to a nearby pub and talked. They talked and talked and talked, until the barman called time and they had to leave. When they did, Carter insisted on walking Nicole back to her college. At the gate he kissed her gently and then they exchanged phone numbers and agreed to call each other the next day.

Carter smiled as he recalled his walk home that night. There had been a spring in his step like never before and on a couple of occasions, he had jumped in the air and let out a loud "YES!" as he punched the air.

And then, after seven months and four days, it had ended. He had become aware that Nicole's father was not happy about their relationship. On the one brief occasion when he had met him, Philippe had made it quite clear what he thought of Carter's suitability as a potential son-in-law and Carter knew that he had given Nicole a lot of grief about it, to the point of threatening to pull her out of Oxford and take her back to the South of France where he could keep an eye on her. But Carter had not expected what happened that day.

Nicole had telephoned him and asked him to meet her by the river in the gardens of Christ Church College. When he had arrived, she had been standing looking across the river, clearly deep in thought. She turned to face him as he walked up beside her and put his arm round her waist, and he saw a tear trickle down her cheek.

"What is it?" he asked, concerned that she was upset about something, "What's wrong?"

Nicole looked down at her feet for a few moments before speaking. When she did speak, all she said was, "I'm sorry, Carter," and shook her head sadly unable to look at him.

He took her in his arms. She didn't need to say more. Carter knew what had happened. She rested her head on his chest for a few moments and then pulled away a little from him.

"It's OK," he said, "I understand."

Nicole burst into tears at this, her face contorting as she did and she looked up at him.

"It is NOT OK!" she shouted angrily. "Who the fuck does he think he is?"

"He thinks he's your father, Nikki. And he thinks he's looking out for your interests."

"Oh, no, no, no, it's not that! No way! The only person he is thinking about is himself. He wants me to go home and marry some nice little Frenchman that he approves of, that's what *he* wants."

She turned away and Carter sighed. "Yeah, maybe. Either way, I guess it's over between us?"

Nicole turned back to look at him, her agony written all over her face. "For now, Carter. Just for now. I want to finish my course and graduate. But I love you and I'm not going to let him beat me on this. Once I've graduated, he won't be able to dictate to me who I can and can't see."

"You serious?" asked Carter, his spirits lifting a little.

Nicole nodded emphatically, her lips set in grim determination. " It's only a few months. Will you wait for me?"

"Why can't we carry on seeing each other and just keep it to ourselves?"

"Because he'd find out about it, he's good at that, and I'd be back in Sainte Maxime before I knew it." Nicole looked at Carter, wishing there was some other way. "And he's my father. I don't want to have to lie to him about it." She looked at him appealingly and asked the question again. "Will you wait for me?"

Carter smiled. "You need to ask?"

But it had been the end of their relationship. A couple months had passed with Carter getting updates from mutual friends to the effect that Nicole wasn't seeing anyone and then, three months after they had broken up, she had met Andrew, and that had been that.

Now, twenty-five years later, as Carter was driving the last few yards to his hotel and parking his car in the car park, Nicole was sitting in the hotel lounge, nervously wrapping a paper napkin round her fingers as she waited for him to arrive. She wondered if she had made the right decision about seeing him but Nicole's hesitance owed more to shock than any reluctance to meet Carter. More than a quarter of a century earlier, she had been in love with him, passionately so. But did she want to see him again now? After all the time that had passed, and after all that had gone on between them? She wasn't sure. And his timing was awful. Coming so soon after Rob's death, she was struggling to come to terms with the memories she and Carter shared, memories which were flooding back as she waited for him to arrive. They had been so close, so very much in love and then, because of her father's strong opposition to the relationship, because Carter was not French and, worse still, he was black, they had broken up.

Despite the passage of the years, Nicole was still a good looking woman, she knew that, but she was over forty years old now and she also knew that time was always kinder to men than to women. He would be older too but with him it would probably mean that he had become more attractive, not less. He would probably look very distinguished, with some grey hair and the lines which the years had drawn on his face would give it character and depth. She had a picture in her mind's eye of how he would look but she couldn't help wondering if he would live up to it. When he had telephoned her from Belize, he hadn't sounded so very different, even though his Caribbean accent had been largely superseded by an American one. When he had asked her if she wanted to meet, it could have been the Carter of long ago speaking to her.

Nicole's thoughts were interrupted by the sound of Carter's voice at the bar. Her heart missed a beat and she got up from her chair.

"I'm supposed to be meeting someone here at twelve o'clock," he said to the barman, "Her name is Nicole Darrington."

By this time, Nicole had reached the bar.

"Would this be the lady?" asked the barman, indicating to Carter that there was someone standing behind him.

Carter swung round to face Nicole and his lined face broke into a wide smile, his white teeth gleaming the welcome she had hoped for.

"Nikki!" He just said her name, the shortened version he had always used when they had been together, and wrapped her in his long arms. Her knees buckled and she hung there. After a few moments, she regained her feet and Carter let go of her. He stood back a pace, the better to look at her, before speaking.

"Sorry!" he said. "It's just *so* good to see you."

"You too," said Nicole, and she meant it. Seeing him, holding him, hearing him were everything she had expected, and more. She was beaming too and just a little flushed.

"Have you got a drink?" asked Carter.

"Yes, it's over there."

"Then let's sit down. We've got a lot to catch up on." Carter asked the barman to bring him a Budweiser and followed Nicole to the table where she had been waiting for him.

"It's been a long time, Nikki, too long."

"I know. I didn't think I'd ever see you again."

The silence was tangible as they both looked at each other. Awkwardly, Carter broke the silence.

"I was sorry to hear about Andrew, even if he did steal you away from me all those years ago." Carter smiled briefly and then looked at Nicole, pity in his eyes, as he continued, “But the news about Rob... well...”

Nicole’s face darkened and she looked down at her hands which were resting in her lap. Carter looked at her and his heart went out to her.

“What can I say,” he said, “You must be devastated?” Nicole nodded and looked away, tears in her eyes. Then, after a few moments, she looked back at Carter. She managed a smile but it was a thin smile.

The barman brought Carter’s drink to the table and disappeared quickly. As Carter lifted his glass and drank from it, Nicole took a deep breath and looked at him, the smile was gone and there were tears in her eyes as she spoke.

“He was a wonderful boy, you know.”

“How could he have been anything else. He had a wonderful mother.”

Nicole pulled a photograph of her children from her handbag and passed it to Carter. “That’s a picture of him, with Eloise, his sister.”

“She takes after her mother, too. She’s beautiful.”

Carter handed back the picture and Nicole replaced it carefully in her handbag. Then she took out a handkerchief and wiped her eyes.

“I’m sorry,” she said, shaking her head sadly.

“It’s OK, don’t worry,” soothed Carter as Nicole dabbed at her eyes again with the handkerchief.

She sniffed and smiled as she looked at him. “So what brings you to England, then?” she asked, changing the subject.

“Two things. One reason I’m here is to promote my book...” Nicole’s eyes widened and her mouth dropped open as she interrupted him.

“Your book!” she said, “Since when did you become a writer? I always had to help you with your essays. Your English was appalling! Even worse than mine!"

"I know," smiled Carter recalling the days when his command of English had lacked the sophistication demanded by Oxford professors, "It started after I quit track."

"I always followed your running career, you know. Right up until you announced your retirement. I was so proud of you when you won the gold in Barcelona. But I didn't know you'd taken to writing books." Nicole lifted her glass to her mouth and waited for Carter to respond.

"No reason why you should," he said, "Apart from a couple of academic tomes of interest only to hardened geologists, the only thing I've written before this, my first novel, is my autobiography."

Nicole spluttered into her drink and an involuntary laugh escaped from her mouth. "You're kidding!" she exclaimed.

"Hey! They made me do it! OK," protested Carter, "But it didn't sell too well, not here or in the States."

Nicole looked at Carter, who smiled at her. She thought for a moment and then picked up her glass. As she drank from the glass, she looked at Carter over the top of it. Then she put the glass down and dropped her eyes as she spoke.

"Am I in it?" she asked, her voice now quiet, almost casual in tone.

"Should you be?" responded Carter non-committally, playing along.

Nicole shrugged and picked up her glass again. She was trying hard not to appear too interested, one way or the other, and Carter grinned.

"Well, you can find out for yourself," he said. "I brought you a copy."

Carter reached into his bag and pulled out a hard backed book with a picture of him running on the dust cover. He handed the book to Nicole. She took it from him and lovingly passed her hand over the picture of Carter.

"Look inside, I've signed it for you," he said.

Nicole opened the book and turned to the first page. Her eyes filled with tears as she read what was there. She looked up at him and shook her head slowly.

"Oh, Carter," she said as the tears ran freely down her cheeks.

Inside the book, Carter had signed 'With all my love for ever, Carter' but it wasn't this inscription which had caught her so off guard, it was the printed dedication which simply read:

FOR NIKKI

THE ONLY GIRL I EVER LOVED

"What does your wife think of that?" she asked when she had regained her composure, "Must have shaken her a bit."

"I'm not married, Nikki," he said, "Never have been. How could I be? The only girl I ever wanted to marry went and married someone else." Nicole looked away as the tears returned. She wiped her eyes quickly with her hand and turned back to Carter.

"Carter, I can't have lunch with you now, not after this," she said, looking at him and shaking her head gently. "It would be too… difficult."

Nicole got up from her chair to leave but Carter reached out and gripped her hand.

"I understand," he said. "Truly, I do! But please, you must stay. There's more."

Nicole resisted for a moment and then sat down again. "What? What more can there be?"

"Nikki," Carter looked at her uneasily. "You remember I said I had two reasons for being here?"

“Yes,” replied Nicole as Carter looked at her, wondering how to bring up the second reason for his trip without destroying her. He would have preferred not to talk about it but he didn’t see how he could avoid it. He decided to press on.

“Well,” he said, ”I think the second reason may have something to do with Rob’s death.”

Nicole sat stonily, too shocked to speak, but when Carter didn’t continue, she forced herself to say something. “Go on,” she croaked and Carter’s eyes began to fill with tears. He fought the tears back, cleared his throat and continued.

“Apart from writing,” he began, “There’s something else I do. I work as an investigator for an organisation called The New York Federation of International Diamond Traders. As you might guess they’re involved in the diamond business.”

Carter leaned forward and put his hands on the table. He looked at Nicole, hoping that what he had to say would not put a brick wall between them. She leaned a little further back in her chair, not really wanting to hear what Carter had to say.

“A few weeks ago,” he continued, “some very good synthetic diamonds were found in a consignment of natural stones and last week I was brought in to find out how they got there. So far, all we know is that they came from a dealer who bought them from a cutting house in France. And, according to their records, the whole batch came from a mine in Guinea.”

“But they couldn’t have, could they?” said Nicole, beginning to recover from the shock of what Carter had said.

“No, they couldn’t. About ten percent of the batch had never seen the inside of a diamond mine.”

Nicole's throat was dry, raspingly dry. She took a drink from her glass. "But what's all that got to do with me, Carter?" she asked, "Or with Rob?"

Carter steeled himself to speak, knowing that he was about to drop a bombshell. "The mine in Guinea, Nikki, belongs to your father, to Philippe Lacoste."

Nicole could feel waves of nausea coming over her but they were repelled by her anger at what Carter had inferred. She looked at him as if he had gone stark raving mad and there was undisguised aggression in her voice.

"Are you, for one moment, suggesting that my father is involved in something illegal?"

"It *is* his mine, Nikki. There's no doubt about that."

"Even if he is involved with something he shouldn't be, which I don't believe he is for a moment, why would that involve Rob? You surely can't think Rob had anything to do with it?"

"No. Not knowingly, anyway. But he may have been drawn into it by accident. Maybe, somehow, he inadvertently stumbled onto something. Maybe he saw something or overheard something. A successful operation like this can net millions of dollars before it gets closed down. That's big bucks. Big enough for the people involved to be willing to do pretty much anything to protect it. Even kill if they think it's necessary."

Nicole gave Carter a searching look. He seemed sincere. What reason could he have to lie? Nevertheless, she moved into defensive mode. If what Carter was saying was right, then her father was implicated in her son's murder and that was unthinkable.

"My father has always had lots of business interests," she said, "I'm sure he knows nothing about these diamonds of yours. He probably doesn't even realise he's got a diamond mine."

"Whether he does or not, the fact remains that's where the stones appear to have come from."

Nicole looked away in disgust. She shook her head and stared out of the window, thinking. Then she turned back from the window and gave Carter a searching look.

"What do you want from me, Carter?" she asked, "You drop in out of nowhere after twenty-five years and tell me my father is responsible for my son's death." Nicole looked away from Carter.

"No! No, I'm not saying that. Just that there may be a link," corrected Carter, "And while you might not want to hear any of this, you might want to find out who killed Rob. And why." Carter and Nicole stared at each other before Carter broke the stare and looked away as he spoke, "And you might be able to help me to do that."

"But I don't know anything about any of it," pleaded Nicole, her anger now replaced by a feeling of impotence.

"Maybe not," said Carter, trying to soothe her, "And I know you probably hate me right now, but…"

Nicole interrupted Carter, raising her hand as she did. "I don't hate you Carter," she said, "You're not responsible for what's happened, I know that. But I don't believe my father is either. And I really don't see how I can help."

"Maybe you can't but can I just ask you, have you noticed anything unusual or strange in the last few weeks? Maybe something you couldn't explain?

Nicole considered the question before responding. "No, nothing," she said, shaking her head. "Except… No, no that couldn't possibly be anything to do with it."

Chapter 5

While Carter was getting reacquainted with Nicole in Yorkshire, back in Port Grimaud, Philippe was holding a business meeting in his living room. Apart from Gilles, there were three other people there, all boat owners who had complaints about how Gilles was running Philippe's charter agency. When, eventually, the meeting ended and the boat owners left, Philippe went to the drinks cabinet and poured himself a cognac. He indicated to Gilles to help himself to a drink and walked across the room to the French window. He stared out towards the Capitainerie, deep in thought, and when he spoke, he did so without turning to face Gilles.

"Are you sure he was the one who killed Rob?" he asked.

"It was him," responded Gilles.

"Then justice has been done." Philippe turned away from the window and looked at Gilles. "But nothing can make up for what he did. Rob was my only grandson."

As Philippe was speaking, his phone rang. He walked over to it and answered it. At the other end of the line was Nicole.

Having returned home from Carter's hotel, Nicole had been uncertain what she should do but it had not been long before she had come to a decision and had picked up the telephone to ring her father. After they had exchanged pleasantries, her voice took on a challenging tone.

"Papa, I've just been speaking to Carter Jefferson; you remember him, don't you?"

"Yes," responded Philippe hesitantly.

Gilles was now sitting in an armchair watching Philippe and he detected some unease on Philippe's part.

"He says you're involved in something illegal, something to do with diamonds," said Nicole.

"I have no idea what you're talking about," responded Philippe, trying to deflect his daughter's interrogation.

"Really?" Nicole left Philippe in no doubt that she did not believe him. "What have you got yourself involved with Papa?"

Philippe decided to try a different tack. "Nicole, he has never forgiven me for opposing your relationship with him, you know that. That's why he is making such a stupid allegation."

Nicole took a deep breath before she spoke.

"So you're not then?" she challenged.

"Not what?"

"Smuggling diamonds."

"No, Cherie, I am not."

"OK. Bye Papa."

"Au revoir Cherie."

Gilles looked at Philippe, a little apprehension apparent as Philippe ended the call and sighed.

"Problem?" asked Gilles.

"Maybe," shrugged Philippe.

A few days after his twenty-first birthday, Jacques, with an envelope in his hand, approached a boat which was moored stern on at the Capitainerie. It was the

Fleur de Grimaud, the sixty-five foot Johnson motor yacht in the saloon of which, only a couple of weeks earlier, Philippe had been sitting with his laptop open in front of him. As Jacques approached the boat, he looked at the stern. Across it, newly painted, was the boat's new name, Esprit de Jacques.

As Jacques looked adoringly at the boat, a man dressed in a suit came to the stern. This was André, the manager of the yacht brokerage in Sainte Maxime, a few miles up the coast towards Nice from Port Grimaud. André addressed Jacques from above.

"Bonjour Jacques," he said, "Venez à bord."

Jacques crossed the gangway and dropped onto the rear deck of the yacht, close to the man, and they shook hands. With a sweep of his hand, André indicated the new name on the boat.

"Comme vous voyez, elle a été rebaptisée conformément à vos instructions," he said.

Jacques nodded and smiled briefly as André continued. "Vous avez la traite bancaire?"

Jacques nodded again. "Oui, certainement," he said and reached out the hand which was holding the envelope.

André took the envelope from Jacques and opened it. He extracted the bank draft that was inside and nodded before returning the draft to the envelope and looking at Jacques.

"Bon, le bateau est le vôtre," he said as he handed Jacques the keys for the boat. They shook hands again before André left the boat. Jacques watched him go, a broad smile covering his face.

After he had watched André disappear along the Rue Grande, Jacques went to the sliding glass doors which led to the saloon of the boat. He inserted one of the keys in the lock, turned it and the catch sprang back releasing the door. With a gentle push, the door swished aside. Jacques hesitated for a moment before going in and looking round the saloon, taking in the sumptuous detail of this, *his* boat.

Tinted windows on all sides gave a clear view of everything outside and on the right of the glass doors through which Jacques had entered, there was a small low coffee table of polished maple inlaid with a band of mahogany. This was bounded on three sides by comfortable, continuous seating upholstered in cream with narrow blue stripes and blue piping. To the inboard side of the table, there were two matching low stools and the floor was covered with a thick pile, dark blue fitted carpet.

To the left, a circular staircase led to the master cabin beneath the aft deck. Forward of the circular staircase, a range of floor cupboards, in the same restful pale colour of polished maple ran along the side as far as the two broad steps which led up from the saloon to the galley, dining area and helm station. On top of the cupboards, at the far end, near the steps, were a television set and a music centre and above them, a shelf for books.

Beyond the saloon, up the steps, the dining area on the left was similarly fitted out. The same striped upholstery and maple joinery complemented each other perfectly. To the right of the dining area, the compact, but well designed, galley was separated from the helm station in front of it by a worktop and in front of the Captain's seat, the helm station bristled with electronic equipment. Switches and gauges crowded into a panel of polished walnut. To the left of the helm station, a flight of steps led down to the forward cabins and on the other side of the steps there was a chart table where navigation maps could be laid out and courses plotted.

Jacques walked slowly across the saloon and then vaulted the two steps which separated the saloon from the dining area. Then he went over to the helm station and lovingly ran his hand over the shining chrome wheel before noticing that propped up behind the wheel, in front of the instrument panel, was an envelope. He opened the envelope and pulled out the contents. It contained the ownership document for the motor yacht Esprit de Jacques made out in the name of Jacques Armand. It was at this point that the reality of his situation really struck home and in an uncontrollable fit of delight, he slapped the sheet of paper to his lips and kissed it. At last he had the boat he had only ever been able to dream of owning. His mind filled with the opportunities and possibilities that opened up before him. Deep in thought, he replaced the document in the envelope and carefully put it into the pocket of his shorts.

With the ownership document safely stowed in his shorts, Jacques turned and went back down the two steps into the saloon. There he saw that the previous owner had left several items on board including a collection of audio CDs next to the music centre and some books on the bookshelf. He looked through the CDs and then briefly at the books. They were mostly modern French paperback novels together with one or two coffee table books about the South of France.

Still revelling in his good fortune, Jacques decided to explore the rest of his boat. He had been round it before, when he had decided to buy it, but now he wanted to explore it again, this time on his own.

Below the forward deck at the front of the boat, reached by the steps between the helm station and the chart table, was the stateroom. Like the saloon, it too was luxuriously fitted out in polished maple with a double bed and en-suite facilities. Either side of the steps from the saloon, more steps leading down in the opposite direction, took Jacques from the stateroom to two further cabins. Each of these had two bunk beds and Jacques wandered round the cabins in a daze, hardly able to take in that it all belonged to him.

Finally, before leaving, he looked round the master cabin, which was beneath the rear deck and which was reached by the circular staircase from the saloon. If he was amazed by the luxury of the stateroom, the master cabin took his breath away. It had its own carpeted lobby with a small door leading to the engine room. A larger door led to the cabin itself. Inside the spacious cabin, there was a large double bed, with a mirrored wall behind. As well as the bed, on one side of the cabin there was a comfortable sofa and, on the other, a range of floor cupboards and drawers incorporating a dressing table, a television and a DVD player. Set into the sound-proofed bulkhead between the cabin and the lobby was a full run of wardrobes and beside the sofa, a door led to the en-suite shower and toilet.

Jacques was still in a daze as he climbed back up the steps to the saloon and walked out onto the rear deck. He was careful to lock the glass doors behind him before climbing the steps to the fly bridge above the saloon. There, he found another helm station, shrouded in a thick white cover to protect it from the elements. There was more seating on the fly bridge, just as comfortable as that in the saloon but made of weather-proof materials.

Deep in thought, Jacques returned to the quayside. He turned towards the Esprit de Jacques and lovingly surveyed the boat for a few more seconds before walking off across the tarmac of the helipad and away from the Capitainerie. As he passed by the hotel, he thought he saw an old man watching him through an open window but he couldn't be sure and by the time he was close enough to have been able to make out the man's features, he had turned away from the window and disappeared.

Outside his hotel in York, Carter was waiting on the steps at the entrance to the hotel. He looked at his watch; she was late but only by a few minutes. When he had invited Nicole to have dinner with him, he had hoped that she would accept the invitation and she had. She hadn't even hesitated when Carter had posed the question and he had been confident that he had done the right thing. But now, as he waited for her, he was worried that she might have changed her mind. There was so much history between them that maybe she had decided not to contemplate renewing their relationship. After all, it had been twenty-five years since they had last seen each other. But Carter hadn't quite been able to let her go and for a few years after they had parted, he had kept up with her news through mutual friends. With time, however, even that had died out and the last he had heard of her had been nineteen years before when Rob had been born.

As he heard the sound of a car approaching, he looked excitedly to his left and saw Nicole's car drive through the hotel gates. A broad smile covered his face as he watched her park the car and walk towards him.

"Thanks for coming," he said as she came up the steps. "I wasn't sure you would."

"None of this is your fault, Carter. And, believe it or not, I still have feelings for you," she confided as they embraced and kissed. Then Carter took her hand in his and led her into the hotel and through to their table in the dining room.

After they had ordered their food, Carter and Nicole, who were sitting opposite each other at the small table, looked into each other's eyes. Neither of them spoke for several moments and it was Nicole who broke the stare first as she reached down to her handbag to retrieve an envelope from it. She handed the envelope to Carter.

"I don't know if it's got anything to do with your case," she began, "but I found this in Rob's room. It's a printout of a very strange email he received a few days before he died. I think he was trying to decipher it."

Carter took the envelope and opened it, removing the sheet of paper which was inside. As he scanned what was on the sheet, he nodded a couple of times. Then he put the paper back in the envelope and put the envelope into his pocket. Reaching out, he put his hand on Nicole's, affectionately, as he spoke.

"Thank you," he said.

"Is it important?" asked Nicole.

"I don't know. It might be."

Nicole smiled as the waiter returned with their food and Carter, slightly embarrassed, withdrew his hand from hers.

Chapter 6

As Jacques lay awake in bed, he could hear outside his bedroom window the early stirrings of the stall holders in the Place du Marché. He still found it hard to believe that his long-held dream, his fantasy, had actually become a reality, that he had become the proud owner of a luxury motor yacht. But he realised that with the boat came many responsibilities. For one thing, maintaining and running a boat of that size would not be cheap. With her fifteen foot beam, the Esprit was far too big to moor in the canal by the apartment. The berth at the Capitainerie alone would cost him around two thousand euros a month. And then there would be insurance premiums, repairs, fuel. His head was spinning with all the things that were going to cost him money.

Buying the boat had taken most of the money he had received from his father and the more Jacques thought about it, the more he realised that he would have to put into practice what he had always told Yvonne; he would have to make the boat earn its keep. More than that, it would have to earn his keep too. His mind eased a little as he worked out in his head that it would not take too many charters to cover the costs and he relaxed, resolving to go that morning to see Gilles at the charter agency in the Place des Artisans. Gilles would be able to advise him.

An hour or so later, Jacques walked into Gilles' office. He was slightly nervous but confident that he would soon have the solution to the problem of how to pay for the maintenance and running of the Esprit de Jacques.

The charter agency's small office was wedged between the tower which kept vigil over the main entrance to the town and a restaurant. Inside there were two desks, at one of which Gilles was sitting going through the papers in front of him and occasionally signing his name. To the right of Gilles, a young man sat at another desk. He was Gilles' assistant and it was he who looked after the agency when Gilles was not there. Between and slightly behind the two desks a flight of stairs led to another office on the floor above. In the window facing onto the Place, there was a large display board covered with photographs and details of boats which the agency had available for charter. Above the centre of the room, a large fan rotated lazily, helping the warm air to circulate.

Gilles looked up from his paperwork as Jacques approached him tentatively.

"Bonjour, Jacques. What can I do for you?" he asked.

Jacques sat on one of the two chairs in front of the desk. "I'm looking for a bit of advice," he said.

"Advice? Advice about what?" asked Gilles as he adjusted his large frame, muscular from regular weight training at the gym in Sainte Maxime.

"About chartering a boat, of course. What else?"

"OK, Jacques. What did you have in mind? An inflatable? A rigid?"

"No, no, you don't understand. I don't want to hire a boat. I want you to arrange for my boat to be chartered."

"You want me to arrange charters for *your* boat." Gilles looked up at the fan as it made a leisurely rotation. "Jacques, it is usual for a person to own a boat before he hires it out. Correct me if I'm wrong, but you haven't got a boat, have you?"

"Yes. Yes, I have. I bought it a few days ago."

"OK, Jacques, so you have a little boat, good. The smallest size we deal with is five metres. How big is yours?"

"It's..." Jacques knew Gilles wasn't going to believe him, "It's a twenty metre Johnson with twin Detroit nine hundred diesels," he blurted out.

Jacques watched apprehensively as Gilles coloured with anger and rose from his chair. He rested his hands on the desk and leaned towards Jacques.

"All right, Jacques, you've had your little joke," he said threateningly. "Now push off back to your petrol pumps and leave me to get on with my work."

"But..." protested Jacques, rising from his seat and backing away slightly. Gilles was a big man and although Jacques was hardly a six stone weakling himself, he had always found Gilles intimidating and never more so than at that moment.

"OUT!" shouted Gilles coming round from his desk and manhandling Jacques out of the office. "And don't come back here wasting my time again!"

Outside the office, Jacques found himself in the midst of a throng of tourists. He wanted to make himself invisible; his face was stinging red with embarrassment and the people in the square were staring at him, some with pitying smiles on their faces, some tut-tutting and shaking their heads sagely. He wanted to shout at them, to tell them that it was true, that he did have a boat and that Gilles was wrong to throw him out. Instead, he shook his fist impotently at Gilles and walked off.

When Jacques got back to the apartment, his neck and ears were still warm from the humiliating experience. He recounted to his mother what had happened.

"Why didn't you show him the ownership document," she said. "It proves the boat is yours."

Jacques slapped his forehead. "Idiot!" he said to himself, "Why didn't I think of that." He swept into his room and hunted for the shorts he had been wearing the day he had got the boat. They weren't where he had left them.

"Have you seen my blue shorts?" he called.

"I washed them this morning. They're drying on the balcony in my room," said Claudine.

A look of consternation came over Jacques' face. What if she had washed them with the document still in the pocket? It might be ruined. Then he would never be able to prove anything to Gilles. He edged into the living room, hardly daring to ask the question. "Did you check the pockets first?"

"Of course I did! I always check your pockets. Never know what I might find." Claudine glanced up from her ironing and smiled. "There was an envelope. I put it over there, by the coffee pot."

Jacques stopped holding his breath and exhaled a long, relieved sigh. He retrieved the envelope and checked inside to make sure the document was there. Clutching the envelope, he kissed his mother and dashed out of the apartment.

As Jacques re-entered the charter office, Gilles stood up behind his desk and a look of barely restrained rage spread across his face.

"Jacques, I warned you…" he said through clenched teeth as he came round in front of his desk to confront Jacques.

He reached out to take hold of Jacques but Jacques, made bold by the document in his possession, held up his hands to fend him off.

"Hold it! *Hold it*!" he said, as Gilles knocked his arms out of the way and moved closer.

"Why? Why shouldn't I throw you out again you mangy little rat?"

Monique, Gilles' tiny secretary, had come down the stairs from her office on the next floor and was watching open mouthed, as was Gilles' assistant, who was still sitting at his desk.

"Because I really do own a boat. *Look*!" Jacques held out the envelope, inviting Gilles to take it and examine the contents.

Still poised to carry through his action, Gilles took the envelope from Jacques and extracted the legal form inside it. As he read the document, he moved back behind his desk and flopped into his chair. The hand holding the document fell onto his desk and he looked up at Jacques. Jacques detected a different demeanour now, not exactly respectful but not hostile either.

"What can I say?" said Gilles, the businessman side of his personality now in control, "I'm sorry. I just never saw you as a boat owner."

Jacques grinned cockily. "You believe me now, then?"

"I do. Sit down, please. Monique!" Gilles looked towards the stairs and saw Monique standing there, "Two coffees. And I think I could do with a Cognac as well. This has been a bit of a shock. What about you, Jacques?" Jacques nodded enthusiastically and Monique scuttled back up the stairs.

Half an hour later, Gilles was examining the Esprit from top to bottom as Jacques followed him round keeping close watch. At one point Jacques noticed him touch one of the books on the bookshelf and glance across at him. The inspection over, Gilles turned to Jacques on the quayside.

"A magnificent boat, Jacques," he said, "How did you come by it?"

"I received some money from my father on my birthday," answered Jacques, "Enough to buy the boat."

Gilles eyebrows raced to the top of his forehead. "Jacques, I have to tell you that I know this boat, I've been on it many times. It belongs to Philippe Lacoste. I arrange a lot of charters for Monsieur Lacoste and I have bookings in hand for this boat. He hasn't told me that he has sold the boat."

"That may be so but I have bought it. It's mine now. You've seen the papers."

Gilles had to admit that this was true and the two of them returned to his office to sign the agency agreement. As Jacques was leaving, Gilles called up the stairs behind him.

"Monique," he said, "Get Philippe Lacoste on the line for me."

Jacques paused and smiled to himself and thought, he still doesn't believe me!

Later that day, the sun shone brightly on the boats moored at the Capitainerie as two men dressed in white tee-shirts and trousers carried cardboard boxes of supplies from a nearby Citroen van onto one of the yachts. This was the Hedonist, the boat that Philippe would use for his own purposes now that the Fleur de Grimaud belonged to Jacques. Philippe watched the proceedings with a critical eye as Gilles approached from the direction of the Rue Grande.

"Philippe," said Gilles tentatively as he reached Philippe's side, "It seems that Jacques Armand has acquired the Fleur de Grimaud. Only now he's calling her the Esprit de Jacques." Gilles raised his eyes heavenward before continuing. "I didn't know you had sold the Fleur."

Suddenly, Philippe's attention was distracted. Unable to believe what he had seen, he marched towards the stern of the Hedonist where one of the men had just dropped a crate of champagne onto the rear deck.

"Not there, idiot!" shouted Philippe, "Stow it below, out of the sun."

The man froze when he heard Philippe's voice. Slowly, he turned to face Philippe and stood, almost at attention. He nodded his head to Philippe as he spoke.

"Oui, Monsieur Lacoste. Pardon."

Philippe continued to watch as the man picked up the crate and disappeared into the boat with it. Philippe turned on his heel and returned to Gilles.

"You were saying?" snapped Philippe.

Just as Jacques was intimidated by Gilles, Gilles was intimidated by Philippe. There was no physical threat from Philippe but the man carried himself in an imperious manner born of his considerable wealth and many years of running his businesses with an iron hand. It had never occurred to him to clothe it in a velvet glove and even if it had, he probably wouldn't have bothered.

Gilles, now even more tentative than before, continued, "The Fleur de Grimaud, Philippe. Jacques is the new owner. I knew she was for sale but I didn't know you had sold her."

Philippe looked away from the two men who had been engaging his attention and focused on Gilles. "Yes, I agreed the sale while you were in Paris. I was going to tell you when you got back but I forgot. What of it?" Philippe returned his gaze to the men loading the boat.

"Well, it's nothing really. Just that he came to see me to tell me he wants to hire her out on charter."

"Well what's wrong with that?" asked Philippe, not looking at Gilles as he spoke.

"Nothing. I've already given him the Baines charter. As you are now using the Hedonist instead of the Fleur, I had planned to switch the boats for that job anyway."

"Good."

Philippe started walking away from the Capitainerie, satisfied that his employees would not transgress again, and Gilles followed him, looking distinctly uncomfortable.

Philippe noticed Gilles at his shoulder and sensed that Gilles had more to say. Becoming a little exasperated, he stopped and turned to face him.

"Was there something else?"

Gilles nodded nervously. "Philippe, you know I always inspect boats before taking them on to my books."

"Of course."

"Well, I inspected Jacques' boat, and…"

Gilles hesitated for a few seconds and Philippe became impatient and irritated by Gilles' reluctance to speak his mind.

"What? What is it? What is it that's worrying you?"

"The book was still there! On the shelf!"

The two men stared at each other, Gilles unsure what to expect from Philippe and Philippe, for once, lost for words.

Carter sat at the desk in his hotel bedroom poring over the printout of Rob's email which Nicole had given him. His mind wasn't really on the strange message; he wanted to be with her. After twenty-five years of pining for her, the possibility of finally getting back together with her again was not something he could easily put to the back of his mind but he was trying to concentrate.

As he stared at the printout, Carter wondered if it would be possible to track down the sender of the email. He thought it surely must be possible but he wasn't certain about it. What he was certain about was that if he could identify the owner of the email address, he would be able to determine whether or not the message was in any way relevant to his case or just an annoying distraction. He decided to speak to Conrad about it. Conrad was much more interested in computers and technical things than he was; Conrad would know the answer. He picked up his phone, found Conrad in his contact list and pressed the button to call him.

"Carter! Hi!" said Conrad as he answered the call. "What's up?"

"Hi Conrad, I'd like to pick your brains about something."

"Good luck!" joked Conrad.

"I've been given a printout of an email that might have something to do with our case and I'd like to find out who sent it. What are the chances of doing that?"

"I guess it's not clear from the email address it came from who sent it or you wouldn't be calling me?"

"The email address it appears to be from is: ljsherwood@hotmail.com. It was sent to Rob Darrington a few days before he was killed but his mother says he didn't know who this L J Sherwood character was. She says he told her that he didn't know anyone with that name."

"There are ways to track the owner of an email address if it's been used to access services or buy something on the Internet but that would mean it's a genuine email account."

"And if it's not?"

"Well, if it's not, if it's someone using a false name and trying to hide his identity, then all the account holder details at Hotmail are going to be false too."

"Not much chance then if that's what we've got here?"

"Well, it's not quite as black and white as that. If you have access to the computer that received the email then it should be possible to find out the IP address of the sender from the full message header. That would identify the computer that the message came from and all the other computers involved along the way. That should at least get you to the country of origin of the message although probably not much further than that. To find out more, you would need a court order requiring Hotmail to give you any information they have about the source computer but even that probably still wouldn't get you any closer to the real identity of the sender."

"OK, so basically, if it's a fake email account, even if I could get the IP address, which I can't because Rob's iPad was stolen when he was killed, I probably wouldn't be able to find out who it came from?"

"That's about the size of it. But I'll check out that email address for you and see if anything comes up."

"Thanks Conrad. See you in a few days."

Carter pressed the button to end the call; he was no further forward. He looked out of the window as he mulled over what he had learned from Conrad. He decided to use the hotel's business unit to scan the printout of Rob's email and send it to John at the FIDT; maybe John could get it deciphered and then he would know if it was of any importance.

Having flown from Moscow to Nice via Paris a couple of days earlier, Eloise had spent the day working with the staff of the Hotel du Promenade in Sainte Maxime, getting the conference suite ready for the gathering of salesmen and customers who would arrive the following day. Apart from a four hour break in the afternoon, when everyone had suddenly disappeared and during which she had gone for a stroll along the sea-front and sunbathed on the beach, the whole day had passed with her directing and advising various workmen in the windowless conference rooms.

Despite the hotel having hosted the event for the past four years, there was still a great deal upon which they required decisions: where to put the lecterns; how to set out the tables and chairs; where to put the advertising banners; how to arrange the exhibition spaces; testing and adjusting the sound and lighting systems, and so on. It had seemed to Eloise that they would never be ready but then, as the French working day drew to a close at seven o'clock, miraculously it had all seemed to come together. After a final check round the empty rooms, she had sat in the bar waiting for Jeremy and Anna to arrive. They had decided to spend a couple of days in Paris while Eloise went on to Sainte Maxime to oversee the preparations for the conference.

An hour later, she had given up and dined alone in the restaurant before returning to her room. She knew that Jeremy and Anna were due to arrive at some point during the afternoon but she had no details of exactly when. She had been expecting them to walk in at any moment and was surprised that they had still not appeared; she was in the shower when the phone rang in her room. She turned the shower off and quickly wrapped a voluminous soft white towel round her wet body before going to answer it.

"Hello? Is that you Eloise? It's Jeremy here."

"Hi, Jeremy. Have you just arrived? I was expecting you earlier."

"Our plane was delayed leaving Paris for four hours because of a bomb warning. But we're here now. Is everything ready for tomorrow?"

"Yes, it's all done," said Eloise confidently, "Do you want to have a look round this evening, just to make sure?"

"Yes, that would probably be a good idea," said Jeremy before adding quickly, "Not that I don't have every confidence in you."

Eloise smiled to herself. "I've just had a shower and I'm dripping all over the floor. It'll take me a few minutes to dry myself and get dressed. How about meeting in the bar in, say, twenty minutes?"

"Fine. See you then."

Twenty minutes later, Eloise was sitting in the bar at a table near the windows gazing out at the brightly lit promenade where courting couples wandered along slowly beneath the line of palm trees. The street lights cast shadows under the trees and from time to time one of the couples would stop under a tree and the pair would turn to face each other before embracing and kissing. Beyond the promenade, she could see the sea glinting in the moonlight as it rippled in the soft evening breeze.

Eloise turned from the window when she heard Jeremy's voice and smiled as Jeremy and Anna approached and sat at the table with her.

"Hi," said Eloise, looking at Anna, "Jeremy said you had to wait for four hours for your flight. What a bore!"

"Oh, it wasn't too bad," said Anna, cheerfully, but she looked drawn and tired.

Jeremy was just finishing ordering drinks for himself and Anna when he noticed that Eloise's glass was empty. "Et la même chose pour la mademoiselle," he added in a hopelessly English accent.

"Oui, bien sûr," replied the waiter as he scribbled down the order on his pad and left.

Jeremy turned to Eloise. "Been enjoying the sun?" he asked, smiling at her.

"Yes, in the afternoons. As you know, they don't work here between twelve and four, so nothing can be done then. I think it's a great way of doing things. It means you can enjoy the beach and the sea every day if you want to. And what's the point of being in the South of France if you can't go to the beach and sunbathe?"

Eloise outlined to Jeremy the arrangements for the conference and, although she was satisfied with her work, she was anxious to ensure that nothing went wrong. When they had finished their drinks, she took both Jeremy and Anna through to the conference rooms and showed them everything. By the time they had finished, it was nearly eleven o'clock.

"How about a nightcap?" suggested Jeremy.

"Not for me thanks," said Eloise. "It's going to be a long day tomorrow so I think I should get some sleep. Goodnight." She waved her hand as she headed for the lifts.

Chapter 7

Two days after Jeremy and Anna had joined Eloise in Sainte Maxime, Jacques awoke on the morning of his first charter with feelings of excitement intermingled with apprehension. He hoped that all would go well and that he would get further business from his new and, for the moment, only client. Gilles had told him to have the boat tied up and ready in the harbour at Sainte Maxime by ten o'clock. There he would be met by Jeremy Baines who would want to inspect the boat and check all the arrangements before his guests boarded at ten-thirty. To achieve this, Jacques knew that he would have to leave Port Grimaud no later than nine forty five, and he still had to collect Yvonne and the buffet lunch which she had agreed to prepare for him.

"Jacques! Are you awake?" he heard his mother calling.

"Oui, Maman," he called back, "I'll be up in a minute."

Although Jacques fully intended to live on the Esprit, he had not yet taken the step of leaving home completely. Sometimes he slept on board and sometimes he stayed with his mother; she was always pleased to have him at home.

A few miles up the coast, in her bedroom at the hotel in Sainte Maxime, Eloise answered the early morning call she had booked and turned over to face the window. She rose from her bed, dressed only in the long tee-shirt which was her normal night attire, and drew back the curtains allowing the sun to burst into the room. It was a beautiful sunny day, as indeed every day had been since she had flown in to Nice airport. There was a knock at the door and she opened it to find a trolley bearing her breakfast waiting outside. She pulled it into the room and poured herself a glass of freshly squeezed orange juice before returning to the bed.

She recalled with satisfaction that the conference had gone well. A minor problem with one of the projectors had given her a few moments of panic but the hotel's technician had arrived almost as soon as she had put the phone down and the fault had been corrected in moments. Many of the delegates had taken the trouble to tell her how much they had enjoyed the day and, all in all, the event had been a success. There only remained the boat trip to Monte Carlo and her first major assignment for Baines Automotive would be over. There was another knock at the door.

"Un message pour mademoiselle," stammered the bell-boy as he thrust the silver salver bearing a small envelope under her nose.

The note was from Jeremy and thanked her for arranging the conference so well. She put the note on the table before stripping off her tee-shirt and going into the bathroom to shower.

At the same time that Eloise was enjoying a leisurely shower, Jacques drove from Port Grimaud to Sainte Pierre des Maures with his usual total disregard for his own safety and that of any other driver who happened to be on the road at the same time although, on this occasion, there was some justification for it. When he arrived, Yvonne answered his knock at the door of the gallery and greeted him with a kiss on the cheek, standing on the tips of her toes to reach him.

"Bonjour, Jacques."

"Is everything ready?" Jacques asked, following her up the stairs to the apartment above the gallery.

"But of course," she replied, "Didn't I say it would be? What's the time?"

Jacques looked at his watch. "Nine-thirty," he said. "We're going to be late."

"Then we'd better get going."

As they drove back to Port Grimaud, the rear seat of the car was piled high with that part of the buffet lunch which would not fit in the boot. Jacques again drove dangerously fast and Yvonne cursed him when he drove over a pot-hole in the road, forcing her to put her hand out behind her to steady the boxes containing the carefully prepared food.

When they reached the seaward entrance to Port Grimaud, Jacques waited impatiently for the guard to raise the barrier which prevents unauthorised cars from entering the narrow streets of the town. The sun was beating down on the car and he was hot and sticky; the back of his shirt was wet with sweat. As soon as the barrier was up, Jacques shot through the archway into the Place des Six Canons, along the Rue Grande past the hotel and across the helipad at the Capitainerie. He screeched to a halt behind the Esprit and leapt out to run onto the boat and open the sliding door. Then he helped Yvonne unload the buffet which was no longer quite so tidily laid out in the boxes. When they had finished, the Capitaine, who was the person responsible for the smooth running of the port, was standing beside the car.

"Vous ne pouvez pas le laisser ici, vous savez?" he barked at Jacques.

"Oui, oui, deux minutes!" shouted Jacques in response before calling over his shoulder, "Yvonne, Adolf says you must move the car."

Yvonne threw up her hands in despair, jumped into the little Peugeot and drove away from the boats, back along the Rue Grande, across the Place des Six Canons, and out through the archway.

Five minutes later she returned, having put the car in the car park and sprinted all the way back. She was holding her sandals in her hands as she ran and every now and then she hopped along on one foot as she brushed a sharp piece of grit from one of her feet. Jacques laughed loudly at her from the fly bridge of the Esprit. He had already started the boat's engines and raised the anchor and was ready to move off once Yvonne had untied the stern mooring warps. This she did as soon as she reached the Esprit, even though she was still puffing and panting from the run.

As the Esprit emerged from Port Grimaud into the bay, Yvonne climbed the steps and joined Jacques on the fly bridge.

Fifteen minutes later, when the Esprit arrived in the harbour at Sainte Maxime, Eloise, with Jeremy and Anna on either side of her, was waiting at the quayside. Although Jacques was only a few minutes late, Anna was tapping her foot impatiently as she watched the boat approach slowly and then turn away from them before dropping anchor and reversing into the berth. Yvonne, already quite accomplished in her duties as a member of the crew despite only having had a few days' practice, had dropped the boat's fenders over the sides and the stern and was standing with her bare feet braced apart waiting for the boat to come close to the quay. She looked very professional as she jumped down from the partially lowered gangway onto the quay dressed in her white shorts and a white tee-shirt with 'Esprit de Jacques' emblazoned across the front of it. Quickly, she wrapped the port side mooring warp twice round the nearest bollard and then, putting one of her feet on top of the bollard, she leaned back on the rope and pulled it in as the Esprit drew ever nearer to the quay. At the same time, Jacques put the engines into forward gear and revved them briefly to stop the backward motion of the boat. When the Esprit had stopped, Yvonne jumped back on board to fetch the starboard mooring warp and attached that to another bollard. Then she stood back and surveyed her handiwork. Jacques came down the steps from the fly bridge, lowered the gangway fully onto the quayside and strode across it to stand beside Yvonne in front of his clients.

"Bonjour, Monsieur Baines," he said holding out his hand to Jeremy, "I am Jacques Armand. The Esprit is my boat and I will be taking you to Monte Carlo today."

"Bonjour, Jacques," answered Jeremy, shaking his hand.

"You're late!" piped up Anna, "You were supposed to be here at ten o'clock and it's ten past now." She tapped the Cartier watch on her wrist with one of her long fingernails to emphasise the point and looked expectantly at Jacques.

"Oui, Madame," said Jacques, cocking his head on one side and looking her straight in the eye, "But we have plenty of time to be ready for your guests." Turning his attention to Jeremy, he said, "I would like to introduce Yvonne who will be looking after your guests during the voyage."

"Bonjour, Yvonne," said Jeremy politely before turning back to Jacques, "This is my wife Anna and this is Eloise, who is responsible for organising our conferences."

"Bonjour Madame," said Jacques coldly to Anna as he shook her perfectly manicured hand. Then he turned to Eloise whose honey blonde hair shone as it reflected the rays of the sun. He took her hand in his and bowed slightly before lifting it to his mouth and kissing it. "Bonjour, mademoiselle. I hope you will enjoy the day." He let go of her hand and stood back, unable to take his eyes off her.

Eloise smiled shyly. "I'm sure I will. And that our guests will too. Perhaps we can inspect the arrangements now?"

"But of course." Jacques swept his arm back directing Eloise and the others on board the Esprit just as the port manager arrived to collect his fee from Jacques.

A couple of minutes later, with the port manager paid, Jacques followed Yvonne back on board the boat and into the saloon. Eloise turned to Yvonne as she came in. "This is excellent!" she said, indicating the buffet Yvonne had prepared. "Much better than I had expected. Thank you."

Jacques heard and smiled at Eloise as he walked past her on his way to Jeremy who was looking out of the front window of the boat. Yvonne, who had spent two days preparing the food, relaxed and her face brightened at the compliment from Eloise.

"Merci," she responded, "I have tried to cater for all tastes and there should be enough for fourteen people. I was told there would be eleven guests plus the three of you. Is that correct?"

"Yes, that's right," said Eloise.

While Jacques was talking to Jeremy, he kept an eye on Eloise and noticed that she was also casting glances at him. Over Jeremy's shoulder, he tracked her with his eyes as she came over to join them at the helm station.

"Jacques, could I go through the programme for the day with you?" she said.

"Of course." Jacques smiled and indicated to Eloise that they should leave the saloon. "Let's go up to the fly bridge," he suggested as they came out onto the aft deck.

Sitting beside Eloise, on the luxuriously upholstered L-shaped bench seat at the back of the fly bridge, Jacques outlined the itinerary for the day to her. While he spoke, he examined her closely. He was trying not to be too obvious about this but it was clear that he found her very attractive.

"That all sounds great. I'm really looking forward to the day," said Eloise when he had finished. "Oh, one more thing, Jeremy has asked me to invite you and Yvonne to join us for dinner at our hotel afterwards, if you can?"

Jacques was surprised by the invitation but he hid it well. "Yes, I would like that very much," he said, "but Yvonne will not be able to come as she will have to return home to close the gallery."

"The gallery?"

"Yvonne runs a gallery in Sainte Pierre, where she lives. It's a little village up in the mountains. There is a woman, her cousin, who looks after the place when she's not there but she likes to close up herself and lock the day's takings away in the evening. But I will be able to accept your invitation."

"But..." Eloise paused and Jacques waited for her to go on, "doesn't Yvonne work for you? Isn't she your crew?"

Jacques laughed. "No, no. Yvonne is my sister. She doesn't work for me. She does this for me as a favour."

A flicker of excitement crossed Eloise's face as she spoke. "Oh, I see. I thought maybe she was your girlfriend."

Eloise smiled and gazed into Jacques' eyes as he gazed into hers. The narrowing space between their faces was alive with unspoken messages, ones they both understood perfectly.

The spell was broken by Jeremy's voice as he climbed the steps to the fly bridge. "What are you two doing all alone up here?" he said as his head appeared.

Jacques and Eloise pulled away from each other sharply and it was Eloise who spoke first, after clearing her throat.

"We've just been going through the plans for the day," she said, "Everything is fine. It's going to be a super day." Eloise and Jacques rose simultaneously from the seat.

"Good," said Jeremy, "Our guests should be arriving soon. Could you greet them for me as they come on board?"

"Yes, of course," replied Eloise.

Followed by Jacques, Eloise went down the steps to the aft deck where Yvonne and Anna were talking about the recipes for some of the canapés.

Before long the guests started to arrive and by a quarter to eleven the Esprit was under way, leaving the harbour of Sainte Maxime behind her. Although there had been nearly a hundred people at the conference the day before, only eleven carefully selected customers and potential customers had been invited on the boat trip. The eleven guests who now milled around on the aft deck were a disparate bunch ranging from a quite attractive and vivacious woman in her early thirties to a grossly overweight middle aged man who would spend most of the trip leering at both Yvonne and Eloise.

Once clear of the harbour, Jacques opened up the throttles and the Esprit began to plane over the sea at her full cruising speed. Several of the guests made their way up to the fly bridge to make the most of the view, while others remained on the aft deck and a few went into the saloon.

After two hours of cruising along the French coast and during which the guests and their hosts enjoyed Yvonne's sumptuous buffet and several bottles of good French wine, the Esprit de Jacques rounded a headland and Monte Carlo came into view. It was a beautiful sight with the palace high up on the promontory and boats of all shapes and sizes moored in the harbour. Behind the boats, skyscrapers rose up, silhouetted against the majestic dark form of the mountains.

With the assistance of Yvonne, Jacques moored the Esprit on the west side of the harbour, near the pink apartment blocks which line the road at that point. The little party would need to walk halfway round the harbour in order to reach the bars and cafés which overlook the boats and face out towards the harbour entrance.

As they ambled towards the cafés, following on behind their guests, Jacques and his three clients stopped at the first café they came to and sat at a table under a straw parasol. Jacques made sure that he sat next to Eloise, almost pushing Anna out of the way to achieve his objective.

When Jeremy had finished his first glass of wine, he summoned a passing waiter and was about to order another round when Jacques suddenly stood up.

"I think I might go for a walk round the town," he said, rising from his seat, "Does anyone want to come with me?"

Eloise rose from her seat quickly, almost too quickly. "Yes, I'd like to do that," she said and Jacques smiled as Jeremy and Anna looked on. "You two don't mind, do you, if Jacques and I leave you to it?"

Jeremy and Anna were not given the opportunity to object as Jacques and Eloise walked off quickly together. As they went, Anna waved them cheerily on their way and smiled knowingly at her husband.

Jacques and Eloise strolled towards the 'centre ville' and soon came to a quiet café, away from the main tourist areas. Jacques suggested they stop for a coffee and Eloise readily agreed. They found a table near the back and sat opposite each other. After the waiter had brought them their coffee, Jacques opened the conversation.

"So, tell me, why does a beautiful English girl like you have a French name?" he asked.

Eloise smiled a shy smile before responding. "Simple. My mother is French."

"No! Which part of France is she from?"

"You won't believe this," said Eloise, still smiling at him as she took a sip from her coffee. Jacques narrowed his eyes and stared intently at her as he waited for her to continue. "My mother grew up in Sainte Maxime. But her father, my grandfather, now lives in Port Grimaud."

Jacques was surprised at this revelation and he eyed Eloise carefully as he drank from his cup before responding. "So, who is he then, your grandfather? Maybe I know him."

"I expect you do. He's quite well known, a prominent citizen, you might say."

Jacques was intrigued. Leaning forward and putting his elbows on the table, he cupped his chin in his hands and raised an inquisitive eyebrow. Eloise sipped her coffee again and looked coquettishly over her cup at him, the expression on her face tantalising and teasing him.

"His name is Philippe Lacoste," she said eventually. "Have you heard of him?"

Jacques' face dropped. He sat back in his chair and rested his hands on the table in front of him as he spoke. "Of course. Everyone has heard of Monsieur Lacoste," he said a little disappointedly.

"Is that a problem for you?" she said quietly, her smile fading slightly as she noticed the change in his attitude but he soon recovered his good spirits.

"No!" he said emphatically, "Definitely not! Philippe Lacoste is just the richest and most powerful man in Port Grimaud. Why should that be a problem? I just need to be careful what I say to you, that's all." Jacques reached into his pocket and slapped some coins on the table before jumping up from his seat.

"Come on, little rich girl! Let me show you the sights of Monte Carlo."

He grabbed her hand and led her out of the café. She giggled as she followed him out into the street, almost falling as she caught her foot on the threshold and tripped.

As they walked along the street, Eloise squeezed Jacques' hand. He smiled and squeezed hers back as she turned her head towards him and looked at him admiringly.

"Your English is very good," she said. "Where did you learn to speak such good English?"

"I have lived all my life in a tourist resort which, in the summer, is full of Americans and English people. It just happened."

"Maybe. But I think you must have a special talent for languages as well."

Jacques let go of her hand and put his arm round her shoulders. She responded by putting her arm round his waist and leaning towards him, resting her head on his shoulder.

Half an hour later, they were still arm in arm as they approached Casino Square. Jacques looked at his watch and then turned to look at Eloise.

"We should be getting back," he said

Eloise looked at her watch. "Wow, is that the time!" she said, "We'll be late."

"Don't worry, nobody is going anywhere without me."

They both laughed at this and when they arrived back at the Esprit, everyone else was already on board. Jacques walked briskly along the quay, over the gangway and up the steps to the fly bridge to start the engines, leaving Eloise trailing along behind him. When the engines were running and the boat was ready to leave, Yvonne untied the mooring warps and ran back onto the boat with them, coiling them quickly and expertly.

An hour after leaving the harbour in Monte Carlo, the Esprit slowed and Jacques took her into the harbour at Cannes. This time it was Jacques' turn to mind the boat while Yvonne went ashore with Eloise.

Finally, with all the guests gathered back on board, Jacques took the Esprit back out to sea and sped along the coast at full speed for forty minutes before easing the throttles back as Sainte Maxime came into sight.

The Esprit continued slowly towards the harbour and once she was securely moored and the guests had left, Jacques saw Jeremy, Anna and Eloise off the boat. On the quay, he turned to Jeremy.

"I will meet you for dinner tonight at eight? Yes?"

Jeremy nodded and the two men shook hands before Jacques returned to the boat where he found Yvonne sitting in the saloon, relaxing. He threw up his arms and sat down beside her.

"Well, it's done. My first charter completed," he declared.

"And I think you have found yourself a girlfriend, maybe?"She looked at him knowingly but he just looked back at her non-committally, pretending not to know what she was talking about.

"Oh, come on! I saw the way you looked at her," she challenged and Jacques smiled and looked down at his hands.

"Yes, well, maybe," he said before looking up at Yvonne, a smile lighting up his face. "She has invited me to have dinner with them tonight."

As Carter parked his car in the car park of the North Yorkshire Police headquarters and walked towards the building, a police car drove past him and stopped in front of the entrance. Two policemen in uniform got out of the car and went into the building. Carter followed them in.

Carter was hoping that Harris would have some information to share with him and that he would be willing to do so. He was still convinced that there must be a connection between the two murders but he wanted some proof of it and that could only come from the police.

As Carter waited for Harris in the reception area, he smiled to himself. Meeting up with Nicole had been special. It had confirmed to him that what he had once felt for her was still there, that it had not faded with time. As he ruminated on the events of the last week during which he had seen Nicole on no fewer than five occasions, a policeman in uniform approached him. A few minutes later, he was sitting in Harris's office on the third floor of the building discussing the results from the forensic examination of the murder scene under the bridge.

"Did they come up with anything?" asked Carter, upon which Harris turned the open file in front of him round so that it was the right way up for Carter.

"Nothing that helps. See for yourself," he said as he pushed the file across the desk towards Carter. Carter started looking at the file, leafing through the papers as Harris continued. "There's a profile of the bullet of course but it doesn't match anything on our files."

"What about Interpol?" asked Carter, looking up from the file.

"We could try them I suppose but we don't have any reason to suspect foreign involvement, do we?"

Carter shrugged and returned to looking through the file. Then he spotted something and looked intently at it, his face moving a little closer to the file.

"It says here that there was some blood on his trousers," said Carter, looking up at Harris as he continued, "Not his own. Have you been able to identify whose it is?"

"Not yet."

"May I offer a suggestion?" The two men stared at each other for a few moments before Harris spoke, they both knew what Carter was saying.

"I'll arrange for a comparison of the samples," said Harris as he picked up the phone on his desk and pressed a button.

Later that day, Carter was standing at the entrance to his hotel as a taxi pulled up. Conrad, a man of medium height in his thirties, got out of the taxi and the two men approached each other. They shook hands vigorously before going into the hotel and making their way to the bar. When they had chosen a table, they ordered themselves a beer each.

The two men had worked together on several previous occasions and they had a healthy respect for each other although it was always understood that Carter was in charge. The cases they had worked on together for the FIDT had taken them all over the world, to places both exotic and drab, but they had always enjoyed the process of solving what were usually complex and interesting cases.

As Carter was filling Conrad in on the latest developments with the current case, his phone rang. He removed it from his pocket, pressed the receive call button and put it to his ear. He listened to what the caller was saying but said very little himself.

"Thanks for letting me know. Goodbye," said Carter as he ended the call. Deep in thought, he put his phone down on the table before looking at Conrad.

"That was Inspector Harris from the local police," he said. "The blood on Spicer's trousers was Rob's."

Carter looked into the distance for a few moments before speaking again. He had been convinced that there was a connection between the two murders and now he knew for sure.

"So, now we know who killed Rob," he said. "We just don't know why."

"And is it any of our business anyway?" Conrad shrugged questioningly as Carter turned his head to look at him.

"I can't pin it on anything concrete but my instinct is telling me that it is. There's a connection between the mine and Rob, that much we know. And my gut says that the timing of his death is more than just a coincidence."

"Then I guess we'd better follow through on it, hadn't we?" said Conrad. Carter smiled and raised his glass. "It's good to have you on board again," he said.

"Well someone's got to keep you out of trouble," shot back Conrad, whereupon they both looked at each other and laughed.

Chapter 8

As Jacques approached the hotel in Sainte Maxime where the Baines party were staying, he was full of anticipation. He was not dressed formally but he had made an effort to look good. He was wearing a smart pair of black jeans and, under a lightweight beige jacket, an open necked black shirt which allowed a few wisps of hair to show against the background of his brown chest. His thick dark hair was swept back and his green eyes shone out from his tanned face.

As he entered the hotel bar and scanned the room, he spotted Eloise sitting at a table near the window overlooking the promenade. He breathed deeply when he saw her. She too was dressed casually but smartly in a pale blue short sleeved blouse which stopped short of the top of her white skirt revealing an inch or two of bare tanned midriff. Around her neck was the only jewellery she was wearing, a simple gold necklace.

As Jacques watched, Eloise turned away from the window and saw him. She smiled as he walked briskly over to the table.

"Bonsoir, Eloise," he said, rather formally.

"Jacques," acknowledged Eloise as he settled into the seat opposite her and glanced at the two empty chairs either side of him.

"Where are the others?" he asked.

"I'm afraid they won't be coming. Jeremy is having to prepare for an unexpected meeting in Frankfurt tomorrow and Anna has decided to have dinner with an old friend. I hope you don't mind."

"No, no, of course not. I would gladly have paid them to stay away." They both laughed. "Especially that Anna! She is a hard woman."

"She's certainly a single minded one," responded Eloise. "She knows what she wants and she can usually find a way to get it. That's how she came to be Yorkshire Woman of the Year last year. Anyway, it seems a shame to waste a free dinner."

Later that evening, after a leisurely dinner during which they avoided probing too deeply into each other's personal lives and talked mainly about the trip to Monte Carlo, Jacques and Eloise were walking along the promenade. The warm evening air, enhanced by the good wine they had enjoyed over dinner, created a feeling of relaxed well-being in both of them. On their left as they strolled along under the street lights was the beach and they could hear the calm sea's little waves breaking gently on the shore. Every now and then they passed a palm tree held up, or so it seemed, by an amorous young couple. Eloise smiled a relaxed smile and hung on to Jacques' arm.

When they reached a gap in the wall which ran alongside the beach, Jacques guided Eloise gently down the two or three steps onto the beach. She stopped and let go of his arm so that she could reach down and take off her shoes. He followed her lead and removed his shoes and socks. He reached for her hand and they walked slowly down the beach, towards the sea. As they moved further and further away from the promenade, the light from the street lamps grew dim and when Jacques turned to look at Eloise, her face was lit only by the moonlight. She looked at him and squeezed his hand, just as she had done in Monte Carlo.

The two of them looked out to sea. In the distance they could see the twinkling lights of a cruise ship anchored in the bay for the night and beyond that, the lights of St Tropez. They turned quietly away from the sea and Jacques removed his jacket and spread it out on the sand for Eloise. She sat down on it and he sat beside her on the soft sand. She pulled her knees up and dug her feet into the sand before resting her forearms on her knees and staring out to sea.

After several minutes had passed in silence, Eloise spoke. "This is such a beautiful place," she said, "I think I could stay here for ever."

"Tell me about your home," he said. "Where you live. Your family. I know about your grandfather of course, but what about the rest? I want to know everything there is to know about you."

Eloise turned to look at his face. "I'm not sure I want you to know *everything*. I must keep a few secrets."

He smiled. "Just tell me whatever you want to tell me."

"OK. Well, I live in a little village in Yorkshire," she began and then stopped and looked at him. "Do you know where that is?"

"It's in the North of England, I think."

"That's right. I'm impressed." Eloise smiled. "Welburn, that's where I live, is a small village in Yorkshire. It's very pretty and our house is on the edge of the village. I've lived there all my life." Eloise paused for a moment before continuing. "As far as my family is concerned, well, my mother is French, as you know. Her name is Nicole. My father was English. Very, very English. His name was Andrew."

"Was?" queried Jacques.

"Yes. He died a few years ago, when I was eighteen." Eloise paused and looked into the distance as her eyes grew moist. “And,” she continued, her voice now faltering, “As well as my Mum and Dad, I had a brother.” She sniffed and her face contorted as she fought back the tears which suddenly welled up. “He died recently.”

Eloise looked away from Jacques and down at the sand beside her. She picked up a handful, letting it run through the tips of her fingers onto her feet as she fought back the tears.

“I’m sorry to hear that,” said Jacques, “How did it happen? Was he sick?”

Eloise shook her head. “No,” she said. “He was murdered.”

Jacques closed his eyes and winced. When he opened his eyes again, he looked at Eloise, her head sunk into her shoulders. Though she said nothing, her pain was evident. Slowly, she lifted her head and in the moonlight he saw a solitary tear run down her cheek leaving a wet trace behind it.

Eloise took a deep breath and turned to look at Jacques. “And I have absolutely no idea why,” she said, the tears now running down her cheeks freely.

Jacques said nothing, there was nothing he could say. He just put his arm around her and pulled her towards him. Eloise let him and gently laid her head on his shoulder as the tears flowed.

“I’m sorry,” she sobbed. “This is the first time I’ve cried since that awful day. I didn’t want Mum to see me crying; she was upset enough as it was.”

Jacques felt her shake and heave as the sadness and misery which had stalked her flowed out freely onto him. He cradled her head with his hand and stroked her hair. He could feel her tears running down his neck and when, eventually, she stopped crying and looked up, her face was stained and her eyes misty.

“I’m sorry,” she said again.

Jacques turned her head towards him gently and kissed her on the forehead. “There’s nothing to be sorry about, Eloise. I’m glad that you trust me enough to let me be here with you, to share your sadness, your grief.”

Eloise let her head fall back onto Jacques’ shoulder.

Eventually, after a while, their inactivity made them feel chilly in the night air and Eloise shivered. Jacques stirred and she lifted her head.

“Cold?” he asked and Eloise nodded.

They both got to their feet and Jacques put his jacket round Eloise’s shoulders to keep her warm as they began to stroll back to the hotel.

When they reached the promenade, Jacques put his arm round Eloise and squeezed her shoulder. She looked up at him and smiled a warm affectionate smile.

“When do you have to go home?” he asked.

“Tomorrow.”

“So soon?” Jacques stopped and turned to face Eloise. “Can’t you stay a little longer. For a few more days at least?”

“I’d like to,” said Eloise. “Really, I would. But I don’t know if it’s possible.”

“I’m sure it would be good for you,” pleaded Jacques. “The sun, the wine, the swimming in the sea…”

Eloise smiled as she turned to continue towards the hotel. “OK, I’ll see what I can do.”

Jacques smiled a broad smile, “Good! Come and tell me in the morning what you have been able to arrange.”

As they approached the entrance to the hotel, a taxi pulled up in front of them beside the steps. The passenger door on the far side of the taxi opened and Anna got out. Although Jacques couldn’t see him clearly enough in the dark to identify him, he knew that the other passenger in the taxi was a man. Anna bent down to the window and kissed him on the cheek before standing again and turning to go into the hotel. Jacques and Eloise looked at each other. Eloise shrugged and held out her arms as if to say 'How should I know?'

By the middle of the next morning, Eloise had not appeared and Jacques was convinced that he had seen the last of her. By the time she did return to the Esprit, having made her excuses to Jeremy and Anna and sought Jeremy's approval for her absence from work, he had given up hope of ever seeing her again and was forlornly preparing the Esprit for the short trip home across the bay. Finally, as he started to untie the mooring warps, he heard a familiar voice.

"Jacques!"

He straightened up instantly and turned to see Eloise's unmistakable form approaching the boat. He ran to meet her, taking her in his arms and swinging her round before putting her down.

"I'm glad you came," he said, "I wasn't sure you would."

"So I see! Looks like you were going to leave without me."

"I have to take the boat back to Port Grimaud," said Jacques, "I've already stayed too long in this berth. Do you want to come with me?"

Eloise nodded. "I can stay another week. But the hotel is fully booked so I need to find another one before tonight."

"There's a good hotel in Port Grimaud. I'm sure they'll have a room for you."

Jacques picked up Eloise's holdall and carried it onto the Esprit before returning to the quay to untie the warps. When he had, he threw them onto the deck of the Esprit and guided Eloise across the gangway before raising it. As the boat began to drift away from the mooring, he made his way to the helm station on the fly bridge and started the engines. Eloise followed him, climbing the steep steps up to the fly bridge. She stood next to him as he raised the anchor and the Esprit began to pull away from Sainte Maxime.

"Is it OK if I go and get my phone, it's in my holdall?" Eloise asked as they left the small harbour behind them and cruised towards Port Grimaud.

"Of course," replied Jacques, "go wherever you want."

Eloise went back down to the rear deck and then into the saloon. Once inside, she went over to the dining area and removed her phone from the side pocket of her holdall.

On her way back through the saloon, she performed a pirouette, clearly enjoying being on the boat, and took the time to have a look round. She saw the bookcase and went over to look at the books that were stacked neatly in it. She pulled one of them out, a travel book, and leafed through it briefly before returning it to the bookcase.

As she scanned the rest of the books, Eloise's eyes stopped and narrowed slightly. She removed the book which had caught her attention and saw that it was a copy of *Robin Hood*. As she held it in her hands, it fell open where a folded sheet of paper had been inserted and the sheet of paper floated down to the floor.

Eloise picked up the sheet of paper and opened it out. Her eyes widened as she saw the rows of numbers on the sheet, just like the email Rob had received, only hand written. She turned from the bookcase and headed for the aft deck.

As the Esprit continued to head towards the entrance to Port Grimaud, Eloise climbed the steps to the fly bridge again and went over to Jacques at the helm, she was holding the book in one hand and the sheet of paper in the other.

"Jacques?" she said when she reached him.

Jacques was concentrating on driving the boat and did not look round as he responded. "Oui?" he said, waiting for her to continue.

"The piece of paper that was in this book," she began, "Do you know anything about it?"

At that moment, a sailing yacht crossed the Esprit's path forcing Jacques to alter course to avoid it. He lost his temper and shouted at it.

"Faites attention! Espèce d'idiot!" Jacques hit the wheel before calming down and turning towards Eloise. "What piece of paper?" he asked and Eloise showed him the piece of paper and the book.

"It was in this book," she said.

"Ah, yes. I have seen the book before," said Jacques, returning his attention to navigating the boat, "But I don't know anything about the paper. The books and the CDs, they were all there when I got the boat. Why?"

"Oh, no reason. Just curious."

Eloise turned away from Jacques and slipped the sheet of paper into the pocket of her shorts while Jacques concentrated on taking the Esprit into Port Grimaud.

Inside the Hotel Giraglia, which is next to the Capitainerie in Port Grimaud, Eloise, with Jacques by her side, booked a room overlooking the channel from Le Lac to the sea. Jacques scowled at the little man who suddenly appeared with the intention of carrying Eloise's bag to her room. The man promptly disappeared and Jacques carried the bag up the single flight of stairs himself. He followed Eloise into the room before depositing the bag on the bed.

"Would you like to go to the beach for a swim after you've settled in?" he asked.

"That would be great," she replied with a smile. "I'd like that."

"Good. I'll come back in an hour. Is that enough time?"

Eloise nodded and Jacques left her to return to the Esprit. After he had gone, she unpacked her bag and put her clothes away before extracting her phone from her shorts and tapping in her mother's number.

"Hello?" Nicole answered.

"Hello Mum. It's Eloise here."

"Cherie, how are you? How did the conference go? And the boat trip to Monte Carlo?"

"Oh, great. It all went really well. But the reason I'm ringing is to let you know that I've decided to stay here for another week. I've..." she hesitated before continuing as she considered how to break the news about Jacques to her mother, "I've met someone."

"Oh, I see." Nicole's disappointment was clear to Eloise from the tone of her voice as she continued, "I was really looking forward to you coming home today. I've missed you so much. It's very quiet here without you."

"I know, Mum, and I'm sorry about that, but this guy... Oh, what can I say. What can I tell you about him?"

"How about his name, for a start?" quipped Nicole, overcoming her disappointment.

Eloise smiled. "His name is Jacques Armand and he owns the boat we hired for the trip to Monaco. Oh, Mum, he is just *so* amazing! I feel as if I've been waiting for him all my life."

"I see. So when *will* you be home then?"

"A week tomorrow, if that's OK?"

"Yes, all right," said Nicole, "And then you can tell me all about this perfect man you've found." Eloise smiled as her mother continued. "And make sure you pay Grandpa a visit while you're there."

"Of course," said Eloise with a nod and then a more serious expression took over as she removed the sheet of paper covered in numbers from her pocket and looked at it.

"Mum, before you go," she said, "You remember Rob's email, the strange one with all the numbers on it?"

"Yes, yes I do. Why do you ask?"

"Well, it's really strange," said Eloise, "but I've found something that looks just like it, only hand written. It was on Jacques' boat. Have you still got the printout of Rob's one?"

Nicole paused before answering. "No, sweetheart, I haven't. I threw it away," she lied. Nicole didn't want Eloise to know about Carter and the investigation he was conducting into Philippe's activities.

"Oh well. Never mind. I don't suppose it means anything anyway. See you in a week. Bye, Mum."

In the lounge at Darrington Hall, Nicole replaced the telephone receiver and thought for a few moments about what her daughter had told her. She shook her head unhappily, picked up the phone again and tapped in Carter's number.

"Carter? Is that you? You sound very faint."

"I'm just driving under a bridge. Hold on a second… Is that better?"

"Much better. Carter, I've just had a call from Eloise. As you know, she's in Port Grimaud. The thing is, she says she's found another of those odd messages. You know, like the printout I gave you."

There was a pause before Carter responded. When he did it was in a matter of fact tone. "In that case, I think I'd better get over there sooner rather than later and talk to her."

"No! Wait!" Nicole was anxious. The thought of Carter rushing over to France and getting Eloise caught up in whatever it was that was going on frightened her. "I don't want her getting dragged into this, Carter. Please! Promise me that you won't let her get involved."

"I can't promise that, Nikki. You know I can't," said Carter, wanting to please Nicole but aware of his responsibility to follow up on this new lead.

"You must! She's all I have left now. Promise me that you won't involve her, that you'll keep her out of it."

Carter took a deep breath as he considered how to reconcile his two conflicting objectives. "Look, I'll do my best, OK?" he said, in the hope that it would put Nicole's mind at rest but it did not.

"That's not good enough, Carter!" she said, beginning to get angry with him. "This is really important to me. I helped you when you asked me to. Now promise me." She paused to give weight to what she was going to say next. "Or I'll never speak to you again."

"OK, OK. I promise," said Carter without hesitation. "I promise I will *try* to keep her out of it. That much I can do."

Nicole relaxed a little on hearing his promise. It was less than she wanted but she knew it was all she was going to get.

"OK, I suppose I can't ask more than that," she said as she breathed a long sigh of relief and ended the call. She hoped Carter would be true to his word. She had already lost one of her children and the thought of losing the other made her tremble with fear, so much so that she decided to make another call.

An hour later, Philippe was pacing up and down his living room as Gilles sat in the armchair and listened.

"I have had another call from Nicole," he said, "asking me again what I am involved in."

"What did you tell her?"

Philippe looked at Gilles as if at someone who had just lost his sense of reason. "What do you think I told her?" he retorted. "I told her nothing."

"Then what is there to worry about?" Gilles held out his hands questioningly whereupon Philippe stopped pacing and turned to look at Gilles.

"Nicole is worried because Eloise, my grand-daughter, is over here. She says she does not want her to be involved in anything illegal that I might be doing." Gilles nodded at this before Philippe continued. "She also let it slip that Carter Jefferson is on his way here. She did not say why but I think he could be trouble; I am not his favourite person in the world. We need to find out how much he knows and who he is working for."

In her hotel, Eloise looked at her watch as she finished unpacking her bag and noted that she still had three quarters of an hour to go before Jacques would be calling for her. Although she didn't really want to visit her grandfather, she knew that it was unavoidable, especially as she was now staying on for another week, and staying in Port Grimaud at that. She decided to get the visit to Philippe over and done with so that, having done her duty, she could relax and enjoy herself.

It took Eloise about ten minutes to complete the U-shaped walk along the Rue Grande, through the Place du Marché, along the Rue Du Ponant and then down the Rue des Deux-Iles to Philippe's house. When she got there, she took a deep breath and then rapped her knuckles on the door. A few moments later, Philippe pulled the door open and a broad smile crossed his face as he saw Eloise standing these.

"Eloise, ma Cherie! It is good to see you. Come in, come in." They went into the living room together as Philippe continued, "How is your mother?"

"As well as can be expected, I suppose," said Eloise and a frown appeared on Philippe's brow.

"Yes, she must be going through hell."

"To put it mildly. I think she'll be glad when I get home."

"Of course she will. It's good that she has you to help her at this time."

Eloise and Philippe continued the polite chit-chat for about twenty minutes before Eloise looked at her watch.

"I must go," she said, getting to her feet. "I have to meet someone at the hotel in ten minutes."

"In Sainte Maxime? I think you will be late." Philippe laughed as he spoke and got to his feet.

"No, I've moved to the Hotel Giraglia, here in Port Grimaud."

"You are staying in Port Grimaud?" Eloise nodded and Philippe added, "But then you must stay here with me, in my house."

Eloise's expression said it all but she tried to find the right words. "That's very kind of you Grandpa but I've booked in at the hotel now and I don't want to impose on you. I know you use the house as your office as well."

"As you wish," said Philippe, accepting her decision, "But if you change your mind..."

Eloise smiled and stood on her tip toes to give Philippe a kiss on the cheek before she left to return to the hotel.

Jacques left the Esprit at twelve o'clock to call for Eloise and as he approached the hotel, he heard someone calling from above.

"Jacques! Up here."

He looked up and saw Eloise leaning over the rough wooden balustrade on the balcony of her first floor room. She was smiling and waving furiously. The sun lit her face from the side and through the rustic balusters, he could see the shape of her legs. He waved back and continued round the corner to the hotel entrance.

Eloise opened the door to her room as soon as she heard Jacques knock. Inside, he saw that she was not quite ready. She had been in the middle of changing into her beach clothes when Jacques had arrived and her legs and feet were still unclad.

"I won't be long," she said. "Sit down a minute."

Jacques sat on the bed. A gentle breeze blew in through the open French window and wafted Eloise's perfume towards him as she reached over and behind him for her shorts which were on the bed. A combination of her own scent and that of her perfume filled Jacques' nostrils but he resisted the temptation to put his arms around her and pull her onto the bed. He watched her put on her shorts and do them up before slipping her feet into her flip-flops and grabbing her sunglasses from the dressing table.

"I'm ready," she said, standing in front of him, a mischievous smile seeming to tickle the corners of her mouth.

As they left the room, Eloise pulled the door shut behind her and Jacques took her hand in his. They walked briskly along the corridor, down the stairs and past the reception desk before leaving the hotel. Together they walked along the Rue Grande in the direction of the Place des Six Canons and through a gap between the apartment blocks onto the beach.

The beach was teeming with people, most of whom were content to just lie in the sun. Their bodies ranged in colour from a very pale couple who had obviously only just arrived from the north, probably Paris, to a man of about thirty who was laboriously, and very obviously, oiling his dark brown skin, very little of which was covered by his extremely skimpy swimming trunks.

Apart from the sunbathers, there were a few couples and groups playing beach tennis and boules, while still others, less energetic, reclined under bright parasols, reading magazines and newspapers. Hardly anyone was in the sea.

Jacques led Eloise to a vacant patch of beach where he laid out his towel before dropping his shorts and pulling off his tee-shirt. He watched as Eloise followed suit. Under her shorts and tee-shirt, she was wearing a white satin bikini with high-cut legs and a brief halter-neck top. Jacques thought she looked stunning in it and proudly puffed out his chest.

"Swim?" he asked when he thought the neighbouring sunbathers had looked at her long enough.

Eloise nodded and kicked off her flip-flops before taking the hand Jacques was holding out to her and walking down to the sea with him. At one point, as they negotiated the sharp shells and pebbles near the waterline, Eloise lurched unsteadily and reached out for Jacques. He caught her in his arms and looked into her eyes. For a few moments, their bodies were locked together. He didn't want to let go of her but she regained her feet and pulled away from him.

"Come on!" she called as she ran the last few yards down the steeply sloping beach and dived into the sea. Jacques ran after her and together they swam out to the sand-bar about fifty yards from the water's edge. For several minutes they larked about, splashing and chasing each other as they laughed freely, in no way inhibited by the mass of people on the beach.

After their swim, Jacques lay on his back next to Eloise enjoying the feel of the sun beating down on him as he dried off. Suddenly he felt something hard land on his stomach. He sat up and looked around him. Eloise was lying on her back, her eyes closed and her left knee raised slightly. Jacques looked around for the object that had struck him; it was a bottle of sun tan lotion. He picked it up and looked at Eloise again. She opened one eye and squinted at him, a smile spreading across her face.

"Did you do that?" Jacques asked.

Eloise nodded. "I need someone to rub it on my back." She rolled over onto her front, undid the strap of her bikini top and stretched her arms out above her head expectantly.

Jacques opened the bottle and squeezed some lotion onto her back. She shivered with the coolness of it. He knelt beside her and started to rub the lotion into her skin. As his hands passed over her body, this way and that, gradually he reached further down towards her bottom and further round towards her breasts, now squashed beneath her body.

"Jacques," he heard her say, "that's enough, thank you."

Jacques didn't want to stop, but he did. He wiped his hands on his tee-shirt and lay back on his towel as Eloise sat up, clutching her bikini top to her chest modestly. She touched his shoulder.

"Don't you want some on? You might get burnt. I can put some on for you, if you like."

Jacques turned his head to look at her. "No, I never use it. It makes you all sticky." He pulled a disgusted face and then smiled.

"OK." Eloise fastened her bikini top in place and put on her sunglasses. "So! Now it's your turn to tell me a bit about you. I don't really know anything about you and I'd like to."

"What do you want to know?"

"Whatever you want to tell me."

Jacques lifted himself onto one elbow and looked into her face. He told her about growing up in Port Grimaud with his mother; about the appalling way she had been treated by some of the town's people; about his absent and anonymous father who gave him expensive presents on his birthday each year. He told her about his poor showing at school and about his job as a petrol pump attendant. He told her about his twenty-first birthday and about the money which his father had given him.

When Jacques had finished telling Eloise his life story, he looked at her and tried to discern, from the expression on her face, what she thought of what he had told her.

"And she's never told you who your father is?" she queried, her tone clearly indicating how strange she felt that was. Jacques shook his head.

"And now you know everything about me," he said.

She smiled. She didn't say anything but her smile voiced her feelings perfectly. It wasn't a smile of pity, nor was it a joyous or seductive smile. What Eloise's smile conveyed to Jacques was intimacy and tenderness, and a depth of feeling known only to those in love.

Then, her smile faded and a serious look came into her eyes. She put out her arm and pushed him back onto his towel before leaning over him, pressing herself against him and kissing him deeply on the lips.

After about a minute had passed, Eloise pulled her head slowly back from him and looked down at him. He smiled and put his hands behind his head in a nonchalant manner.

"I have another charter tomorrow," he announced. "Will you crew for me?"

"Why? Is Yvonne not available?"

"No. It was a last minute booking and Françoise is away, so she has to work in the gallery." Eloise smiled and nodded.

"Then of course I will," she said, "I'd like that."

Jacques sat up, a happy smile on his face. "Good!" he said. "Shall we get some lunch?"

Eloise nodded as Jacques stood up and started gathering his things together. She followed suit and before long they were walking along the beach together towards the Capitainerie and the hotel.

"I have a suggestion," said Jacques as they reached the Capitainerie and came to a stop near the Esprit. Eloise looked at him enquiringly before he continued. "It doesn't make any sense for you to spend money on a hotel. Why don't you come and stay on the Esprit?"

A little surprised by his suggestion, Eloise gave him a shocked look, not sure what to say. "On the Esprit?! With you?!" she said and Jacques realised what she was thinking. He reacted quickly.

"I didn't mean...." His face broke into a smile. "Although that would be nice. No, there's a spare cabin. You could stay in the forward cabin. Yes?"

Eloise looked at him intently and a smile spread across her face. "OK. Why not?" she said. "I'll get my stuff together and check out of the hotel. I'll be back in about half an hour, OK?"

Jacques nodded and smiled and Eloise gave him a quick kiss on the lips as they parted. Jacques watched her as she headed for the hotel, a noticeable spring in her step.

Chapter 9

Very early the next morning, Carter and Conrad, dressed in their suits, were seated side by side on Jet2 flight 202 from Leeds to Nice.

"The guys in New York say they think the code is some sort of alphanumeric substitution, probably based on a key text," said Carter. "It's a simple but effective coding system."

"So what use is another message we can't decode?" questioned Conrad.

"None. But where we find a message there's a good chance we might also find the key text. The message is useless without that, so it must be somewhere. We just have to find it, that's all."

"Simple," said Conrad jokingly as Carter settled back into his seat and closed his eyes to review, mentally, the progress he had made over the last week.

Initially, he had been unable to get beyond Philippe Lacoste and the mine in Guinea. He had satisfied himself that the synthetic diamonds were not being made there; it just wasn't practical. In any case, he knew that it would not be the appropriate point at which to feed them into the distribution system. He had seen enough synthetic diamonds over the years to know that they look more like cut diamonds than uncut ones and that the best point at which to introduce them into the system would be at the cutting house stage. That meant they were much more likely to be making them somewhere else.

Carter also knew that the creation of man-made diamonds could only be achieved effectively in two ways. One of these required the construction of a pressure chamber made up of several large pyramid shaped pieces, with their apexes meeting in the middle of the chamber. Then, enough pressure had to be applied to the base of each pyramid such that the cumulative pressure at the apex of the pyramids was enough to push the tiny quantity of graphite in the small container at the centre of the chamber over the conversion pressure barrier. But to reach the necessary pressure, the ratio between the base area of the pyramid and the area of the apex meant that the pressure chamber had to be at least ten feet across. And the process was slow, requiring the pressure to be applied for several days to produce a one carat diamond.

The other method involved taking a tiny crystal of diamond and placing it in a solution of graphite such that the tiny crystal grew into a gem sized diamond. This method did not require the large bulky equipment that the first method needed but it still needed a chamber the size of a wardrobe in which to conduct the process and it took even longer than the high pressure, high temperature method. Using the chemical vapour deposition method, it could take several weeks for the crystal to grow to a size where it could be used in jewellery.

Although Carter was very well acquainted with the theory of synthetic diamonds, their atomic construction and the ways in which they could be synthesised, Conrad was the Federation's technical expert on the case. As well as being very handy with a gun, which had come in useful on more than one occasion in the past, Conrad was the one with detailed first hand experience of the latest technology being used for the manufacture of synthetic diamonds. He had told Carter that even with the most advanced equipment available, it would still require a very large space to house enough units to produce the diamonds in significant quantities.

And then there was the coded message. There would surely be some clues in that. But they would have to find the key text before they could decipher the message and the experts in New York had told him that the key text could be any book as long as both the sender and the recipient of the message were using exactly the same edition of the same book. It didn't even need to be a published book, any sufficiently large body of text would do although it was more usual to use published works as these were less obvious. The experts had also said that if the key text could be found, then decoding the message would be a simple task with each group of numbers representing the page, line, word and letter in the text.

Then Nicole had told him about Eloise finding another message on Jacques' boat. Did that mean that the book could also be on the boat? If it was, it should be fairly easy to find. How many books could there be on a boat? But Nicole had told him that if he wanted her continued co-operation, he must not let Eloise get involved. That would make things more complicated, especially as she had also told him that Eloise was spending a lot of time with Jacques. What if she was on the boat with him? How could he avoid involving her? Especially if Jacques was mixed up in what was going on?

As he pondered these things, Carter's brain grew tired and before long he was asleep. The next thing he knew was his arm being shaken by a stewardess as the plane started its descent into Nice airport.

"We'll be landing in a few minutes, sir. Please fasten your seat belt."

Carter looked out of the window as the plane turned east after crossing the coastline of southern France. As it did so, Carter was able to see the French Riviera bathed in the early morning sunshine. The deep blue sea running up to golden beaches, and bordered by hotels and palm trees, was a beautiful sight. Inland the holiday scene gave way to the mountains of the Alpes Maritimes. Before long they were passing the Cap d'Antibes and Carter could see the runway at Nice airport reaching out into the sea. A minute or two later, the plane turned north and the runway disappeared beneath it.

It was a few minutes past nine o'clock when Carter and Conrad stepped off the plane onto the steps leading down to the tarmac and as they did, the heat enveloped them, reminding them that it was the height of summer. Inside the airport buildings, air conditioning provided welcome relief from the heat and Carter turned to Conrad.

"We'll need to find a taxi to take us to Sainte Maxime," he said.

"How far is it?" asked Conrad.

"About fifty miles, as the crow flies."

"Then I'd better pay a visit before we leave," said Conrad, as he headed for the public toilets.

Soon Carter and Conrad were in the back of a taxi, racing along the Autoroute la Provençale which runs from Nice to Marseille. At Fréjus the driver turned off the autoroute to take the coast road to Sainte Maxime. It was a Sunday and the volume of local traffic was somewhat reduced so the journey took only a little over an hour but the absence of air conditioning in the car meant that by the time they arrived at the Hotel du

Promenade, their shirts were wet with perspiration and they were tired and irritable.

"Pay the man," said Carter as he got out of the taxi. "I'll go and check in."

Ten minutes after they had checked in, Carter and Conrad were sitting in the hotel lounge, close to where Eloise had been sitting only a couple of days earlier. They had changed into more casual clothes and were starting to cool down as they enjoyed a refreshing glass of ice cold coca cola.

"Ah, that's better," said Conrad as he downed the last drop before putting his glass on the table and turning to Carter.

"So, what's the plan from here?" he asked.

"First, we check out Jacques Armand's boat," responded Carter. "New York say someone called du Bois, from an agency in Sainte Maxime, should have hired it for us for the afternoon. He's supposed to be meeting us here at one to take us to Port Grimaud."

"Then what?"

"Then..." Carter was thinking hard but no plan presented itself, "Then we play it by ear. Somehow we have to try and search Jacques' boat and find the book, if it's there, without him being aware of what we're doing."

"It's not much of a plan," said Conrad matter-of-factly. "Wouldn't it be easier to just tell him what we want and ask him for it?"

"I agree it's not much of a plan. And that it would be easier to come straight out with it and ask him if we can search his boat. Except for one thing, we don't know who's involved and who's not and it's entirely possible that Jacques is involved. So I think it would be better for us to keep our powder dry for now. And for another, according to Nicole, Eloise is seeing him and I promised her I would try to keep Eloise out of it. So, that's what we'll do, if we can." Carter paused to allow Conrad to consider his plan. "But if you've got a better plan, taking all of that into account, then let's hear it."

Conrad did not have a better plan, he was an engineer not a detective and was there mainly for his technical input and to provide Carter with back up. He let the matter drop.

"Let's go and find ourselves some lunch," suggested Carter as he drained his glass and got up.

After Carter and Conrad had finished their lunch at a café in Sainte Maxime, they returned to the hotel lounge to await the arrival of du Bois. While they were sitting there enjoying a beer, in front of Carter was a folded letter from the FIDT which he had removed from his pocket, re-read and put on the table. It had been emailed to him before he left the UK and provided him with the name and contact details for the private detective they had hired to assist him as necessary in Sainte Maxime. He had printed the letter out at the hotel in York so that he would have the information easily accessible when needed.

As they relaxed in the lounge, Conrad drained his glass and called the waiter over. He ordered two more beers just as a short man dressed in cream trousers and a colourful patterned shirt appeared at the entrance. The man was also wearing sunglasses and a panama hat and Carter spotted him looking in their direction. He changed Conrad's order to three beers, acknowledging Conrad's enquiring look with a nod towards the man.

"Is that him?" asked Conrad.

"I think so. He looks like he could be our man in Sainte Maxime," answered Carter.

The man approached the table and removed the hat he was wearing. He also removed his sunglasses as he addressed Carter and Conrad who were sitting expectantly at the table.

"Monsieur Jefferson?" he asked.

"Oui, c'est moi," said Carter, standing up and offering his hand. "You must be Monsieur du Bois."

"Yes, that is my name." The man took the offered hand. "But please, call me Antoine."

"OK, Antoine," said Carter, "This is Conrad. He's working with me on this case."

Antoine acknowledged Conrad and sat in the empty chair beside Carter. The waiter appeared with their beers and placed them on the table.

"I took the liberty of ordering one for you when I saw you come in," said Carter, "I hope you drink beer."

"Thank you. It is most acceptable," replied Antoine lifting the glass and draining it at one go.

"Would you like another?" asked Carter as he watched in amazement.

Antoine raised his hand as if he were trying to stop traffic. "Thank you, no. We must get on with business. Time is short." Carter nodded in agreement as Antoine continued. "I have spoken to Jacques Armand, as you requested, and his boat is booked for you for this afternoon, commencing at two o'clock. It will take half an hour to get to Port Grimaud from here; the traffic is bad at this time of year, you know. So many tourists! So we must leave now. I have a car and a driver waiting outside to take us there."

"That's excellent. Thank you," said Carter.

"Monsieur Jefferson..." said Antoine hesitantly.

"Carter, please call me Carter."

"Ah, bien. Carter. Are you able to tell me what this is about?"

Carter shook his head. "I'm afraid not. Information about this case is strictly on a need to know basis."

"I understand." Antoine's disappointment was clearly written on his face. "Shall we go?"

Carter and Conrad sat in the back of the Citroen while Antoine sat in the front with the driver. When they reached Port Grimaud, the driver stopped at the entrance to deposit his passengers.

"Wait for me at the Café Poisson," instructed Antoine as he got out of the car. The driver nodded and swung the car round the small roundabout and into the town car park.

Antoine led Carter and Conrad to the Capitainerie where Jacques was on the quayside, casually coiling excess rope from one of the Esprit's mooring warps as he waited for his clients to arrive. When they did, he greeted them warmly.

After the introductions were complete, Antoine took his leave. "I will await your return with the driver. We will be at the Café Poisson in the Place du Marché."

"That's great. Thank you." Carter took an envelope from his blazer pocket and passed it to Antoine. Without looking inside, Antoine folded the envelope and put it into the pocket of his trousers before leaving them.

"Where do you wish to go?" asked Jacques when Antoine had gone, "Monsieur du Bois did not say when he made the booking."

Carter had expected the question and was ready for it. He knew it would be necessary to have some pretext upon which to base the charter if suspicions were not to be aroused unduly.

"The Ile du Levant," he said, "We'd like to see the old fort."

"Yes, I know it," said Jacques, "It will take about an hour and a half to get there."

On board the Esprit, Jacques introduced his clients to Eloise. Carter knew from what Nicole had told him that Eloise might be there but he had still hoped that she wouldn't be.

As Jacques prepared the Esprit for departure, Eloise crewed for him, as she had promised. She was surprisingly adept at it and clearly enjoyed the role.

When the Esprit was under way, Eloise went up to the fly bridge to be with Jacques, leaving his two clients to themselves on the aft deck. Carter watched her legs disappear up the steps and waited a few moments to see if she returned. When she did not, he motioned to Conrad to follow him into the saloon where they began their search. They soon found the bookshelf and noticed the copy of *Robin Hood* amongst the other books, most of which were in French. Carter grabbed it eagerly and began to leaf through the pages.

"Do you think that's the one?" Conrad asked.

"It must be! Look," Carter pointed to the shelf where the other books were, "it's the odd one out. All the others are either modern novels or reference books, and they're all in French. It's got to be the one."

Up on the fly bridge, Eloise was standing beside Jacques as the Esprit sped across the bay. "I'd better go and see if our guests are all right," she said, "They seemed a bit strange to me."

"Strange?"

"Yeah, you know, a bit odd."

Jacques shrugged. He had clients who were paying good money to use his boat; he didn't really care if they were a bit odd.

When she entered the saloon, Eloise saw Carter and Conrad hunched together near the bookshelf, intent on examining the book they had found. She looked at them suspiciously.

"Can I help you?" she asked.

They froze. Carter closed his eyes and swore under his breath. Slowly he turned and looked at Eloise.

"We were just saying that this is kind of a strange book to find on a boat in the south of France. Don't you think?"

Eloise saw that the book Carter was holding was the copy of *Robin Hood*, the one in which she had found the sheet of paper, and she sensed that there was more to it than that, especially as the two men were not behaving like tourists; tourists would have been out on the deck or up on the fly bridge enjoying the view, not in the saloon.

"Maybe," she said, walking over to them. She took the book from Carter and put it back on the shelf with the others, "but I don't really think you're interested in literature, are you?" She stepped back from them and folded her arms defiantly. "Are you going to tell me about it? Or shall I tell Jacques to turn the boat round and go back to Port Grimaud?"

"Tell you about what?" asked Carter.

Conrad tried to get round behind Eloise but she moved quickly to the door, blocking him and turned to face them.

"About why you're here. About why you hired this boat. And about why you're so interested in that book."

"I don't know what you mean," Carter protested.

"Oh I think you do."

For a few moments Eloise held Carter in a fixed stare. Then, still keeping her eyes on him, she leaned back and shouted out through the door, "Jacques! Can you come down here, please."

Jacques only just heard her over the noise of the wind and the engines but he could hear enough to pick up the sense of urgency in her voice. He cut the engines, leaving the Esprit to drift with the current, and was soon standing beside her.

"What's going on?" he asked.

"I don't think these people are who they say they are," said Eloise as she stood defiantly in the doorway with Jacques looking over her shoulder into the saloon.

Carter tried again to calm her fears. "Look, we're just a couple of guys looking for a day out from a boring conference, OK?"

"Oh, is that right?" snapped Eloise. "Well guess what? I don't believe you. And we're not going anywhere till we find out the truth. Right, Jacques?" She looked at Jacques for support and he nodded his agreement emphatically.

"OK you guys! Playtime's over!" Conrad moved forward menacingly as he spoke and Eloise saw him draw an automatic pistol from where it had been tucked into the back of his trousers. Jacques saw it too and moved round in front of Eloise to protect her. As Conrad passed in front of Carter, Carter reached out, took hold of the barrel of the gun and twisted it out of Conrad's grasp.

"Where the hell did you get that?" he asked as he stared at Conrad.

"Well, you remember when I went to the bathroom at the airport…?"

"You're kidding me?"

Conrad shook his head slowly. "Someone's got to watch your back."

"Well, I don't think there's any need for that here," he said as he put the gun down on the table. "We're not back in the US of A now, you know. This is France, and they don't take too kindly to people carrying concealed weapons here."

"In that case, maybe you should tell them," said Conrad.

"Sounds like good advice to me," said Eloise, trying very hard not to sound scared.

"Let's all just cool down for a second, shall we?" said Carter, "Why don't we all just sit down and keep calm, huh? No one's going to hurt anyone. Right, Conrad?"

Conrad nodded and sat down at the table. Carter looked at Eloise and Jacques standing in the doorway. "You too," he said.

"No way! I'm not moving till you tell us who you are," retorted Eloise, loudly but a little unsurely.

Carter sighed. Slowly, he took his wallet from his pocket and showed Eloise his FIDT identity card. She looked at it carefully.

"So what are you? Some sort of private investigator?" she asked

"Something like that," replied Carter as, reluctantly and slowly, Eloise and Jacques walked forward and sat at the table in the saloon. Carter sat down facing Jacques from the other end of the table whilst Eloise and Conrad were side by side with their backs to the boat's starboard window. Eloise shuffled as close to Jacques as she could and as far away from Conrad as possible.

"You know, there's no reason for you to be afraid of us," said Carter. "We're the good guys. It's the ones we're trying to track down that you need to watch out for."

"So who are they? And what's it got to do with us anyway? And what the hell is the FIDT?" questioned Eloise.

There was something about Carter which made Eloise believe him, even trust him; his voice was quiet and reassuring and his manner relaxed, almost tired.

"Well, it's a long story," began Carter, "but I guess you're entitled to hear it. Maybe you should secure the boat, Jacques. This could take a while."

Jacques nodded and went to the helm station at the front of the saloon. The others sat in silence as they heard the anchor chain rattle over the bow of the Esprit.

"OK," Carter took a deep breath as Jacques returned to his seat, "Conrad and me, we're working for an organisation called The New York Federation of International Diamond Traders, the FIDT, like on my identity card." Jacques stared at Carter as he continued. "The Federation works with other national and international organisations which, together, are responsible for the distribution of most of the diamonds produced in the world. It's our job to track down people who try to cheat the system, usually by feeding fake diamonds into the market and passing them off as the real thing."

"But surely there are ways of detecting fakes aren't there?" Eloise's fear had subsided, to be replaced with interest and curiosity, but Jacques kept throwing a glance at Conrad. Each time he did, Conrad smiled back at him and patted the gun which he had reclaimed from the table and pushed into his waistband.

"Yes, that's true. And it's easy enough to detect diamond substitutes. Zirconia for instance. Our members don't have too much trouble distinguishing between substitutes and the real thing. No, where the trouble starts is with synthetic diamonds. These are real diamonds. They have all the properties and attributes of real diamonds, except that they've never seen the inside of a diamond mine."

"I didn't think it was possible to make diamonds artificially," said Eloise

"Most of the commercially produced synthetic diamonds in the world are very small, poor quality and easily distinguished from the real thing. They can only be used for industrial purposes. Drill bits, glass cutters, that kind of thing. Not for jewellery. And their value is relatively low. But for a while now, people have been trying to make bigger, better, gem quality stones and some of them have succeeded. The Russians, for instance, have been making gem quality synthetics for quite a few years and synthetic diamonds are now getting so good that it takes special, very expensive equipment to detect them, equipment that jewellers just don't have."

"And you think someone's been feeding some of these synthetic diamonds into the system illegally?" queried Eloise, "Mixing them in with natural diamonds at some point?"

"Yeah! That's right! " Carter looked pleased. "Your mother was right. She said you were bright."

The silence was deafening.

The only sound was the gentle lapping of the sea against the hull of the Esprit as all eyes turned to look at Carter. He closed his eyes, realising what he had done. In a moment of carelessness, he had got carried away and had said something stupid. He cursed himself and opened his eyes again to find Eloise staring at him, her face challenging him. After several seconds of silence had passed, she spoke.

"What did you just say?" she asked, daring him to try to extract himself from the hole he had just dug for himself. Carter cleared his throat.

"About the diamonds?"

"About my mother. How come you know my mother?" Eloise tilted her head threateningly as she spoke.

"Your mother? Oh yes. Didn't I tell you? Your mother and I, we were at university together."

"No, you didn't tell me. And, anyway, that was twenty-odd years ago. I wasn't even born then. So how do you know about me. And about how bright I am? When did you last speak to my mother?"

"I spoke to her yesterday."

"About this?"

"Yes."

"But what have synthetic diamonds got to do with her? Or me, for that matter?"

"Well, they appear to be coming from a mine owned by your grandfather."

Eloise's mood changed from one of intellectual interest to one of apprehension. But she was angry too.

"Are you trying to tell me that you think my grandfather is involved in this… this scam?"

"I don't know for sure but it's possible, yes. Likely, even."

Eloise got up from the table. "I think I've heard enough of this rubbish," she said and stormed out of the saloon onto the aft deck.

Moments later, she was standing at the aft guard rail, staring out into the distance as Carter came up behind her and touched her on the shoulder. She shied away from his touch.

"What about your brother Eloise? What about Rob?" he said, desperate to get her back on side.

Eloise rounded on him, her eyes bright and challenging. "What about him?" she said. "I suppose you're going to tell me that he was involved as well. Well if he was, you're never going to know because he's dead!" She glared at him and went to hit him with her clenched fist but he caught it in mid-air and held her with a stare. She grimaced and a lonely tear trickled down her cheek. Carter let go of her fist and her hand dropped to her side.

"No, Eloise, I'm not going to say that. But I do believe he died because of it. I think, somehow, by chance, by accident, unknowingly, I don't know how but somehow, he got caught up in it. He probably wasn't even aware of his involvement."

"You haven't got a shred of proof of any of this, have you?"

Carter stood silently and looked away into the distance. The atmosphere bristled in the silence that followed before Carter suddenly turned back to face Eloise, his face animated and lively. He grabbed her by the shoulders, frightening her.

"Maybe there *is* a way I can prove it to you," he said. "Come back into the saloon with me and let me try." He looked at her intensely and she backed away from him. As she did she could feel the Esprit's guard rail behind her.

"Come on, Eloise. Let me try. Please?" pleaded Carter as he gently guided a hesitant Eloise towards the saloon. Jacques and Conrad, who had come out onto the deck behind Carter, followed them back inside and took their seats again, waiting expectantly.

"If I'm right," said Carter, "this will convince you."

Slowly he took an envelope from his jacket pocket and removed the printout of Rob's email from it. Eloise's eyes widened as he unfolded it.

Carter spread the document out on the table. "Conrad, the book please." Conrad went to the bookcase and extracted the copy of *Robin Hood* and passed it to him.

Carter looked at the first group of numbers on Rob's email, it read 161893. He turned to page sixteen. They all watched Carter as he ran his finger down the page counting the lines as he went.

"Line eighteen," he said to himself as he got to it, "and word number nine, and the third letter. That's a C." He looked at Conrad. "Well go on, write it down."

Conrad reached into his pocket for the ball point pen and small note pad which he always carried with him. "C," he said as he wrote it down on a fresh page.

Carter leafed quickly through the book to find the next few letters. "O … N … F … I … R … M … Confirm. That's the first word of the message," he said. "Looks like maybe I was right!"

As Carter read out each letter, Conrad repeated it and wrote it down. When, ten minutes later, Carter got to the end, he looked up.

"OK, that's it. Read it back to me," he said.

Conrad looked at his pad and began to read the decoded message. "Confirm transfer of merchandise at three pm Friday eighth July on board Hedonist in Nice."

Carter looked at Eloise. "That do it for you?" he asked.

Eloise knew Carter was right but she didn't want to admit it, at least not to him. She searched for a flaw in his argument.

"The message doesn't say anything about diamonds," she said. "The 'merchandise' could be anything."

Carter looked at her. He raised his eyebrows and cocked his head to one side as if to challenge her to admit what she knew to be the truth. She looked away from him through the window into the distance, hating to believe him but knowing that he was right. She reached into the pocket of her shorts to see if the sheet of paper she had taken from the book the previous day was still there. It was. Slowly, she extracted it and held it out to Carter.

"I suppose you'd better see what this one says too."

As Eloise got up to leave the saloon, Carter looked at her with compassion in his eyes. She noticed and knew for sure then that he did not wish her any harm but she still found it difficult to accept that her grandfather was involved in anything illegal. Especially if, as Carter had suggested, Rob had been killed because of it. It was hard for her to believe that Philippe would be a party to the murder of his own grandson. She went out onto the aft deck again.

When Eloise had left the saloon, Carter opened up the sheet of paper she had given him. He looked at it for a few seconds and then compared it with the printout of the message Rob had received.

"It's the same as the other one," he said. "Except handwritten."

Carter got up and went out to join Eloise at the stern of the boat where she was standing quietly and looking out to sea.

"I'm sorry," he said quietly. "But surely you must believe me now?"

Eloise looked round at him, resigned to the truth but still trying to pick holes in his argument.

"There's still nothing there to connect my grandfather to all of this," she said.

"I'm afraid there is," replied Carter. "Apart from the mine in Guinea, this used to be one of his boats."

Carter looked round and saw that Jacques had come out onto the deck and was standing watching them. He motioned to Jacques to come closer and they passed each other as Carter returned to the saloon. Jacques came up behind Eloise. He didn't say anything, he just put his arm round her.

"You're not involved in any of this are you, Jacques?" she said, turning and looking into his eyes as she spoke.

"Of course not. This boat used to belong to Monsieur Lacoste and now it's mine, that's all."

Jacques pulled her closer to him and kissed her on the forehead as Carter came back out onto the deck.

"We can go back to Port Grimaud now," he said as he approached Eloise and Jacques. "We have what we came for."

Jacques nodded his acknowledgement to Carter but waited until Eloise was ready to let go of him before leaving her to go to the helm station and get the Esprit under way.

"I'm sorry you had to find out about all this, Eloise," said Carter as the Esprit made her way back to Port Grimaud, "I promised your mother that I would try to keep you out of it and I would have liked to have kept my promise to her." Eloise gave a brief nod of her head, accepting what Carter had said, before he continued. "But, now that you do know about it, is there anything you can tell me that you think might help?"

Eloise shook her head." No," she said, "I've told you everything I know."

"OK, but if you think of anything, please call me. I can always be contacted on this number." Carter held out a card and Eloise took it. "Your mother has the number too. Can I trust you not to speak to anyone else about this?"

"Yes, but..."

"No buts, Eloise. You must promise me. I know Philippe is your grandfather but if he *is* involved then he's also involved in your brother's death. Please remember that."

Chapter 10

The basement room smelt of years of disuse. Long ago, the stench of rotting vegetation had deserted the place leaving only a slight tell-tale impregnation in the stone walls. Now, the solid floor was covered in a fine film of dust and grime which, in the more remote parts of the room, had remained unmolested for many years so that even the centipedes, en route to more fruitful pastures, left footprints.

At one end of the room, a collection of old and broken furniture was piled high, reaching the joists of the floor above. At the other end, even the stone steps from the kitchen above looked tired, an indent in each one marking the thousands of footsteps it had withstood.

The rest of the room was bare except for a sturdy wooden high backed dining chair with arms, which looked much too solid to have been reclaimed from the pile, and which had been placed in the middle of the room under the single light bulb hanging from a hook screwed into the joist above it.

Sitting on the chair, and tied to it with thin ropes which bit into his wrists and ankles, was Antoine. He looked up pleadingly at Henri, a small but mean looking man, who was standing over him. Behind Antoine stood Albert, a large and muscular man, and to one side, in a corner of the room where he was almost invisible, stood Gilles.

Henri was not getting the information he wanted but both he and Gilles were determined to find out everything Antoine knew. Henri drew back his hand and, with all the force he could muster, struck the little man. Antoine's head moved to the right as the blow landed and he felt a searing pain in his cheek.

"This is not a game, du Bois," Henri said. "You will tell me what I want to know."

Antoine was not a strong man, physically or in any other way. He had already taken all the punishment anyone could expect of him and blood was running down his face into his mouth from the cut left by Henri's ring.

"Are you ready to talk yet?" Henri's voice was menacing.

"OK, OK," said Antoine, his voice shaky and faltering. "What do you want to know?"

"That's better. Why did you make me hit you?" Henri smiled insincerely and turned away from Antoine. "Now then, first of all, who were those people you took to see Jacques Armand?" He turned back to Antoine, his face hard again. "What do you know about them?"

Antoine shrugged. "Not much," he said.

"Who are they?" insisted Henri as Albert struck Antoine from behind on the back of the head.

"I don't know anything for sure," he said. "I got the job through the agency and I was paid in cash."

Henri prepared to hit Antoine again, pulling his arm back over his shoulder. As he saw this, Antoine hurriedly added, "But I saw a letter one of them had. I only saw part of it but at the top of the letter I think it said The New York Association… or was it Federation? Yes, it was Federation. The New York Federation."

"The New York Federation!" snapped Henri, "What sort of a name is that?"

"I… I don't know. That was all I could see. Just The New York Federation."

Henri turned away from Antoine and threw his hands in the air in frustration. "OK, Antoine. So they are something to do with an organisation called The New York Federation… maybe The New York Federation *of* something. Have I got that right?"

Antoine nodded enthusiastically, looking more frightened than ever as Henri turned back to face him, putting his hands on the arms of the chair and leaning forward so that his nose was almost touching Antoine's.

"Why did they want to hire Jacques' boat?"

Antoine tried to move his head back, away from Henri, but his freedom of movement was limited by the back of the chair.

"They wouldn't tell me anything," he said, closing his eyes and screwing up his face in anticipation of another blow from Henri or Albert. When neither of them struck him, he opened one eye and looked at Henri through it. "All they said was that they wanted to charter the boat today."

Gilles came out of the shadows and motioned to Henri to join him by the steps.

"He's no use to us," he said. "He doesn't know anything." Gilles looked at Antoine and lowered his voice. "Get rid of him."

Henri nodded as Gilles climbed the steep steps to the door at the top and left the basement of the old farmhouse.

Once the Esprit had returned to Port Grimaud and berthed, Carter and Conrad disembarked and set out to walk from the Capitainerie to the café where they were to meet Antoine and his driver. As they did, Carter turned to Conrad.

"I want you to watch them. Eloise isn't involved, I'm sure of that. But I'm not so sure about Jacques. Hire a car in case you need it; I'll get another one for myself when I get back to the hotel. And don't let them out of your sight; I want to know every move they make, as soon as they make it. OK?"

"Yeah, sure. No problem," replied Conrad and turned to go back to the Capitainerie.

When Carter reached the café in the Place du Marché where he had agreed to meet Antoine and the driver, he found only the driver there. Sitting at a table in the shade of a parasol, he was gently stirring his coffee and watching the pretty girls walking to and fro in front of him. When he saw Carter he stood up immediately and bowed slightly.

"Where is Antoine?" asked Carter.

"Je ne sais pas. He has not been here. I have been here since I park the car but Monsieur du Bois…" he shrugged, "Je ne sais pas."

Carter looked around but there was no sign of Antoine in the immediate vicinity. "You'd better take me back to Sainte Maxime and then come back here and wait for him," he said to the driver.

In the living room of his house, Philippe was pacing up and down as usual while Gilles sat in an armchair.

"Beyond this partial name," said Gilles. "The New York Federation. Beyond that Antoine doesn't know anything."

Philippe stopped pacing and turned to face him.

"You are sure?" he challenged.

"He said he was just asked to book Jacques' boat for Jefferson," said Gilles as he nodded his confirmation.

"And you believe him?"

"Yes. Yes, I do."

Philippe walked over to the drinks cabinet at one end of the room and poured himself a large cognac before sitting in the armchair close to the French windows so that he could look out over Le Lac. Still sitting in the other armchair, Gilles watched him.

After a few minutes deep in thought, an idea occurred to Philippe. He got up from the chair and fetched his address book from the drawer of his bureau. He flicked through it until he found what he was looking for and then picked up the phone and dialled the international code for the USA followed by the number in the book.

"Hello, Randolph," he said cheerily when he heard a man's voice at the other end of the line, "This is Philippe here, Philippe Lacoste in France."

"Hi there Philippe, how *are* you? How's business?"

"Good, thank you, very good… How about you?"

"Can't complain. Managing to make a buck or two. What can I do for you, old friend?"

"It is a small thing. I don't really like to trouble you with it."

"Just name it Philippe. You know I'd do anything for you."

"Well," said Philippe, choosing his words carefully, "I have been asked to rent a boat to some people from an organisation called The New York Federation but I prefer not to charter my boats to people I do not know and I have never heard of them. I wondered if you knew anything about them?"

"Not off hand, Philippe. But I'll check and call you back as soon as I find out anything."

"Thank you Randolph. I owe you one."

"You don't owe me a damn thing! I haven't begun to repay you for what you did for me."

"You are very kind," said Philippe and rang off.

An hour later, Philippe and Gilles were sitting quietly, waiting for the phone to ring. When it did, Philippe answered it.

"Lacoste," he said.

"Philippe, it's Randy here. I think I've found out what you wanted to know."

"Good, good."

"There isn't an organisation called The New York Federation but there are a few whose names start with those words."

"I see," said Philippe, his voice conveying his disappointment.

"But most of them are associations of teachers and nurses, that sort of thing. In terms of hiring one of your motor yachts, I think there's only one that would be likely to be doing anything like that."

"Yes?" said Philippe eagerly as he waited for Randolph to continue.

"Yeah. It's The New York Federation of International Diamond Traders. I haven't been able to find out much about them but they are kosher, a sort of trade body for the diamond business here in New York. Does that help?"

Philippe's worst fears had been realised. "Yes," he said pensively, "Thank you for your help with this matter. We must meet up next time you are in France."

"Yeah that would be good. We could tie one on and reminisce about old times. Hey, do you remember that dame in Auxerre, the blonde one that couldn't do enough for us. Hot damn! She was gorgeous, wasn't she? Anyway, so long Philippe. See you soon."

"Bye Randolph." Philippe put the phone down and looked at Gilles. "It is bad," he said and repeated what Randolph had told him. As he did, Gilles' face fell.

"I know of the FIDT," said Gilles, "They are powerful, and well funded."

"We need to find out how much they know. Maybe Jacques could tell us."

Gilles nodded. "I will take care of it. Leave it to me."

"OK, but no more accidents, like with Rob. You understand?" Philippe fixed Gilles with a stare and Gilles stared back at him for a few seconds before turning away and leaving.

Night had fallen and Carter was deep in thought as he looked out of the window of his hotel room in Sainte Maxime but when his phone rang, he picked it up off the table immediately and answered the call.

"Nicole, Hi," he said.

"Carter, I've just had Eloise on the phone."

Carter sensed Nicole's anger and knew what was coming. He had been expecting to get a call from her and he had already decided that when it came, he would get in first and try to minimise the damage to his relationship with her.

"I didn't have any choice, Nikki," he pleaded, before she had a chance to say anything more, "She had already worked out for herself that all was not as it seemed. I had to tell her. It was the only option"

"Well, I'm worried about her."

"I know you are."

"Please, Carter, make sure nothing happens to her. I'm depending on you. She's all I've got left now."

"Can't you get her to come home? That would be the best solution."

"I tried. But Eloise has never been one to do as she's told and right now she seems to be more concerned about this new boyfriend of hers than she is about anything else."

"I'll do everything I can to make sure she's safe, I promise. I already have someone keeping an eye on her."

"OK, Carter. Thank you."

Carter rang off and threw his phone onto the bed. Then he went back to the window and stared out over the sea. He desperately hoped that his investigation wouldn't get in the way of his renewed relationship with Nicole but he knew it probably would. All he could do was try to convince her that his involvement would, if anything, make things better; make it more likely, not less, that Eloise would come out of it unscathed.

Chapter 11

Yvonne woke to the soft but unmistakable sound of footsteps climbing the stairs from the gallery to her apartment. She looked at the alarm clock beside her bed and saw that it was three o'clock in the morning. She shook her head and wiped the sleep from her eyes before listening again. Through the open door between her bedroom and the living room, she was sure she could hear someone on the wooden steps outside the apartment. But who? And how had they got into the gallery without setting off the alarm?

She threw back the sheet and rose from her bed. As she was naked, preferring not to wear anything in bed during the summer months, she instinctively reached for her bathrobe. She put it on quickly and went to the corner of the room where she kept a baseball bat she had once accepted from a customer in payment for a painting by a local, rather indifferent, artist. She picked up the bat and silently closed her bedroom door. Almost as soon as she had, she heard the living room door open and the sound of voices whispering. Her heart was racing as she backed away into a corner of the bedroom, hoping they would just take what they wanted and leave.

Then, suddenly and noisily, the bedroom door was thrown open and the sight that met her eyes filled her with panic. Standing in the doorway were two men, one large and muscular, the other smaller and slighter. They were dressed entirely in black and their faces were set stony, expressionless, as they looked around the room. Yvonne lifted the bat above and behind her right shoulder. She was trembling from head to toe, terrified by the presence of the two intruders, but she was ready to defend herself.

As they came into the room, Henri and Albert saw Yvonne in the corner of the room and moved slowly and menacingly towards her; she noticed that one of them was holding a gun and was pointing it at her. As they got closer to her, she swung the baseball bat with as much force as she could in an arc in front of her but they had halted their approach and were out of range. The bat swished harmlessly in front of them and as it completed its journey, Yvonne's arms were stretched out to her left and she was defenceless. At precisely the right moment, Albert, using his size and strength, leapt forward and grabbed her, putting his big hairy arms around her shoulders from behind and smothering any further swings of the bat. Yvonne dropped the bat and tried with all her strength to use her elbows to fight back but Albert had her arms pinned to her side. She looked at Henri, who was standing directly in front of her, and swore at him as she continued to struggle to break loose. She thought about screaming in the hope that a neighbour would hear and come to her rescue, but when she opened her mouth, no sound came out.

Henri moved towards her and when he was close enough, he slapped her face, quickly and firmly but not with any great force. "Manners!" he said mockingly, wagging a finger in front of her, "You must remember your manners."

Henri's counterfeit smile reminded Yvonne of pictures she had seen of Great White sharks about to bite into their prey. She tried again to wriggle free but it was hopeless.

Henri reached out his hand and took hold of her firmly under the chin. "You should try to be more welcoming towards your guests," he said, so lasciviously that he was almost drooling, and with that, he adjusted his grip and held her face tightly by the jaw as he kissed her.

Yvonne clenched her teeth and tried to disengage from the kiss but it was useless. Instead, she relaxed, opened her mouth and pretended to give in to him. Then, moments later, she took his bottom lip between her teeth and bit deep into it.

He pulled back immediately and as he did, she lifted her knee sharply; it found its mark and Henri gasped and bent over in agony. Still holding Yvonne tightly, Albert smiled but when Henri had recovered, he was furious and his eyes flashed with anger.

"Bitch!" he said and slapped her face again, this time much harder. "I think you need to learn to be more friendly."

Yvonne's blood ran cold. She realised that these men were not burglars at all; they had not broken into her apartment to rob her; they were there for a different reason. She struggled again with even more vigour than before, but Albert was too strong for her and his grip did not slacken at all. She might as well have been wrapped in bands of steel.

"Put her on the bed," said Henri as he looked round the room. His voice was cold and hard and threatening and the uncontrollable trembling returned to Yvonne's body.

Albert looked at Henri, obviously reluctant to obey the order.

"Go on! Do it!" barked Henri.

Albert changed his hold and grabbed Yvonne's arms. His huge hands easily closed round her biceps and he pushed her towards the bed. Unwillingly, and to avoid stumbling and falling, she got onto the bed. He changed his grip once more and, stretching her arms out above her head, pinned her firmly by the wrists.

In the corner of the room, where Yvonne had found the baseball bat, Henri noticed a length of coiled washing line. He went over to it and picked it up. As he walked round to the bottom of the bed he tested its strength by snapping it taut between his hands a few times. Then he faced Yvonne and smiled. It was the Great White smile again.

Albert looked on impassively, merely grunting acknowledgement of the instructions he was given as he kept Yvonne pinned down on the bed.

"Now Mademoiselle Bitch, you will learn why you should be better mannered," said Henri as he made a loop with the washing line before grabbing one of Yvonne's flailing feet and deftly slipping the loop over it. He pulled the loop hard, stretching out her leg and Yvonne winced as the rope bit into her ankle. As he tied the rope to the bedpost, Henri looked at Yvonne, no smile anymore just a hard cold look in his eyes.

"Now the other one," he said, as if he were talking to a child, and, using the other end of the rope, tied her other foot to the second bedpost.

Throughout, Albert never relaxed his hold on Yvonne's wrists though she struggled with all her might. When she realised what was going to happen, Yvonne stopped struggling, it was no use anyway. Slowly and deliberately, Henri removed his trousers and boxer shorts before climbing on top of her. Roughly and without any pretence of finesse, he undid her bathrobe and pulled it aside. Involuntarily, he passed his tongue over his lips as he looked at Yvonne's vulnerable body beneath him.

"You bastard," she said quietly as his face came close to hers, "I'll get you for this." She could feel him probing between her legs and wanted to be sick but she couldn't.

"*BASTARD!*" she screamed as he found his mark and thrust home.

After that, for several minutes, the only sound was that of Henri panting as he pumped in and out of Yvonne before climaxing and falling on top of her.

Traumatised, Yvonne fell silent and her body went limp. Albert let go of her but she had no more fight in her and when he did, she just lay there, her hair matted with sweat. Henri got up off the bed and put his clothes back on before giving Albert another instruction.

"Untie her and put some clothes on her," he said in a matter-of-fact tone.

Yvonne started to cry and Albert began to feel sorry for her. Gently, he untied her feet, pulled them round off the bed and lifted her into a sitting position. Between the tears, she looked at her attacker, anger in her eyes, and repeated "You *bastard*."

Henri laughed at her as he tightened his belt. "Maybe next time you won't be such a little bitch."

Albert passed Yvonne the clothes she had put on a chair to one side of the room when she had undressed the night before and silently indicated to her to put them on. Quietly, she dressed while they waited and watched.

When she was dressed, Henri forced her mouth open and pushed a large handkerchief into it almost choking her. Then, before she could spit it out, he removed the red scarf she had put round her neck and tied it tightly to hold the handkerchief in place. When he had finished, Albert took her arm and, noiselessly, they led her out of the Gallery, into the street, and out of Sainte Pierre.

Henri drove out of the car park with Yvonne sitting in the back next to Albert. She stole a glance at the man who had held her down whilst his accomplice had violated her; he was staring straight ahead, his face impassive as the car sped along the unlit country roads in the inky, moonless night.

Within a few minutes, though it seemed longer to Yvonne, they came to a halt outside a farmhouse at the end of a long track. Albert took Yvonne's arm and pulled her, unresisting, out of the car. Henri fumbled for a torch in the glove compartment and led the way. When they reached the farmhouse, he took a key from his pocket and unlocked the front door.

Once inside, Henri switched on the ceiling light and Yvonne could see that they were standing in the hallway of what must once have been an imposing residence. She looked round and saw that on each side, a door led off the hall into what she supposed must be the two main reception rooms. Directly in front of her, a broad flight of shallow stairs rose to a galleried landing. On each side of the staircase, a corridor led to another door.

It was obvious from the general state of disrepair all around, that the house was no longer occupied. The red glass shade of an electric lamp designed to look like an oil lamp was broken and bare wires hung sadly from the wall where once there would have been expensive wall lights. To one side of the front door stood a small table bearing only an ancient bakelite telephone and a hopelessly out of date and dog-eared directory. Yvonne doubted if the telephone were connected but thought she would like to have the chance to test it. The carpet in the middle of the floor had obviously once proudly welcomed visitors to its tasteful owners' home, but now, weighed down with dust and debris, it might as well have been a cheap special offer from a mass market furnishing store.

The two men led Yvonne along the passageway to the left of the stairs and into the kitchen, switching on the kitchen lights as they entered. If the hall had spoken to Yvonne of disuse, the kitchen bellowed of misuse. The sink was piled high with dirty pans and crockery. Filthy cutlery, undoubtedly teeming with wildlife of the microscopic variety, stuck out from the pile like the spines of a porcupine. On the floor, months of dropped crusts and bits of food littered the black and white checked linoleum and, apart from a few rickety wall and floor cupboards, the kitchen was unfurnished.

Yvonne looked round quickly when she heard the pile of crockery clatter. She was sure she saw a rat scamper behind the electric kettle, the flex of which showed signs of having been gnawed. A shiver ran down her spine at the thought; she hated small rodents and she hated big ones even more.

Henri opened the door next to the one through which they had come into the kitchen and flicked the light switch on the wall beside it. It looked to Yvonne as if the door would lead into a cupboard underneath the staircase in the hall, but as she got closer she saw that it led down some steps. The three of them descended the flight of stone steps into the basement of the house.

The switch had turned on a single light bulb hanging in the centre of the room and Yvonne was totally unprepared for what she saw. There, in the middle of the windowless room, beneath the light, was a chair, and tied to the chair was Antoine with his head resting limply on his chest.

Henri motioned towards Antoine. "Untie him and get rid of the body," he said and Albert, keen to do as he was told let go of Yvonne and approached the chair.

Yvonne saw her chance and without hesitation swung round on her heel and darted up the steps. Albert turned as he heard her go and looked at Henri, who quickly jerked his head towards the steps indicating that he should go after her. Defying his great bulk, he took the steps two at a time as he followed Yvonne and chased her through the kitchen, passageway and hall, finally catching up with her about fifty yards from the house. He reached out and seized the collar of her blouse, bringing her to a standstill. Yvonne choked as a button bit deep into her throat and she started to cough. The big man was panting with the effort of running after her and his face was red. Yvonne turned to look at him. Still gagged, she stared at him as he stood there, catching his breath, and implored him with her eyes to let her go. Then, in a desperate attempt to win her freedom, she brought her knee up, aiming for his groin, but he was ready for the move and stepped back quickly without letting go of her collar. He smiled weakly and wagged a finger at her.

Yvonne pleaded again with her eyes for her freedom, and for a moment she thought she might succeed; that Albert might relent and let her go. But he didn't. All she got was a sympathetic look, the smile fading from his round face as he shook his head sadly.

Still holding the collar of her blouse, Albert half led, half dragged Yvonne back into the farmhouse and down to the basement. When they re-entered the depressing room, Antoine's body lay crumpled on the floor and Henri was coiling the thin rope which had been used to tie him to the chair. He looked round as they came in and walked over to where Albert was holding Yvonne.

"You just won't learn will you?" he said, and as he spoke, Yvonne noticed that his eyes, like his voice, were cold and hard. In his hand, he held the knife he had used to cut Antoine free. He put it behind her head and cut the scarf which held the gag in place allowing

Yvonne to spit it out. Then he lifted the knife to her face and slowly turned it this way and that in front of her. "Obviously my last lesson taught you nothing. Perhaps this one will."

Yvonne wondered what he meant; she hoped she would never find out. She knew what pleasure it gave this animal of a man to hurt others; she had experienced his vicious nature already. As the seconds passed, she became more and more gripped by panic and there was a terrified look on her face as, in a single deft movement, Henri whipped the knife up across her face. Her cheek gaped open and blood poured from the wound. Yvonne gasped and put her hand to her face. She felt the warm sticky blood flow down her wrist and looked at her hand.

"*You bastard*!" she hissed, her eyes alive with fury despite the tears which filled them from the pain. Albert winced as the knife cut through her cheek and his face expressed his silent disapproval.

"Tie her to the chair," said Henri throwing the rope to Albert and, at the same time, handing Yvonne the scarf. "You'd better hold that to your face or you'll bleed to death and we don't want you to die, do we?... Not yet, anyway."

Yvonne took the scarf reluctantly and did as she had been told. Then Albert led her gently to the chair and sat her down in it before using the rope to tie her wrists and ankles to the chair's arms and legs, just as Antoine had been tied to it. She looked at him when he had finished and could see in his eyes the distaste he felt for Henri's actions.

When he had finished tying Yvonne to the chair, Albert lifted Antoine's body off the floor and with remarkable ease, put it over his shoulder. He made his way to the bottom of the steps where he picked up a shovel that was resting against the wall and began, slowly, to climb the steps. Henri followed and when they reached the top, he switched off the light, leaving Yvonne alone in the dank darkness.

The blood from Yvonne's wound had stopped running down the side of her face but her cheek still stung with pain and the ropes hurt as they bit into her wrists and ankles, even more so when she attempted to wriggle free. Eventually, she gave up trying to free herself and sat still in silence surrounded by the total darkness of the room. She felt sick at the thought of what might be going to happen to her and the sweat from her armpits ran down the sides of her body as she contemplated what the future had in store for her.

In the silence, she thought she heard the scuffling of another rat, or perhaps the same one, in the pile of furniture at the far end of the room. She tried to lift her feet out of its reach but the ropes kept them firmly anchored to the floor.

Chapter 12

When his phone rang at eight o'clock the next morning, Jacques was still asleep in the master cabin of the Esprit. Even though he had left the phone in the saloon, the incessant shrill ringing eventually woke him. He looked at Eloise who was fast asleep next to him. Trying not to disturb her, he got up from the bed and threw on a towelling bathrobe before climbing the steps to the saloon. Standing in the saloon he ran a hand through his hair and yawned before picking up the phone and speaking into it.

"Hello," he said.

"Jacques?... Jacques Armand?"

"Oui."

"Bon! Now listen to me, Jacques. Your sister, Yvonne, she is my guest. A little unwillingly, perhaps, but she is here with me."

"Who *is* this?" asked Jacques. He was still half asleep but he was rapidly waking up.

"It doesn't matter who I am. What matters is that I have your sister and if you don't do *exactly* as I say, it will not go well for her."

Jacques was alarmed now. It was beginning to sound as if someone had kidnapped Yvonne.

"Listen," said the voice on the phone.

"Jacques? Jacques?" Yvonne's voice was strained but unmistakable. "Jacques, don't listen to him he's going to kill…" Yvonne's voice was cut short and Jacques could feel the panic rising in him.

"What do you want?" he asked in measured tones trying to hide his unease and keep himself under control; mouthing off at this unknown person wasn't likely to accomplish anything.

"Be ready to leave the next time I call."

The line went dead and Jacques slowly and deliberately put his phone down next to the music centre on top of the cupboard unit. Absent-mindedly he went to the galley, spooned some coffee into the cafetière and switched on the kettle. Then he began to pace up and down the saloon trying to work out what to do.

A few minutes later, Jacques was still walking up and down the saloon wondering what to do when a sleepy Eloise came up the steps from the master cabin. She saw Jacques deep in thought.

"Are you all right?" she asked, rubbing her eyes with the backs of her hands.

Jacques looked up and shook his head.

"What's the matter? What's wrong?" asked Eloise as she put her hand on his arm, her sleepiness rapidly giving way to concern.

"They've got Yvonne," said Jacques, his voice flat, simply passing on information.

"What do you mean, they've got Yvonne? Who's got Yvonne?"

"I don't know. Maybe it's the ones those diamond people are looking for."

"But why? What would they want Yvonne for?"

"I don't know. They said they would ring again and that I must be ready to do what they tell me when they do. Yvonne sounded very scared and she doesn't scare easily. She tried to tell me something but they stopped her before she could say much."

"What did she say?"

"Something about them going to kill someone."

"Who?"

" I don't know. They shut her up before she got to that." Jacques began to rub his hands together anxiously. "I don't know what to do," he said, looking helplessly at Eloise.

"You must tell the police," insisted Eloise but Jacques disagreed. His experience of, and involvement with, authority had not left him with any confidence in either the motives or the abilities of public officials, especially the police.

"They'll hurt her, kill her maybe, if I contact the police," he said

"But they'll know what to do," pressed Eloise.

"I am not so sure about that."

"Well what about Jefferson then? Maybe he can help?"

"That also is too dangerous. I am not going to take a risk with Yvonne's life."

Jacques knew that he had little option but to do exactly what he was told to do by Yvonne's kidnappers; the alternatives were all too risky.

"I'll do whatever they say," he said, "It's the only thing I can do." He pushed past Eloise and headed for the circular staircase. "I must get dressed and be ready for when they call again."

Almost exactly an hour after the first call, the phone rang again. Jacques was dressed and ready when it did and he answered it immediately.

"Bon! Tres bon, Jacques," said the caller, "I believe that you are now taking this seriously. I hope you haven't done anything stupid, like speak to the police?"

"No. I haven't done anything, as you said. I've just been waiting for you to call again."

"Good. Now listen carefully. Get in your car and take the road to the west." Jacques grabbed the pen and paper he had put on the table in readiness and started scribbling down the instructions he was being given. He repeated each instruction back to the caller to make sure he had heard it correctly and Eloise listened intently as he did.

"Road to the west," he said as he wrote it down.

"The one leading to La Garde-Freinet," continued the caller, followed by "to La Garde-Freinet," from Jacques.

"Precisely six and a half kilometres after leaving Grimaud, you will see a small road to the left. Take that road."

"Road to left after six and a half kilometres," echoed Jacques.

"After two hundred metres, there is a turning to the right. Turn onto it."

"Two hundred metres, then turn right."

"Follow the road for half a kilometre, and then stop."

"Stop after half a kilometre."

"You will be in front of a farmhouse. Go into the farmhouse and wait. You will be contacted."

"Wait in farmhouse."

"Oh, and Jacques, make sure you come alone. We will be watching you."

Jacques put the pen down. "OK. But if you have harmed her, I will kill you," he said, trying hard not to give away how scared he was.

The phone went dead again before he could say anything more. He looked at Eloise.

"I have to go," he said.

"Was it them?" asked Eloise, already knowing the answer to her question.

Jacques nodded. "They want me to go to a farmhouse up in the hills."

"You're not going to go, are you? It could be a trap," warned Eloise with some dismay, her resolve not to interfere breaking down momentarily.

"What choice do I have? They've got Yvonne."

"Then I'll go with you."

"Are you mad! I don't want to put you in danger as well."

"But I might be able to help," said Eloise. She didn't want him to go but if he was going to go anyway then she wanted to be at his side, to help in any way she could.

"No! Absolutely not," he said firmly, "They said to come alone."

"But Jacques..."

"*No*! And another thing, don't phone the police after I've gone. Understand?"

Eloise nodded as Jacques reached for his car keys. She watched him, pleading with her eyes for him not to go. He kissed her on the cheek before running out of the saloon, across the gangway and onto the jetty.

Eloise watched and waited until he had disappeared along the Rue Grande before taking her phone out of her pocket. She dug into her pocket again and retrieved Carter's card. Then, with only a moment's hesitation, she tapped in his number and put the phone to her ear.

Carter was sitting in the dining room at his hotel in Sainte Maxime enjoying his breakfast when Eloise's call came. He had always liked the French idea of breakfasting on warm croissants and jam, preferably apricot jam. The smartly dressed waiter had looked askance at Carter as he had been asked to replenish the supply of croissants in the basket on his table and

Carter was about to start his fourth one when his phone rang. He answered it immediately.

Eloise told him about the call Jacques had received, that Yvonne had been kidnapped and that Jacques had set off to rescue her.

"Do you know where he's gone?" asked Carter.

"Yes, he repeated all the instructions as he wrote them down."

Carter grabbed a pen and a piece of paper which were on the table next to him. "Give me the directions," he said.

Carter began scribbling as he listened to what Eloise said. When she had finished, he got up from the table and walked quickly out of the dining room as he finished the call. "You stay where you are. I'm on my way."

Carter came out of the hotel running. He pressed the button on the key fob and the car's indicator lights flashed as its doors unlocked. He pulled the door open and jumped in. Almost before the door had shut, Carter had started the engine but before driving off, he called Conrad on his phone.

"Where are you? I just had a call from Eloise," he said when Conrad answered.

"I'm following Jacques. He left the boat a few minutes ago," said Conrad, "I think he's heading for the car park."

"I'm on my way. Meet me at the main road."

"What about Jacques? Don't you want me to follow him?"

"No. Too dangerous, they'll be watching. And I know where he's going anyway."

Jacques watched the numbers roll round on the odometer as he drove along the road to La Garde-

Freinet. A turning to the left came into sight and he swung the car into it, hardly slowing down at all. Once on the new road, he slowed down and referred to his notes.

"Two hundred metres," he said to himself before slowing down even more and then turning right onto a farm track.

After Jacques' car has passed by, Albert emerged from behind a tree. He watched the car travel along the track and then put his phone to his ear.

"Il est seul," he said and then turned and looked along the road where Jacques had come from. "Et personne ne suit," he continued before starting to walk down the track towards the farmhouse.

Jacques' car crawled up to the brow of the small hill and stopped about fifty yards from the farmhouse. He looked intently and nervously at the farmhouse. It was quiet; nothing moved.

Several miles behind Jacques, Carter's car followed the route Jacques had taken earlier. Conrad was in the car with him, sitting in the passenger seat with a map laid out on his lap next to the piece of paper on which Carter had written the directions. Carter listened as Conrad spoke to him.

"It's the next one." He said and looked up as the car came to a crossroads. "Yeah, that one."

Conrad put out his hand to steady himself as Carter veered off to the right onto a road into the mountains, tyres screeching.

Up ahead of Carter and Conrad, Jacques' car slowly started moving again, towards the farmhouse and then stopped when it got close to it. Jacques got out of the car and approached the farmhouse. He looked all around as he did, uncertain of what he was about to discover.

When he reached the farmhouse, Jacques opened the front door and went in. The man on the phone had told him to wait there and that he would be contacted, but as he entered the hallway, he saw Yvonne through the open doorway at the end of the passageway beside the staircase. She was gagged and tied to a chair placed in the middle of the kitchen floor. Behind her was the farmhouse's back door.

Framed by the doorway from the hall, a shaft of light from the kitchen window highlighted Yvonne in the comparative darkness of the rest of the room and Jacques could see the cut on her cheek, which ran from the corner of her mouth almost to her eye. He walked hesitantly along the passageway and stood in the doorway, not sure what to do. Yvonne tried to signal to him with her eyes. As he watched her, the sight of the blood from the cut on her face and the terrified look in her eyes made his heart beat faster. He looked in the direction he thought she was indicating and as his eyes became accustomed to the dim light in the recesses of the kitchen, Henri stepped forward out of the shadows.

"Welcome, Jacques. It is good to see you," he said, looking at his watch. "You made good time. Obviously Yvonne is even more important to you than we thought. That will make things much easier for all of us." He moved towards Jacques and, at the same time, Albert came into the kitchen from the hall, pushing Jacques aside as he walked past him and took up position behind Yvonne. Jacques was struck by the immense bulk of the man but quickly turned his attention back to Henri who was speaking again.

"Yvonne and I got to know each other very well last night. Intimately, you might say." He laughed out loud but Jacques controlled himself, his fear overcoming his temper. Then, in a moment, Henri's expression turned mean and threatening. "Sit down!" he said sharply.

Jacques was too scared to do anything but obey and he sat down on a chair set at right angles to Yvonne's. "If you touch her again, I'll kill you," he said angrily trying to hide his fear.

Henri's face broke into a smile again as he approached Jacques. "Oh… no… you… won't," he said, slapping Jacques hard across the face between each word, first with the palm of his hand and then with the back of it.

Jacques reeled under the blows and his anger welled up inside him as his hands gripped the sides of the chair tightly. He threw a glance at Yvonne and saw that Albert was now holding a knife in his left hand. When Albert saw Jacques look at him, he placed the knife against Yvonne's throat and shook his head slowly, warning Jacques not to try anything. Struggling to control his temper, Jacques sat still and waited to see what would happen next.

Henri turned away towards the grimy window above the sink before speaking in a low tone, "Now that I have your attention, Jacques, there are some things I wish to know." He continued to face the window. "Your two visitors yesterday. What did they want?"

Henri's voice was quiet but menacing and as he finished speaking, he turned to face Jacques and looked him straight in the eye.

"What visitors?" answered Jacques, swallowing and trying to play for time.

Henri nodded to Albert who was still standing behind Yvonne with the knife in his hand. Albert sighed as he grabbed Yvonne's hair and pulled her head back putting the knife to her throat again. Jacques steeled himself. He was sure they wouldn't kill her, at least not until he had told them what they wanted to know.

"I certainly will not tell you anything if you kill her," he said in as even a tone as he could manage.

Henri put his finger to his mouth and gently tapped his lips as he walked to and fro in front of Jacques. "OK, Jacques, I believe you. So we will try something a little different." He turned and looked at Albert. "Undo the lady's blouse," he instructed.

Putting the knife between his teeth, Albert reached down with both hands and ripped Yvonne's blouse apart roughly, causing a couple of buttons to fall to the floor. Yvonne's exposed breasts rose and fell and her breathing became heavy as Albert took Yvonne's left breast in his hand and held the knife next to it. Henri smiled and looked at Jacques.

"Now, Jacques," he said, "Let me ask you again. What did your visitors want?"

It was beginning to dawn on Jacques that these men would never let him and Yvonne go. Once they had found out all they wanted to know, they would kill them both. All he could do was play for time and hope for a moment when their guard was down. But he didn't want to see Yvonne mutilated any more. He waited, and they waited, looking at him expectantly. Then Henri grew impatient and nodded to Albert indicating that he should proceed. Albert was about to comply when Jacques interrupted.

"No! Wait!" he said, a desperate tone to his voice, "OK, you win. I will tell you what you want to know." Albert relaxed and let go of Yvonne's breast as Jacques continued. "They were interested in a book which they found on my boat."

"Ah, very good, Jacques. Now we are getting somewhere. I knew you loved your sister more than that." Henri leaned towards Jacques and, with his face only a few inches away from him, he added, "Having had the pleasure of her myself last night, I can understand why." He stood back and laughed out loud again. Jacques could hardly control himself; he was shaking with rage. That seemed to please Henri and he continued to goad Jacques, taunting him with every word, "If you tell me everything, maybe I will let you watch next time."

That was it! Jacques could take no more. His temper finally got the upper hand and he snapped. He shot out of the chair and grabbed Henri by the throat. The two of them fell backwards against the sink and the pile of filthy crockery clattered as it readjusted itself.

Astonished by Jacques' action, Henri looked at his bewildered accomplice. "Albert!" he croaked as Jacques' grip tightened, "Kill her! Do it!... *Now*!" he wheezed as Jacques' hands tightened round his throat.

Without releasing his grip, Jacques looked towards Yvonne as Albert slowly lifted the knife to Yvonne's throat and started to draw it firmly across her windpipe.

"NO! WAIT!" he shouted in desperation as he let go his grip and moved towards Yvonne. But it was too late and Albert's hand finished the job it had begun. Blood poured from the gaping wound on Yvonne's neck and a gurgling sound confirmed that Albert had cut through her windpipe. A gunshot rang out and one of the glass panes in the back door shattered as Jacques instinctively dropped to the floor.

Responding quickly, Henri, now free of Jacques, took out his gun and fired in the direction of the back door. The bullet from his gun missed its mark and lodged in the door frame. He scurried quickly out of the kitchen and into the hall as, almost in slow motion, Albert fell to the floor with a thud, a small round hole in the back of his head showing where the bullet from Conrad's gun had entered his brain.

Jacques looked up and the awful, horrifying look on Yvonne's face burned itself into his memory. "*NO-O-O*!" he screamed agonisingly as he saw Yvonne's eyes staring at him in disbelief. He closed his eyes to shut out the scene before him. When he opened them again, Yvonne was staring at him vacantly and then her head fell onto her chest.

"*Yvonne*!" cried out Jacques in despair as he turned his face to the floor, sobbing, his whole body shaking and heaving with the strength of the emotion running through him.

Conrad shouldered the back door open and he and Carter came into the kitchen. Carter looked down at Albert and then at Conrad.

"Did you get a look at the other guy?" he asked. Conrad shook his head as Carter continued. "Too bad. But Jacques will be able to identify him."

Jacques slowly managed to control himself and, with Carter's help, got up from the floor. He went over to Yvonne and knelt beside her before taking her head in his hands and gently lifting it a little. Her lifeless eyes stared back at him and he let her head drop back onto her chest.

Chapter 13

Eloise was pacing up and down the aft deck of the Esprit when she saw Carter walking towards the Capitainerie with Conrad beside him. She looked intently but couldn't see Jacques. Then, as Carter and Conrad drifted apart, a pace or two behind them, shuffling along the road with his head down, she saw him. She ran across the gangway onto the quay and raced towards the men as they slowly approached the boat.

"*Jacques! Jacques!*" she called out as she ran.

Jacques looked up as he heard her calling and she almost knocked him over in her haste to embrace him. She kissed him on the lips as he took her in his arms, more as a reflex action than anything else. He kissed her back but without any great enthusiasm and then gently pushed her away.

Carter and Conrad looked on anxiously as it dawned on Eloise that all was not well, that something bad had happened.

"What is it?" she asked looking first at Jacques and then at Carter. "Is it Yvonne?… What's happened?… Please, *someone*, tell me." She saw the tears in Jacques eyes and looked from him to Carter. "*Please!*"

Eventually, Conrad spoke, his tone almost apologetic. "Yvonne is dead," he said.

Eloise's mouth dropped open in horror and her hand went to cover it. "Oh no!" she said, "Oh Jacques, I am so sorry."

Jacques looked away into the distance and Eloise turned to Carter, her eyes pleading with him to tell her what had happened but he said nothing. The little group made its way slowly onto the Esprit and into the saloon.

Jacques and Conrad sat down at the table while Eloise led Carter to the galley. She switched on the kettle and, hoping they were out of earshot of Jacques, she turned to Carter and whispered, "What happened? Please tell me."

Carter glanced at Jacques to check that he was not listening and then filled Eloise in on everything that had happened at the farmhouse. When he had finished, she was stunned. As if by remote control, she poured the boiling water into the cafetière. Carter watched her, concerned that he may have given her more detail than she could cope with but when she had finished pouring the water, she looked at him.

"Have you any idea who they were?" she asked, a grim determination to be strong coming through in her voice.

"We're not sure," said Carter, shaking his head, "You can see how Jacques is. All we've been able to get out of him is that they were asking him about us. And the French PI who was working with us has disappeared. Could be he's dead too."

Eloise shook her head slowly as she put some mugs on the tray. "I can't believe all this is happening," she said. "And what makes it even worse is that according to you, my grandfather is involved." She looked up at Carter before continuing. "What do the police think? Do they have any idea who the men were?"

Carter coughed and looked over towards Jacques. "We haven't spoken to the police, yet," he said, lowering his voice.

"*You haven't...*" began Eloise in a loud voice but Carter put his finger to his lips to quieten her and she continued in a softer tone, "You haven't told the police? Why not for goodness' sake?"

"Because it would take too long to explain it all to them. We're getting close. If we go to the police now, everything will come to a grinding halt while they get up to speed and then these guys, whoever they are, will have time to cover their tracks and get away. The trail we're following doesn't end here in Port Grimaud, you know. We only know a small part of the story so far, there's a lot more for us to find out yet."

"But there's a dead body in a farmhouse up in the hills somewhere, in fact two dead bodies, maybe even three!"

"I know, and..." Carter removed a small polythene bag containing a bullet from his pocket and held it up. "...this came from the gun used by one of the men who kidnapped Yvonne. It wouldn't come as a total shock to me if it matched the one used to execute Rob's killer."

"All the more reason to tell the police," insisted Eloise and Carter raised his hand to try and calm her.

"All in good time," he said as Eloise looked at him disbelievingly. "We just need a little more time. Another day or so, maybe less, that's all. By then we'll have all the evidence we need. Then we can tell the police. I'm asking you not to do anything for twenty-four hours, that's all. If the police get involved now, we'll never catch them."

"I don't know," said Eloise, unconvinced, "As far as I'm concerned, Jacques comes first. I'll do whatever I have to do to protect him. Even if that means reporting my own grandfather to the police."

"Please! Just trust me a little longer," pleaded Carter, "I do know what I'm doing and I will contact the police when the time is right."

"OK. But only for twenty-four hours, no more. Then you tell the police, or I will."

Eloise stared challengingly at Carter for a few moments before picking up the tray and carrying it through to the saloon. She put the tray on the table and then sat down beside Jacques. He was still staring blankly in front of him, largely unaware of anything going on around him. Eloise looked at him intently; he was going to need a lot of support and she wanted to be the one to give it to him. She began to rub his arm gently. Jacques turned his head slowly and looked at her for a moment, then he turned back and continued to stare ahead.

From time to time Carter, who had followed Eloise into the saloon, asked Jacques a question, but the blank look did not change and Jacques didn't even acknowledge his presence.

When Carter had finished his coffee and had no more questions to ask, he put his cup down and signalled to Conrad that they should leave but before they did, he turned to Eloise.

"Will you be all right?" he asked. Eloise nodded and Carter continued, "You've got my number. Call me if you need anything. I'll come back tomorrow. OK?" Eloise nodded again.

When they had left, Eloise put her arm round Jacques' shoulders and pulled his head towards her. She felt a tear trickle onto her shoulder and she held him close, stroking his head gently.

After about half an hour, during which Eloise did her best to comfort him, Jacques took a deep breath and sat up straight. Eloise looked at him, concerned.

"How are you?" she asked quietly.

"OK," answered Jacques, forcing a feeble smile as if to reinforce what he had said.

"You sure?"

He nodded and looked deep into her eyes. "Thank you for being here for me today. I love you so much."

Eloise smiled. "I love you, too," she said and gave him a peck on the cheek.

A few more minutes passed with Jacques and Eloise holding each other close before Jacques spoke.

"I need to go and tell my mother what has happened," he said as he got to his feet. "Someone has to tell her that her daughter is dead. Will you come with me? It will make it easier for me and I want her to meet you anyway."

"Of course I'll come with you," responded Eloise.

Jacques saw the pity in her eyes. "It will be all right," he said. "She is a strong woman, she has had to be."

As they walked up the steps to his mother's apartment Jacques was holding Eloise's hand and he felt her squeeze his hand as he knocked on the door.

"Maman, it's me, Jacques," he called, opening the door and going in.

"Jacques! How nice to see you." Claudine swept into the room. "You haven't been home for days." She threw her arms round Jacques, hugging him tightly. He hugged her back and they kissed each other on the cheek before separating.

"Maman, I have some bad news to tell you."

"Bad news? What do you mean?" Claudine frowned and looked from Jacques to Eloise, a mystified expression crossing her face fleetingly. Then she looked back at Jacques. "What has happened?"

Jacques noticed how the frown made her look so much older. He wanted to see the smile that had cheered him up so often in the past but he knew that the news he bore would not bring it to her face. He steeled himself.

"It's Yvonne, Maman… She is dead."

Claudine's knees gave way and Jacques stepped forward quickly to catch her as she fainted. "Help me to get her onto the settee," he said to Eloise who was standing watching, not at all sure what she should do.

"I'll get a damp cloth," said Eloise once they had laid Claudine on the settee.

Jacques removed his mother's shoes carefully and a few moments later Eloise returned with the cloth and placed it on Claudine's brow. Jacques knelt down beside his mother and patted her hand gently.

When Claudine came round after a couple of minutes, Jacques was still kneeling and Eloise was standing beside him, bent over her.

"What happened?" she asked.

"You fainted," answered Jacques.

Claudine sat up slowly. "I thought you said Yvonne was dead?"

"Yes, it's true; Yvonne is dead."

"But how? Why? Tell me, Jacques. What has happened to her? I don't understand."

Jacques sighed. "It's a long story," he said before proceeding to tell Claudine about the shattering events of the last forty-eight hours. To spare his mother's feelings, he left out the more gruesome details of what had been done to Yvonne but even so, when he had finished, his mother looked pale.

Jacques and Eloise stayed with Claudine while she recovered from the devastating news they had given her and Jacques insisted that she drink all the glass of cognac he had poured for her.

About an hour later, Claudine seemed to be getting her equilibrium back and Jacques asked Eloise to stay with her while he went to fetch her closest friend, Colette, who lived in the apartment next door.

After Jacques had returned with Colette, he and Eloise stayed a little longer, long enough to be sure Claudine would be all right, before taking their leave and promising to return to see her very soon.

While Jacques was giving his mother the bad news about Yvonne, Carter and Conrad were sitting in the lounge of the Hotel Giraglia next to the Capitainerie. Conrad was looking intently at Carter, who was on the phone.

"OK. Thanks. I'll do that." Carter switched off the phone and put it on the table in front of him as Conrad looked at him expectantly.

"Nothing new," said Carter, "Harris said he would forward the forensic analysis on the bullet that killed Spicer to the Sainte Maxime police so that they can compare it with the one we got from the farmhouse." Carter looked at Conrad, trying to gauge his reaction to the news before continuing. "I'd prefer not to, but I think we'd better go and see the French police and bring them up to speed. Before they receive the analysis from Harris and get the idea we're trying to keep something from them."

"Do you think that's a good idea?" asked Conrad, challenging Carter's questioning look as he continued. "Lacoste is a prominent citizen in these parts. He may have, in fact I'm guessing he almost certainly does have, connections within the local police force."

Carter considered what Conrad had said for a few moments before responding. "Good point. What if we tell them about the farmhouse and what we are investigating but leave Philippe out of it for now?" Conrad nodded his approval of this compromise as Carter continued, "That way, if he does have a source within the local police, he won't know we're onto him and start covering his tracks. But we still get the police on our side."

Carter and Conrad looked at each other for a few moments before Carter looked away and stared through the window, mentally going over their plan and checking his thinking. He knew that he had no choice but to tell the police what had happened at the farmhouse. His promise to Nicole meant that he couldn't take any risks with Eloise's safety; he had to play it safe. Telling the Sainte Maxime police would mean getting round the clock protection for Eloise and Jacques and that would put his mind at rest about her safety even if it did prejudice his investigation a little. But not telling them about Philippe's possible involvement would enable him to pursue that line of enquiry without hindrance, for a little while at least.

Chapter 14

Gilles was standing with his back to the French window in Philippe's living room as Philippe paced up and down, clearly very angry with Gilles about what had happened at the farmhouse.

Although Gilles was his most trusted ally, things had got out of hand and now they had gone horribly wrong. He had always known that Gilles mixed with some very violent people, he had grown up with them after all, but he had not been aware that Gilles was involving them in *his* business.

"The one who killed Rob," he began as Gilles looked at him, "Was his death arranged by you?"

Gilles turned away before answering. "You know it was. You said you wanted him to pay for what he had done."

"I meant I wanted him to be convicted of the murder and sent to jail for the rest of his life. Legally!"

"That would have resulted in him telling the police everything." Gilles fixed Philippe with a stare as he continued, "Including who he was with at the time. I could not permit that."

"So you had him killed?" challenged Philippe, "And now the same people have killed again. Only this time that was not the plan, was it?"

Gilles shook his head. "No. It went wrong."

"It went wrong!" shouted Philippe, "Two people ended up dead!" He looked at Gilles in disgust. "Where do you find these idiots?"

"Philippe, it went wrong, that's all," Gilles responded, "It happens. Sometimes things go wrong. But Henri says neither of them got a good look at him."

Philippe turned away from Gilles, his disgust clearly apparent.

"Which just leaves Jacques," continued Gilles, quietly, "Jacques could identify Henri. And that could lead back to me. And to you."

Philippe's head whipped round at this and he looked at Gilles fiercely, staring him in the eyes and pointing at him with his forefinger to emphasise his words.

"You don't touch Jacques! Do you understand? You leave him alone. He is not to be harmed. No more killing!" Gilles looked at Philippe as he continued. "This business has already cost too many lives. Including that of my grandson."

The two men stared into each other's eyes for a few moments before Gilles looked away. "As you wish. I will take care of it," he said and headed for the door as Philippe watched him, shaking his head.

Gilles closed the door behind him as he left Philippe's house. He paused for a moment and looked back at the door before shaking his head and walking off. As he made his way towards the Place du Marché, Gilles took his phone out of his pocket and made a call.

When he reached the Place du Marché, Gilles went into the café which overlooks the boules court and ordered a coffee. As he sat watching the boules players toss the heavy boules in the air in the hope that they would land somewhere near the little target ball, Henri approached the café from the direction of the Place des Artisans. When he reached Gilles, he flopped into the chair next to him. He looked at Gilles for a few moments before speaking.

"Problem?" he asked.

"Philippe says not to touch Jacques," said Gilles.

Henri threw his hands in the air. "So how are we supposed to deal with this then?"

"I need to think about it. I think I am missing something here."

"Well don't take too long. I am happy to help you make your problems go away but I am not so happy about being exposed like this. We need to do something and we need to do it now."

Gilles stared at Henri, his look telling him to hold off and not to question his decision. Henri stared back for a few moments and then stood up.

"Enjoy your coffee," he said dismissively, "I will wait to hear from you."

Henri walked off across the Place, leaving Gilles staring contemplatively at the boules players.

An hour after Gilles had left him, Philippe, wearing a lightweight grey suit and an open necked white shirt with the collar outside the jacket, was sitting on a bench at the Capitainerie, near the Esprit.

As Jacques approached from the direction of the Rue Grande, Philippe got to his feet.

"Bonjour Jacques," he said, holding out his hand. "I am Philippe Lacoste."

Jacques shook the hand cautiously. If Carter were to be believed, this man was in some way implicated in the death of Eloise's brother, and for all Jacques knew, also in Yvonne's death. But, if that were so, it made no sense that he would be there. Jacques was puzzled as to why Philippe had been waiting for him.

"Bonjour," he answered, "I know who you are, of course, but how do you know my name?"

"I know more about you than you might think," replied Philippe. "I would like to talk to you. Can we go on board your boat?"

Jacques was far from certain that it was a good idea for him to be alone on the Esprit with Philippe but if Philippe was prepared to approach him openly and in broad daylight, then it was unlikely that he had anything sinister in mind. It would probably be safe for them to go on board.

"Follow me," said Jacques, leading the way onto the Esprit. He unlocked the glass door to the saloon, slid it open and ushered Philippe in.

When they had settled themselves at the table in the saloon, Jacques looked intently at Philippe. "Well, Monsieur Lacoste, what do you want to talk to me about?"

"This is a fine boat, Jacques," said Philippe, "It was my favourite. Where did you get the money to buy it?"

"What business is that of yours?" Jacques shot back, wondering why he had been asked the question.

"Oh, none. I was just curious, that's all," replied Philippe nonchalantly.

There was a few moments pause before Jacques decided to answer Philippe's question. "My father put some money into an account for me when I was born. I used that to buy the boat," he said.

"Tell me, Jacques," said Philippe, interlocking his fingers and resting his hands in his lap, "Who is your father?"

Jacques looked down, clearly uncomfortable with the question. "He... He's..." Jacques struggled to find something to say. "He's dead," he blurted out eventually.

"Really? Is that what your mother told you?" said Philippe bluntly. Jacques looked at him angrily as he continued. "If she did, then she lied to you."

Jacques fought to control his temper and Philippe quickly raised his hand to stop Jacques from responding violently. "The truth, Jacques, is that *I* am your father."

Jacques drew back, stunned.

"*You*? *You are* my father? No, no. That's not possible. My mother would have told me if you were my father."

"The money came from me, Jacques."

Jacques had always wanted to know who his father was, he was ceaseless in asking his mother to reveal his identity but she had steadfastly refused to do so. He looked at Philippe and when he spoke there was anger in his voice.

"How could you treat her the way you did?" he began. "You got her pregnant and then you dumped her. How could you do that?"

At this, Philippe's mood changed. "You know nothing about it," he countered. "And, in any case, who appointed you as my judge? It was a very difficult situation for me, for both of us."

"I think it was more difficult for my mother," retorted Jacques sarcastically.

"Perhaps, but I have always provided for her, and for you."

"Oh, yes. Out of your wealth, you gave her enough to live on. But only as long as she never revealed to anyone, not even to me, that you were my father."

"That was a necessary condition."

"Was it?" Jacques' eyes blazed at Philippe's apparent indifference. "If it was necessary to keep your identity a secret for over twenty years, why have you decided to tell me now?"

"Because now it is important that you know." Philippe paused and adjusted his position on the seat. "I know I have never been a father to you, but now you are in danger and I want to help you. You must believe me."

Jacques' eyes narrowed. "What makes you think I'm in danger?"

"Jacques, I know about Yvonne. I know about what has been happening. I know about everything."

"How could you know about that?" challenged Jacques, giving nothing away about what he had learned from Carter concerning Philippe's possible involvement with synthetic diamonds.

Philippe sighed. "The men who kidnapped Yvonne," he said, speaking quietly, "they were hired by someone who works for me."

Jacques opened his mouth to speak but Philippe raised his hand to stop him.

"Please! Let me finish," he said, "I didn't know what they were doing. They were just supposed to find out who Carter Jefferson is working for and why he is in Port Grimaud, that is all."

Philippe paused and looked at Jacques to see if he was accepting what he was being told before continuing. "No one was supposed to get killed. But it went wrong, and that's the sort of people they are."

There was regret in Philippe's voice and Jacques sensed it. He looked at Philippe and Philippe looked back at him, the remorse now also showing in his eyes. "I am very sorry about what has happened, truly I am. If I could turn the clock back and change it, I would. But I can't. And now? Well, now I'm more concerned about you, and your safety, than I am about anything else."

Jacques slumped in his seat, exhausted. It was all too much for him to take in; his newly discovered father was admitting to being responsible for the abduction, rape and death of his sister.

"This is a nightmare," he said, more to himself than to Philippe as he turned away.

The two men sat in silence for several seconds before Philippe spoke.

"Jacques," he said, "I know this has been a shock for you." Jacques gave him a disgusted look and then turned away again. "But there are things you need to know. You are in terrible danger. The people who killed Yvonne…"

"And raped her!" interjected Jacques angrily before looking at Philippe accusingly.

"Raped her?" Philippe looked ashamed, "I'm sorry, I didn't know that. But it doesn't change what I have to tell you. One of the men who kidnapped Yvonne, he got away. And he knows you can identify him. The rest of them, the other people involved, think that you should be dealt with so that you can't identify him. Do you understand what I'm saying?" Jacques was impassive, tight lipped, but Philippe pressed on, "I told them no! But I'm still worried that they will come after you. You must get away from here quickly and hide somewhere for a while, somewhere where they can't find you."

Jacques stared at Philippe, uncertain of how to react to what he had said. After a few moments, he decided to voice his thoughts.

"What a great father you are," he said acidly. "Missing for twenty-one years, and now that I *have* found you, I wish that I hadn't. I wish I had never even heard of you."

"Listen to me, Jacques," said Philippe, "You must take what I have told you very seriously. You are my son, my *only* son, and you are important to me. I have watched you grow. From a distance, I admit, but I have watched. And I don't want anything bad to happen to you now. Especially not because of me. That's why I have come to warn you."

Eloise heard Philippe's last few words as she entered the saloon of the Esprit carrying two bags of food which she had bought at the supermarket. She looked at Philippe and then at Jacques waiting for one of them to speak. Eventually, Jacques broke the silence.

"This is..." he started.

"I know who he is, Jacques," interrupted Eloise, "He's my grandfather, remember? And possibly responsible for my brother's death. So why is he here?"

"But..." began Jacques and then stopped. His brain had just realised something and was trying to process it.

"But *what*?" demanded Eloise as she dropped the bags of shopping and put her hands on her hips.

"Er..." continued Jacques uncertainly, "Your grandfather, is..."

"Is *what*? For goodness' sake Jacques, what are you trying to say?"

"I'm trying to tell you that your grandfather... is my father."

Eloise stared at Jacques for a few moments and then looked at Philippe, disbelief in her eyes.

"That can't be true!" she said, her eyes flicking between the two men, "Tell me it's not true. It isn't, is it?"

Philippe got up from his seat. "I was not expecting to see you here, Eloise."

"You haven't answered my question. Is it true that you are Jacques' father?"

"Yes, it is true," Philippe confirmed.

"But that would make me..." said Eloise hesitantly, her anger quelled by the significance of the revelation.

"Jacques' niece, or half niece to be precise," said Philippe.

Jacques looked at Eloise; she looked as if she was about to be sick and he got up from his seat quickly as he saw her eyes roll upwards and her knees start to give way. He ran to her side to catch her and gently led her to a seat. She came round after a few moments and stared up at Jacques as he leant over her.

Suddenly it dawned on Philippe why Eloise had reacted so badly to the news, the reason why she was on board Jacques' boat.

"Are you and Jacques… ," he began.

Eloise ignored the implied question, she was in no state to respond and she had nothing to say to her grandfather anyway, but Jacques flashed him an angry and disgusted look.

"I'm sorry. I had no idea that you two were…," began Philippe, his bushy grey eyebrows almost meeting as he frowned. "But you are still in grave danger. This other complication, it doesn't change that." Philippe got to his feet and headed for the saloon door. "I should leave now," he said, "but please, Jacques, remember what I have told you. Get away from here, for your own safety. And do it soon!" Philippe straightened his clothes, took one last look at his son and his granddaughter, and left the Esprit.

The farmhouse where Antoine and Yvonne had died had never known so many people gathered in the small field next to it. Three of the men in the field were carefully removing earth from a small patch where the grass had obviously been disturbed recently.

Carter and Conrad were amongst the group watching as one of the men who were digging suddenly threw his spade to one side and pulled at an arm which had appeared from the soil. The other two stopped digging and everyone else moved in closer to see what they had found.

Slowly and carefully, the diggers uncovered the face of a dead body. It was Antoine.

One of the men watching, a middle aged man of medium height dressed in a suit, was Inspecteur Le Grande of the French police. He leaned over and looked at the body before straightening up and turning to Carter.

"Is it him?" he asked.

Carter looked a little closer and then nodded before the two men turned away from the scene.

"I think we had better go to the Gendarmerie," said Le Grande, "Then you can tell me everything." He looked at Carter challengingly before continuing, "And I mean everything." Carter nodded as he, Conrad and Le Grande started to walk back to the farmhouse.

On their way back to the Gendarmerie, Carter decided to broach the question that was on his mind.

"Inspecteur," he began, "I expect you will want interview Jacques Armand about this?"

"Yes, we will. But that can wait until tomorrow. For now, all I need from him is a description of the man who got away. I will ask him about that and then I will arrange for him to be watched, partly for his own safety but also so that I know where he is when I am ready to talk to him."

"Good idea," said Carter, happy that Jacques and Eloise would have some protection and also that he would have at least another twenty-four hours before the police became aware of Philippe's involvement.

Chapter 15

Eloise was still in a state of shock following Philippe's revelation that he was Jacques' father and she stared blankly in front of her as Jacques gently helped her off the seat in the Esprit's saloon and guided her down the circular staircase to the master cabin. He pulled back the bed cover and sat her down on the bed before pushing her back onto it and removing her shoes. Then he pulled the cover back up over her and she closed her eyes.

Jacques returned to the saloon and paced up and down wondering what to do. He knew he would have to confront his mother about what Philippe had told him, if only to check if it was true. He decided to go and see her but first he wanted to be sure that Eloise would be all right so he went back down to the master cabin and peeped round the door. She was fast asleep.

Jacques knew his mother would be pleased to see him despite the grim news he had brought on his last visit but he also knew that she was probably not in a good state to find out that he now knew who his father was.

"I wasn't expecting to see you again today, Cherie," said Claudine as she opened the door and Jacques went into the apartment.

Once inside the apartment, Jacques quickly established that Colette had gone and that Claudine was on her own; that would make it easier for him to raise the subject of his father. He went over to the window and looked down at the canal below pensively, unsure how best to open the conversation.

"I've just had a visit from Philippe Lacoste," he said, eventually, continuing to look out of the window as he spoke.

"Really," said Claudine cautiously, "Why on earth would Monsieur Lacoste call on you? What did he want?"

Jacques took a deep breath and turned to face his mother. "He came to tell me that he was my father." Claudine looked away immediately and Jacques took that as confirmation of what Philippe had told him. "So, it's true then," he said.

She turned to look at him, "Yes, it's true," she said.

Jacques nodded slowly, finally accepting that there was no other explanation, no reason why Philippe might have lied about it, that Philippe really was his father. When he spoke, his tone was faltering, shaky.

"He says I'm in danger from the people who killed Yvonne, that I must get away from here. He says that's why he told me, because he wanted to warn me." Jacques fought to hold back the powerful surge of emotion he felt. "Tell me, Maman, did you know he was a murderer when you were sleeping with him?"

"No! It's not true! Philippe is an honourable man. He would never kill anyone. I don't believe it."

"Oh, he doesn't actually do it himself." Jacques' voice faltered again as a wave of anger ripped through him. "He pays other people to do it for him. I know it's true because he told me himself. He told me that, ultimately, *he* was the one responsible for Yvonne's death!"

Claudine dissolved into tears from the force of Jacques' attack and her tears melted his heart. He stepped towards her and took her in his arms.

"I'm sorry, Maman. I didn't want to upset you. I know you loved Yvonne as much as I did. But I had to ask you about this. I hope you will understand."

They hugged each other tightly for a few moments before Claudine pulled back from Jacques.

"What is it, this danger you are in?" she asked hesitantly, as she dried her eyes, "What exactly did Philippe say to you?"

"He said that because I can identify one of the men who kidnapped Yvonne, the one who was not killed, some of his… his associates, they want to kill me. They think that if they kill me they will be safe. He said he told them not to, that he would not agree to it, but he thinks they might try anyway. He says I must get away from here; go somewhere where they cannot find me."

"You must tell the police everything, Jacques. There is no alternative. Maybe they can give you some protection."

"Monsieur Jefferson has asked us not to speak to the police yet. He wants a little more time to try and solve the case."

Jacques looked at his mother and saw the pain in her eyes. He wondered if he could go on and tell her about the sting in the tail of what he had told her. He decided, having got this far, that there was no point in holding anything back.

"There is something else," he said, "You remember Eloise, my new girlfriend, the girl I brought with me when I came to tell you about Yvonne?"

"Yes, of course. What about her?"

"Well, Philippe Lacoste is her grandfather."

Jacques waited for his mother to work out the implications of what he had just told her. When she did, a look of concern spread over her face.

"But that would mean…" Claudine put a hand to her mouth, "Oh, Jacques. Oh no! I am so sorry," she said, taking both Jacques' hands in hers.

They looked into each other's eyes and then hugged each other. When they broke, Jacques' mind was back on practical matters.

"What do you think I should do?" he asked, "If Monsieur Lacoste was telling the truth, they are going to try to kill me; that hasn't changed. What do you think I should do?"

"The most important thing is for you to get away from here, out of danger."

"Then I will leave Port Grimaud. I will take the Esprit and go."

"Where will you go?"

Jacques turned back to the window. "I don't know," he said, "And it's probably better that you don't know where I am. But I'll keep in touch, I'll let you know that I'm safe."

Tears filled Claudine's eyes again as Jacques prepared to leave the apartment. He took his mother in his arms and hugged her. "I hate to leave you like this," he said, "But I'll be back, when this terrible business is all forgotten."

Jacques left his mother at the door to her apartment and ran down the steps to the canal side below. He took one last look up at his mother's window; she was there, leaning out over the balcony. She waved to him and smiled.

"Take care of yourself," she whispered to herself.

Jacques waved back and was gone, lost in the milling crowd of tourists.

Although Eloise had closed her eyes when Jacques had pulled the bed covers up, she had not gone to sleep and soon after he had left the boat to go and see his mother, she had got up and climbed the stairs to the saloon.

In the saloon, she found the pad and pen Jacques had used to write down the kidnappers' instructions. She picked them up and then sat at the table as she wrote a note to Jacques. It didn't take long, there wasn't much to say but as she wrote, there were tears in her eyes and one spilled onto the note. She took her handkerchief from her pocket and dabbed at the damp spot with it, smudging the writing, and then used the handkerchief to mop her eyes as she sobbed quietly to herself.

Having left a note for Jacques on the Esprit, Eloise gathered up her things from the master cabin and from where they were scattered around the saloon, packed them all into her holdall and left the boat. On the quayside, she turned and took a long look at the Esprit before heading down the Rue Grande and past the hotel on her way to the Place du Marché. Once there, she found the road leading from the Place to the Rue des Deux Iles, the narrow road that led to Philippe's house. When she reached the house, she knocked on the door, her knock a little apprehensive. Moments later, the door was opened by Philippe.

"Eloise! I was not expecting you." He smiled at her briefly but the smile faded quickly; he knew his granddaughter had been devastated by the news that he was Jacques' father.

"I think we need to have a talk," said Eloise tersely as she pushed past him into the house. Philippe watched her, noticing that she had her holdall with her. Slowly, he closed the door and followed her into the living room.

"I'm guessing that you need somewhere to stay," he said, pointing at her holdall, which she had dropped next to the sofa before sitting down. He sat in the armchair beside the sofa and looked her in the eye as he waited for her to respond.

"Well, I can't really stay with Jacques any more, can I?" She threw the words at him, clearly disgusted with the situation in which she now found herself. Philippe nodded his understanding of her predicament.

"I'm sorry that you had to find out the way you did. If I had known that you and Jacques were seeing each other, I would have done it differently." Eloise looked at him, her heart softening a little, but only a little.

"Well, what's done is done. And it wouldn't have changed anything anyway. Jacques would still be related to me."

There was a few moments pause as Philippe and Eloise considered this and then Philippe spoke; he wanted to make amends in some way.

"You must stay here with me until you go home," he said and smiled a weak smile.

"That's kind of you Grandpa, but I think I'll check in at the hotel again. I need my own space right now."

"OK, but you must think of this house as your own. Come here whenever you want to. It doesn't matter if I'm here or not. I want you to think of this as your second home. OK?"

Eloise smiled. "OK," she said. "Thanks."

Philippe got to his feet and went into the kitchen. Eloise watched him, not sure why he was doing so but when he returned a few moments later he handed Eloise a key ring with a key on it and a piece of paper.

"This is the key to the front door. I want you to have it so that you can come in whenever you wish, and maybe sit on the canal side watching the boats; there's a good view from there. And on the paper is the code for the alarm system."

Eloise smiled and took the key and the paper from Philippe. She put them in her bag and then looked at Philippe, her expression changing to a serious one.

"Grandpa, I want to know what's going on, what you are involved in. I think you owe me that."

Philippe sighed. "You are right. I do owe you that. But first, we will have a drink." He got up and went to the cabinet in the corner of the room and removed a bottle and two tumblers. "Whisky, I think. For you too." Eloise smiled as he poured the whisky into the glasses and handed one to Eloise. "So, where to start?"

In the Place du Marché, Carter was sitting at a table outside the Café Poisson reading a newspaper when his phone rang. He removed it from his pocket and answered it.

"Inspecteur. Bonjour," he said cheerily and listened to what Le Grande had to say before ending the call.

By the time Conrad found him at the café, Carter had folded the newspaper and put it on the table. Conrad walked quickly towards Carter and sat in the chair next to him before looking at him enquiringly. "Well," he said, "What news?"

"Well, firstly, Inspecteur le Grande says he will overlook the fact that you had an illegal firearm in your possession."

Conrad nodded. "Good. Anything else?"

"It was the same gun," replied Carter.

"Which links the guys here to Rob's murder."

"And that's another link in the chain connecting Rob to this case. It's not just the coded email any more. I never thought his death was just a coincidence and this proves it." Carter paused for a moment. "I think it's time we checked out Lacoste's place. I don't know how, or how deeply, he's involved but I know he's involved." Just as he said this, Carter's phone rang and he answered it.

"Eloise. Hi."

Leaving Conrad to contemplate what he had told him about his escape from being prosecuted by the French police and about the bullets matching, Carter took the two minute walk from the café to the Hotel Giraglia and went into the hotel. He really had no idea why Eloise wanted to see him but even if his curiosity had not got the better of him, he would have wanted to see how she was getting on after all that had happened, and Nicole was expecting him to look after her.

As he entered the hotel bar, Carter saw Eloise sitting alone at a table with a drink in her hand. He went over to her and greeted her before sitting in the seat next to her.

"Would you like a drink?" she asked.

"I'm good thanks," he responded, not wanting to commit himself to staying any longer than he needed to. "You wanted to see me."

Eloise adjusted her position and sat forward as she spoke. "I went to see Grandpa today. There were things we needed to talk about." She glanced at Carter. "About Jacques and me."

Carter nodded, although he didn't really understand why Eloise would need to talk to her grandfather about her relationship with Jacques.

"My grandfather is not a criminal," continued Eloise, "He is just a business man who has got involved with something that he never should have. But he has never done anything illegal before, I want you to understand that." Eloise looked into Carter's eyes and he looked back into hers, not wanting to give any indication of what his thoughts about Philippe were.

"And the only reason I'm here now is because I want to clear him of any involvement with Rob's death."

"Please. Just tell me what you know," responded Carter non-committally.

"I don't know much, he wasn't particularly forthcoming but I did find out that the diamonds are coming from England."

"Any idea who is supplying them?"

"No, he wouldn't tell me that. He just wanted me to know that he is very unhappy with the way things have turned out. It wasn't meant to be like this. It was supposed to be a harmless little enterprise, perhaps sailing a little close to the wind, legally, but no one was supposed to get hurt."

"Well, people have got hurt, Eloise. And not just your brother," said Carter.

Eloise nodded as she looked down at her hands. "I know, but it wasn't his doing and I don't want to see my grandfather get into trouble because of something he didn't have anything to do with," she said as she looked him in the eye again, "Mum couldn't cope with that right now, not on top of everything else."

Carter relented a little, he knew that Nicole was already struggling to come to terms with Rob's death and that the last thing she needed was for her father to be implicated in his death. He leaned forward and returned her look.

"I can't keep him out of it, Eloise," he said. "Things have gone way too far for that. But I will try to soften the blow for your mother. I care about her too, you know." Eloise smiled softly at this.

"Yeah, I know," she said. "She told me a bit about you guys."

Carter looked down as he spoke, wondering if he was sharing too much about his relationship with Nicole but deciding to be honest with her daughter. "I love her very much, always have," he said. "But I have to get to the bottom of this."

Eloise nodded her agreement with that sentiment and reached into her pocket. "Then you might need this," she said as she handed Carter the key to Philippe's house. Carter took the key and turned it over in his hand as she continued. "He told me to use the place as my own, as a second home. And this is the code for the alarm system." She handed him the piece of paper with the alarm code written on it. "The panel is just inside the door." She looked at Carter wondering what his response to what she was doing would be. "We're having dinner together tonight at a restaurant in Sainte Maxime, so that we can get to know each other a bit better." Eloise gave Carter a knowing look. "That will be your chance."

After Jacques had left his mother's apartment, he had gone for a walk along the beach to try to clear his thoughts. He had walked and walked and walked, hoping things would start to clarify in his mind but it had been hopeless.

As the sun began to set, he decided to go back to the Esprit and talk to Eloise. Keen to get back to her, he emerged from the shade of the Grande Rue, half walking half running, and crossed the helipad. He strode over the Esprit's gangway, across the aft deck and opened the saloon door. Once inside, he called to her. "Eloise? Eloise, where are you?" There was no response.

Jacques walked leadenly towards the helm station and sat in the helmsman's chair. He rested his hand on the gleaming chrome of the wheel and stared out at the fuelling station opposite.

As his eyes dropped from the scene, they fell upon a small white piece of paper folded in half and propped up in front of the instrument panel. It had his name written on it. He picked it up and opened it.

Jacques sighed as he read the note. The contents did not really come as any surprise but he had hoped that he would have the opportunity to talk to Eloise before she left. Still clutching the note, he rested his hand on the wheel and stared again at the petrol pumps.

Under cover of darkness, Carter and Conrad followed the same route that Eloise had followed earlier in the day. When they reached the front door of Philippe's house, Carter knocked on the door. He wanted to be absolutely sure that no one was in so when there was no response, he knocked again. When there was still no sign of movement from within the house, Carter tried the key Eloise had given him. The door opened and they went inside, closing the door quietly behind them. As the alarm bleeped the warning that it had not been switched off, Carter went over to the source of the noise and tapped in the code Eloise had given him.

The bleeping stopped immediately and Carter and Conrad began their search, looking briefly round the kitchen before moving into the living room. Conrad began to search methodically through everything in the living room while Carter looked into each of the other rooms which led off from it. One of the doors he opened led to a room which was obviously Philippe's study. He turned to Conrad.

"Hey, Conrad, let's take a look in here," he said gesturing with his hand for Conrad to join him.

Conrad followed Carter into the study where Carter saw Philippe's laptop on the desk. He opened it and pressed the button to turn it on while Conrad began opening the desk drawers and searching them.

When the laptop had fired up, a smile appeared on Carter's face and he shook his head as he spoke. "Careless. Very careless," he said, "No access security."

Carter proceeded to open Philippe's email system and began looking through his messages. Conrad came over to join him and watched over Carter's shoulder as he worked his way through them. When he found the one Philippe had sent to Rob, Carter smiled.

"Gotcha," he said as he opened the message and saw the groups of numbers, identical to Rob's printout.

Carter searched the laptop's email system for other messages which had been sent from the same address and when he saw the list, he smiled again.

"You can see how it could have happened. Most of the messages from ljsherwood@hotmail.com were sent to robin@bainesautomotive.co.uk. Rob's email address was robid@hotmail.com so typing in the first few letters would bring up both addresses. Get distracted for a moment and click on the wrong one and the message goes to the wrong person. We've all done it."

Conrad nodded. "So now we need to find out who robin@bainesautomotive.co.uk is. That would give us the next link in the chain and it should be easier to trace than ljsherwood@hotmail.com was. Unless of course bainesautomotive doesn't exist either."

"Time for us to do a bit of research," said Carter as he got up from the desk. "Can you download these messages so that we can go through them later?"

Conrad nodded and held up the memory stick he had already taken out of his wallet in anticipation of Carter's request.

Chapter 16

Early the next morning, Carter and Conrad were in Carter's hotel room. Carter was on the phone to Inspector Harris while Conrad sat on the bed, waiting expectantly.

"All the coded messages were addressed to someone called Robin at baines automotive.co.uk," said Carter.

"What do you need from me?" asked Harris.

"Well, we did a quick Internet search which showed that there is an engineering company called Baines Automotive based in York. Is there any chance you could arrange for all the information you have about the company to be available for me at the airport when we get there?"

"I'll see what I can do. And if anyone's available, given that it's Saturday, I'll get them to meet you and hand it over to you."

"Thank you, that's great."

Carter took the phone from his ear and ended the call. He looked at Conrad.

"He says he'll get what he can together for us."

"Time for us to make arrangements to head back to Yorkshire then," suggested Conrad and Carter nodded.

Later that day, the plane carrying Carter and Conrad touched down at Leeds Bradford airport in Yorkshire. Having collected their bags, Carter and Conrad came out of the baggage collection area of the airport into the arrivals area. There, they saw a man wearing a suit who was holding up a piece of paper with Carter's name on it. They approached the man and Carter introduced himself.

"Hi, I'm Carter Jefferson," he said, whereupon the man folded the sheet of paper and put it in his pocket.

"Detective Constable Green, from the West Yorkshire Police," he said, identifying himself and shaking hands with Carter and Conrad. "DI Harris, one of our colleagues from the North Yorkshire force, asked me to meet you and give you this file," he continued, indicating the file he had under his arm, "But before I do, please could I see some ID."

"Of course," said Carter as he reached into his jacket pocket for his ID wallet and handed it to him. DC Green looked at Carter's ID, nodded and then returned it to Carter along with the file.

"Please could you return the file to DI Harris in York when you've finished with it," he said.

"Of course, no problem," said Carter as he took the file.

"Oh, one other thing, DI Harris said to ask you to contact him when you arrived."

"I'll give him a call," said Carter.

After DC Green had left, Carter and Conrad went to find the car rental desk. Once they had found their hire car in the car park and were on their way to their hotel, Carter telephoned Harris. He told him they had arrived and thanked him for the file.

"We could do with a briefing," said Harris, continuing the conversation, "To bring us up to date with the case. Perhaps when you've settled in at your hotel you could come down to headquarters and fill us in on what's been happening?"

"Be glad to," responded Carter, "Say in about an hour?"

"Fine."

Carter ended the call and as Conrad drove them to their hotel, Carter leafed through the file DC Green had given him. As he did so, he came across a plan of a building on which were marked all the security systems which had been installed. He opened the plan out in front of him and saw a room denominated as the New Product Development Room. He nodded sagely to himself as he noted that this room had no windows and additional security in the form of a steel door operated by a combination lock.

When they had arrived at their hotel and unpacked, Carter and Conrad met in Carter's room to discuss their next move. Carter had the file on Baines Automotive in his hand.

"Before we go and fill the Inspector in," began Carter, "let's just remind ourselves what we know so far."

The two men sat down in a couple of armchairs which were by the window before Carter began his review.

"First off, we know that Philippe's contact here is someone at Baines Automotive. Secondly, we know that Baines Automotive is an engineering company manufacturing auto parts, so it's in the right line of business to be able to construct the kind of equipment needed to make synthetic diamonds, especially if they're using the high pressure high temperature method. And finally, we know, from the security details in the police files, that the company has a development room, which, for some reason, has been provided with a three inch thick steel door."

"If they *have* been making the diamonds there," suggested Conrad, "the equipment will most likely still be there. Even if they knew we suspected them, which hopefully they don't, the set-up we're talking about, a pressure chamber capable of producing synthetic stones of gem size and quality, is not the sort of thing you fold up and put in your briefcase. It wouldn't even fit through the door. And even dismantling it and moving it in pieces would be a non-trivial exercise. Even if they're using the chemical vapour deposition method, getting rid of the equipment in a hurry would not go unnoticed. And, if they're doing this on a commercial basis, which they appear to be, we're not talking about a single piece of equipment. Each diamond would take weeks to produce using the CVD method so they would need a lot of machines."

Carter nodded at Conrad's accurate summary. "So, let's go and see the Inspector, shall we, and see if we can get to the bottom of this today."

Half an hour later, Carter, Conrad, Inspector Harris and Harris's assistant, Detective Sergeant Grimshaw, were all seated round Harris's desk as Carter concluded his summary of where the case had got to.

"And that brings you right up to date," said Carter.

Inspector Harris had listened intently as Carter had described everything that had happened since their meeting a few days earlier.

"What can we do to help?" asked Harris.

"This is the plan of the company's premises," said Carter opening out the plan on the desk in front of Harris. "It was in the file you gave us."

Carter pointed to one of the rooms marked on the plan. "We'd like to take a look in there, the New Product Development Room. Can you arrange that? If they are making diamonds in that factory, and all the evidence points to it, then that's where they're most likely to be doing it."

"That shouldn't be a problem," said Harris, "I'm sure Grimshaw here can find us a JP to sign the warrant." Harris looked at Grimshaw who nodded and left the room.

"Could take a little while though," added Harris when he had gone. "It is Saturday, after all. Tell you what, why don't I introduce you to our local beer while we're waiting for him to get back."

"Sounds great," said Carter.

Later, when Grimshaw returned, having accomplished his task successfully, he found the little group in his boss's favourite pub across the road from the police station. Harris looked up as he came towards them.

"Did you get it OK?" he asked.

Grimshaw nodded and handed the search warrant to Harris who looked at Carter as he spoke.

"Are you ready then?" he asked, as he drained his glass and got up to go.

"Sure, let's do it," responded Carter, also getting to his feet.

The group returned to the police station where Harris went to speak to the Desk Sergeant.

Once they were all in the police car travelling towards the factory, which was on the outskirts of York, Harris said, "The factory is closed at weekends, so I've arranged for a car to fetch Mr Baines. He'll meet us there."

When they reached the locked factory gate, they sat in the car and waited for the second police car, carrying Jeremy, to arrive. The factory building was deserted and Carter could feel the hairs on the back of his neck bristle as he anticipated the culmination of his investigation. The adrenalin began to flow and he became edgy just sitting there. He opened the car door and stepped out in front of the gate. Harris joined him.

"They won't be long," said Harris. "A few more minutes at the most."

Just then a police car pulled up beside them and Jeremy got out of the back seat. "Which of you is Harris?" he demanded, storming towards them.

"I am," answered Harris. "I have a warrant to search these premises. Could you open up for us please," he added bluntly as he handed the search warrant to Jeremy.

"I don't suppose I've got a lot of choice, have I?" responded Jeremy, after he had looked at the document and confirmed its contents. "But I intend to lodge a formal complaint. I've done nothing that could possibly justify such an intrusion."

"Yes sir," said Harris wearily.

"And what the hell are you looking for anyway?" continued Jeremy angrily.

"I'm not at liberty to say, sir," responded Harris as Jeremy shook his head and began opening the factory gates.

"Where do you want to start?" he asked once they were inside the factory.

"How about the New Product Development Room?" suggested Carter; there was only one place he was interested in searching.

"You can't go in there, it's full of our latest inventions. Our competitors would love to know what's in there. No, no. You can look everywhere else but not in there."

"I think you'll find, sir, that we can look anywhere we like," said Harris coldly. "But you really don't need to worry, we won't spill the beans to your competitors."

"Well, you can't go in *there*. It's on a time lock until Monday morning."

"Not according to our records, it isn't. So, be a good chap, and open it up for us, would you?"

"What about him?" Jeremy pointed to Carter, "He doesn't sound like one of yours."

"He isn't. He's from New York, but Scotland Yard have vouched for him. So you don't have to worry, your secret formulas will be quite safe."

Jeremy gave up resisting and led the group towards the far end of the factory where the development room was located. They walked through the laboratory, where products produced by the company's many competitors were taken apart and examined and tested, and stopped at the big grey metal door to the development room.

Jeremy pulled a bunch of keys from his pocket and unlocked the combination wheel. Slowly and methodically he spun the wheel a few times and lined up the first number of the combination with the mark. Then the next, and the next, and finally the last number. He turned the wheel again and they all heard the click as it locked open. Next, Jeremy used both his hands to turn the big heavy handle and slowly he pulled the thick steel door open. When he had finished, he went in and switched on the lights before emerging and inviting the group to go in.

"After you," said Harris.

As they entered the large room, Carter whistled at the high tech equipment that seemed to fill every part of it. His heart began to race as he contemplated finding the high pressure chamber and solving the mystery of where the diamonds were being made.

Conrad quickly scanned the room and then leaned towards Carter and whispered into his ear. "There's nothing in here that is even remotely like the size or quantity of equipment that would be needed."

As Carter surveyed the room, he knew Conrad was right. His heart plummeted to the soles of his shoes and he felt that hollowness in the pit of the stomach that often signals the realisation of some unwelcome truth. Carter touched a finger to his lips to warn Conrad not to say anything to Harris.

"Maybe they've developed a new process that uses much smaller equipment," he suggested, desperately clutching at any explanation which would mean that he had not been wrong about the room.

"Maybe," agreed Conrad, "It's conceivable. But it's very unlikely."

Carter was dismayed; surely he couldn't have got it so wrong. If the diamonds weren't being made there, then they must be being made somewhere else. But where?

Harris strolled over to them. "Something the matter?" he asked.

"No, no," lied Carter smoothly, taking a tight rein on his anxiety. "Let's get on with it, shall we."

Even though Carter and Conrad no longer believed that the development room was being used as a diamond factory, Carter insisted that they search it thoroughly, just in case he was right and Jeremy had found a means of producing high quality diamonds without the need for a huge high pressure chamber or a collection of CVD units.

At one point, Carter found a supply of graphite, the essential raw material for making synthetic diamonds and got quite excited about it until Jeremy informed him that graphite was an essential ingredient in the manufacture of brake linings and that, amongst other things, his company was developing a new high performance braking system.

When they had finished searching the development room, and had found nothing more incriminating than the stock of graphite, they routinely examined the rest of the factory. As they entered each area, Carter looked at Conrad who, after briefly scanning the space, shook his head.

An hour after they had begun the search, they called it off and as they were about to leave the factory, Jeremy looked at Harris.

"Satisfied?" he asked.

Harris looked at Carter who nodded reluctantly.

"Yes, thank you, sir," said Harris, "I'm sorry to have troubled you. It seems our information was incorrect."

"Yes it does rather, doesn't it? And I can assure you that you will be sorry for this. I wouldn't be surprised to find you directing traffic next week. What the hell were you expecting to find in there, anyway? Gold bullion from a bank robbery? Or perhaps a clutch of white slaves?"

"I'm afraid it's not for me to say," replied Harris, refusing to respond to Jeremy's sarcastic gibes.

Jeremy reset the alarm system before pushing the big main door of the factory shut and locking it. Then he followed Harris, Carter and the rest of the group through the gate and closed it, snapping the large padlock shut, before getting into the back seat of the police car in which he had arrived. He glared angrily at Harris before pulling the car door shut. Harris signalled to the driver and the car drove off. Carter watched and shook his head before speaking to Conrad who was standing close to him.

"There's something we're missing here," he said and Conrad nodded his agreement, "And I don't trust that guy, he's much too sure of himself. I think we should keep an eye on him, stake out his house, see what he does. Could be he's just a staging post, a middle man."

Harris watched Jeremy drive off before walking towards Carter, clearly furious about the embarrassment he had just been subjected to.

"Anything else I can do for you," he asked, barely restraining his anger.

"Not right now, thank you," said Carter.

"In that case, I'll give you a ride back to the station so you can pick up your car. Although, given what has just taken place here, maybe I should let you catch a bus!"

Carter smiled weakly as he and Conrad got into Harris's car. He knew he deserved the taunt and he probably would have reacted in the same way if the roles had been reversed; he had made a bad call and he knew it. Whether or not Harris would still be willing to help him after what had happened at the factory was doubtful but he was still convinced that he had the solution to the case within his grasp, that Jeremy Baines was in some way involved.

Chapter 17

It was early evening as the ferry inched slowly across the inky black sea towards the dock. The woman in the raincoat watched the ship and pushed herself as far back into the doorway as she could. There was no reason why anyone would recognise her, even if they saw her, but she still tried to make herself as inconspicuous as possible as she waited for the person she was there to meet. The rain was a little heavier now; even in her doorway, she had to wrap her raincoat tightly round herself and raise the collar to protect herself from the large drops of water.

Before long cars were rolling out of the ferry, their crossing from Zeebrugge in Belgium to Hull on the East Yorkshire coast completed. One by one the cars passed through the customs shed and drove past the woman until one of them pulled out of the line and stopped a few yards away from her. Its headlights flashed twice. She ran towards the car and got into the passenger seat.

Inside, Dimitri was beaming from ear to ear. “Anna! Hi!” he said, greeting her warmly, ”Your English weather, it gets worse!” he laughed heartily, his broken Russian accent impossible to hide, “One day, I will make this trip and it will not be raining. But maybe I will be old man by then.” Dimitri laughed again as he pulled back into the line of cars.

Anna laughed too, but she was more tense and the tension found its way into her voice, “It’s good to see you again, Dimitri. You're always so bloody cheerful. You cheer me up."

"What is not to be cheerful about?" asked Dimitri, "You make lot of money, I make lot of money and nobody get hurt. What could be better, my friend?"

Dimitri put the car into gear and they drove out through the gates and away from the docks.

"Only bad thing is long journey I have to make to bring diamonds to you. I could have give them to you in Moscow," he said as they drove along the road.

"But then I would have had to get them out of Russia. And if I'd been caught with them at the airport, I could have ended up in a Siberian prison camp."

"Siberia not so bad!" They both laughed at this before Dimitri asked, "Where you are parked?"

"Not far. Quite near your hotel actually," answered Anna before taking a deep breath. She looked straight ahead as she continued. "Dimitri, I've decided to close the operation down."

The silence that followed Anna's revelation was leaden. Dimitri looked shocked and amazed, so much so that he turned his head to look at her, taking his eyes off the road.

"No? But for why? Isn't it good for all of us?"

"Dimitri! Watch the road!" shouted Anna, concerned that he would crash the car.

Dimitri pulled in to the side of the road and switched off the engine. He looked at Anna sitting beside him and she looked back at him.

"What is it?" he asked, "What is problem?"

"Things have been going wrong and people *have* got hurt," said Anna, a serious look on her face. "And now the police are getting too close. Jeremy's factory was searched by the police today. We must stop before we get caught."

Dimitri slammed his hands against the steering wheel angrily. Then, a few moments later, he looked at Anna and he was smiling again, "What the hell! We already make lot of money. So why worry? We live well for rest of our lives, no?"

"You know the money wasn't for me," said Anna, quietly and reflectively.

"Of course not! Always the Robin of the Hood, eh? Always, you are wanting to help others. Taking from rich and giving to poor," replied Dimitri, shaking his head. Anna looked at him and smiled as he continued, "So what I do now with these?" he asked, taking a black pouch from his pocket and holding it up, "I take big risk to get these out of factory, you know. But without you arranging distribution they are worthless."

Anna opened the car door. Where the car had stopped, there was a waste paper bin fixed to the railings between the road and the bank of the Humber estuary. She took the pouch, got out of the car and dropped it into the bin. Back in the car, she looked at Dimitri and smiled.

"Problem solved!" she said. "And now there's no evidence that either of us have done anything we shouldn't have."

At first Dimitri looked aghast and then, after a few moments, he smiled back.

"OK, we have drink now?" he said and started the car as Anna nodded her approval.

The two of them drove to a pub where they were soon sitting together enjoying a drink. Dimitri talked animatedly and every now and then, he laughed good humouredly. The Russian's good humour was infectious, something Anna had always liked in him.

When, after a couple of drinks, they left the pub, the two hugged and kissed each other on the cheek several times until, at last, Dimitri said, "OK. Enough. It has been good doing business with you, Anna. I see you at Fair in Moscow next year. And I hope your charities can survive without all money you have been giving them since we work out this little plan."

"Goodbye, Dimitri. And who knows, by the time I see you next year, I just might have worked out a new way of getting the stones to market."

Dimitri and Anna parted company and went their different ways, Anna to return to her car and Dimitri to register at his hotel, which was only a few yards away.

Partially hidden in a doorway across the road, Carter heard their last exchange and watched them go. He made a mental note of Dimitri's name and of the name of the hotel he was staying at before stepping out of the doorway. He took his hand out of his pocket and held in front of him the black pouch which Anna had thrown into the waste paper bin. Then he put it back into his pocket and set off briskly towards the car where Conrad was waiting for him.

"Let's go see the Inspector," said Carter with some satisfaction as he got into the car.

A couple of hours later, Carter and Conrad were sitting in an interview room at police headquarters waiting for Harris to see them. They had not parted on the best of terms and it was more than half an hour after they arrived that the door opened and Harris walked into the room with Grimshaw.

"What can I do for you, gentlemen?" he asked. It was Saturday evening and the impatience in his voice was not lost on Carter.

"We came to tell you that we've solved the case," Carter said confidently.

"Really?" Harris showed little interest in what Carter had to say. "And did the butler do it?" Harris didn't laugh at his own feeble joke, but his sergeant dutifully did.

"No. As a matter of fact, it was the wife."

Harris pulled out one of the chairs and sat down opposite Carter. "Whose wife? And what exactly did she do?"

"Do you think we could get a drink?" asked Carter, feeling that he had said enough to justify better treatment from Harris, maybe even an apology. "Conrad and I had to stand in the rain for hours to get the information we're about to share with you."

Harris looked hard at Carter. "Very well," he said, "we can go to my office. I keep a bottle of scotch there, for emergencies."

Harris's office was not a great deal more comfortable than the interview room but at least he was true to his word. He served up the whisky in two glasses, which he passed to Carter and Conrad. He himself had to make do with a plastic cup while Grimshaw missed out altogether.

"Thanks," said Carter as he swallowed the small tot he had been given and held out the glass waiting for another. Conrad followed suit and Harris poured them both a second measure.

"So, what have you found out? I hope you don't want to search that factory again?" Harris warned.

"No. There's nothing to be found there. The diamonds aren't being made there. They've been coming in from abroad, via Belgium."

Dramatically, and savouring the moment, Carter pulled the pouch from his pocket and emptied it onto Harris's desk. The pile of diamonds glittered under the bright light of the desk lamp and Harris leaned forward, his excitement apparent from his changed demeanour. Slowly, using his pen to separate them, he began to count the tiny sparkling stones.

"I've already done that," Carter said, smiling. "There are fifty seven.."

"Hmm." Harris stroked his chin. "And coming in from Belgium, you say?"

"Through Belgium," Carter corrected. " My guess is that they're coming from Russia; we know the Russians have the technology to make them, they've been doing it for years, although not to this standard. I think what we've probably got here is someone cheating on his employer."

"Can you prove it?" asked Harris.

"Possibly, if you can catch Dimitri before he shuffles off home."

"Dimitri?" Harris's ears pricked up at the mention of a name.

"He's the guy who's been bringing the diamonds in from Russia. He's staying in a small hotel in Hull, The Regency. Do you think you can arrange for him to be picked up?"

"Of course, but I'm not sure what we can charge him with. There's no proof that he's done anything."

"You have my testimony, and the diamonds," said Carter, unable to hide his exasperation; what would it take to move this man to action? He leaned forward as he continued. "If you don't pick him up tonight he'll be on his way back to Russia on the first boat in the morning."

"What about his contact? 'The wife', I think you said. What did you mean by that?"

"The Baines woman of course. His contact is Baines's wife. When we didn't find anything at the factory, I decided to watch the Baines house; see if our poking around at the factory would make him do something stupid, maybe make a mistake. Then, when Anna Baines left the house, it occurred to me that maybe it wasn't him after all. What if *she* was robin@bainesautomotive, and not him? What if it was his wife all along? We followed her to Hull, where she met Dimitri. And he gave her those." Carter pointed at the diamonds. "But if we want to get her for fraud, and possibly for having something to do with Rob Darrington's murder, we need to get Dimitri as well so that we can prove that the diamonds were obtained illegally and that they were both involved in a scam of massive proportions." Carter hoped that Harris understood.

"Very well. I'll arrange for this Dimitri fellow to be picked up. And then I suggest we visit Mr and Mrs Baines." Harris could not hide his distaste for another run in with Jeremy. "Even if the diamonds aren't man made, we should be able to make a smuggling charge stick."

"Good." Carter was relieved and drew a deep breath before getting up. "Thank you," he said sincerely, offering his hand to Harris who gave him a half embarrassed smile and took the hand.

Jeremy was sitting in the lounge holding a brandy glass and classical music was playing softly in the background when the doorbell rang. Jeremy looked towards the door and moments later, Anna came in looking very serious. Trailing behind her were Carter, Conrad, Harris, Grimshaw and a female police officer in uniform. They all crowded into the room, and then Harris stepped forward from the group.

"You again! And at this time of night!" Jeremy rose to his feet belligerently and faced up to Harris. "I've had enough of this. I'm going to ring your superior." Jeremy tried to push past Conrad and Grimshaw who were still standing near the doorway.

"I think you should hear us out first, sir," said Harris patiently.

"Why? Don't you think this... this harassment has gone far enough?"

"It's your wife we want to talk to this time, sir."

Jeremy pulled up short. "Anna! Why on earth would you want to talk to Anna?" He threw a glance at Anna who was standing beside him. She looked back at him non-committally and shrugged.

"Do you have a computer, Mrs Baines?" asked Harris but before Anna could answer, Jeremy jumped in.

"Of course she has a computer. And a printer, and a photocopier! What of it? She does a huge amount of work for charity, you know. She was voted Yorkshire Woman of the Year last year. She needs a fully equipped office."

"And where is this office?" asked Harris, raising his eyebrows slightly.

"Here in the house, just across the hall," answered Jeremy, still choosing to speak for his wife.

Harris turned to face Anna directly as he spoke the next few words. "Would you mind telling us the user name and password for your computer?" Anna looked at Jeremy as Harris continued, his tone condescending. "Please."

"Robin and Hood."

Harris looked at Carter who nodded and indicated to Conrad to go and check out Anna's computer.

"Excuse me for asking, Mrs Baines," continued Harris, "but would one of the charities you help be a hostel called... " Harris paused as he took his notebook out of his pocket and looked in it, "...Jailbreak?"

Anna cleared her throat and Jeremy was about to speak again when she held up her hand to stop him.

"It's all right, darling, I don't mind telling him," she said. "Yes, that is one of the organisations I try to help. They think, as I do, that youngsters coming out of prison should be given a break, not that you would understand that. Why do you ask?"

"Do you have any contact with any of the, er, clients?"

"Some, yes. Why?"

"Carl Spicer, perhaps?"

Anna looked away guiltily at the mention of Spicer's name. "Quite possibly. I don't know their names."

"I see."

"For heaven's sake Inspector, what's this all about?" asked Jeremy as he moved to position himself between Anna and Harris.

Before asking his next question, Harris gathered himself to his full height. He looked at Jeremy and then at Anna.

"Perhaps Mrs Baines wouldn't mind telling us where she's been this evening?" he said.

"She's been to her bridge club," said Jeremy moving back beside his wife as she smiled sweetly at Harris.

"I'd like to hear that from your wife, sir."

"Anna, tell him," Jeremy urged but Anna did not speak.

"Perhaps Mrs Baines would like to explain what she was doing in Hull earlier this evening?" The boot was on the other foot now and Harris was clearly enjoying kicking Jeremy with it.

Anna's expression changed and she cleared her throat. "Hull?" It was more of a croak than anything else.

"Yes, madam. Why were you in Hull this evening?"

"If you know I was in Hull then I expect you know why I was there."

Jeremy's face reflected his astonishment and, at that moment, Conrad came back into to the room. Carter and Harris looked towards him. He nodded his head and held up a copy of *Robin Hood*, identical to the book they had found on Jacques' boat. Harris took a deep breath and approached Anna. He stood in front of her as he spoke.

"Anna Baines," he began, "I am arresting you on suspicion of the murder of Robert Darrington. You do not have to say anything but it may harm your defence if you do not mention when questioned something you later rely on in court. Anything you do say may be given in evidence."

Jeremy was speechless. Anna seemed in a daze, yet she remained in complete control of herself.

"I'll get my coat," she said as she left the room and went into the hall followed by Harris and the policewoman.

Jeremy trailed after them. "I'll ring Tom Benedict," he called out to Anna, as he found his voice and tried to reassure her. "He'll meet you at the police station. Don't say anything, darling, not until you've spoken to him."

Jeremy looked at Harris who was now also in the hall. "Benedict is our solicitor," he said.

Harris nodded and indicated to the policewoman to escort Anna to the car. As they left, Jeremy gave Carter a menacing look. He'd kill me if he could, thought Carter.

As they came out of the house and Anna was helped into the police car, Carter stopped and turned to Conrad. "Well, that's this end wrapped up," he said, "Just Philippe and his cronies to deal with now. But that can wait until tomorrow. I think we both deserve a night off before we go back to Port Grimaud and deal with Monsieur Philippe Lacoste. And I have a date, so you'll have to find your own amusement." Carter smiled as Conrad looked at him questioningly.

It was late and Darrington Hall was in darkness as Carter approached the front door after a long day and rang the bell. Moments later the door was opened by Nicole and he went in.

Carter followed Nicole across the hall and into the lounge where he spotted a bottle of wine open on the coffee table with two glasses beside it. Nicole sat on the sofa and patted the cushion next to her as she smiled at him. His heart soared.

Trying his best not to convey the strength of emotion he was feeling at finally, after so many years, being able to spend time with her again, Carter sat beside her as she poured the wine and handed him a glass.

"Is it all over?" she asked.

"Pretty much, I think," he answered.

"Just Dad to deal with?" Carter nodded as she continued, "I don't suppose there's any way to leave him out of it, is there? I mean I know he was involved in something which ultimately led to Rob's death, and for that I will never be able to forgive him, but I don't believe he had any idea what sort of people he was dealing with or how far they would go to protect their interests. And as for Anna… Well…!"

Carter shook his head. "I'm sorry," he said, "I wish there was some way I could overlook his involvement, for your sake. But the reality is that he *was* involved. And while I can accept that it wasn't his doing, at least not directly, the fact remains that three innocent people are dead because of what he was mixed up in."

"I know. But it's hard, you know. He's my father and I love him."

Nicole put her glass on the table and looked up at Carter, pleadingly. He could see the pain in her eyes and he put his arm around her. He tilted her head onto his shoulder and stroked her hair gently as he spoke, trying to soothe her.

"I'll do what I can to help him, whatever I can," he said, "But I have to ask you not to speak to him about what has happened tonight. Can you promise me that?"

"If you can promise me that you'll get the French police to go easy on him."

"I promise," he said quietly, as she closed her eyes.

Chapter 18

Early the next morning, having spent the night with Nicole for the first time in more than twenty-five years, Carter was sitting at the kitchen table as she made them some coffee. She took the coffee to the table and sat down as Carter took her hand in his and looked into her eyes.

"There's something I want to ask you," he said and Nicole looked at him enquiringly. "We have been apart for far too long and I don't want to lose you again."

Carter paused trying to gauge what reaction he was going to get to the suggestion he was about to make.

"Why don't you come and stay with me for a while, in Belize?" he asked, "It's a beautiful place and it would give us a chance to get to know each other again."

Nicole dragged her hand back and looked away from him, this was not the response he was hoping for and his heart sank.

"I can't do that, Carter," she began, "What about Eloise? She's due back soon and she's going to need me to be here."

Carter took her hand again and smiled at her. "From what I saw in Port Grimaud, I don't think you have to worry too much about Eloise," he said and Nicole smiled back but her smile was weaker than Carter would have liked. He decided to press on. "Just say you'll think about it. OK?"

"OK, I promise I'll think about it," she said and Carter sensed that there was a chance that she would go along with his suggestion; a chance that after all the time that had passed, they could, at last, be together.

As Carter and Conrad flew back to Nice, Carter recalled the way the case had worked out. The spur-of-the-moment decision to follow Anna had been inspired and Carter was proud of himself. And yet she had nearly got away with it. The tiny fact of the email address she was using being on her husband's company's Internet server had nearly saved her; it had certainly embarrassed Carter. It was with some satisfaction that he had heard from Harris that Dimitri had told the police everything in exchange for a guarantee that he would not be sent back to Russia where, almost certainly, he would have finished up in a Siberian prison camp.

He had explained how the scientists at the scientific institute where he worked had developed the CVD process to its ultimate conclusion, the production of large gem quality diamonds; he had explained how, as head of administration, he had managed to increase production of these diamonds without anyone noticing and he had explained how he had systematically diverted the increased production into his own hands.

There was still a lot of work to be done bringing all the threads of the investigation together so that a cast iron case could be prepared before Anna's trial started, and there was also the matter of the charges relating to the murders of Antoine and Yvonne, not to mention the massive fraud which had been perpetrated on unsuspecting jewellery buyers.

But Carter would leave all of that to be sorted out by the British and French police; he had done what he had been brought in to do. He had traced the source of the synthetic diamonds, and now it was time for him to bow out. All that remained for him to do before going home to Belize was to return to France and ensure that the French police had all the information and evidence they needed from him although, for Nicole's sake, Carter also wanted to make sure that Philippe was given a fair hearing.

After the plane had landed at Nice airport, Carter and Conrad came out of the airport building and got into a taxi.

"Sainte Maxime, s'il vous plait," said Carter to the taxi driver, followed by, "Le Gendarmerie."

As they drove along the road to Sainte Maxime, Carter decided that he should make sure that Philippe was being watched. He wanted to help him if he could but he was acutely aware that the French police were still unaware of Philippe's involvement; a call to Le Grande had confirmed that Jacques had yet to be formally interviewed by the police and that apart from giving them a description of the man who had got away from the farmhouse, he had told them nothing. If Philippe were to suddenly disappear now, Carter would have a lot of explaining to do and his explanations would probably not be acceptable to the French police. He decided to give Conrad the job of watching Philippe.

"After we get to the Gendarmerie," he began, "Could you go on to Port Grimaud and keep an eye on Philippe. I'd like to be sure that we know where he is at all times. He's quite capable of disappearing without trace."

Conrad nodded and when the taxi pulled up outside the police station in Sainte Maxime, he stayed in the car. After Carter had got out, Conrad instructed the driver, "Continuez a Port Grimaud, s'il vous plait," and the car pulled away as Carter approached the entrance to the Gendarmerie and went in.

Half an hour later, Carter was sitting opposite Inspecteur Le Grande in his office and was concluding his summary of the case with an evaluation of Philippe's involvement.

"Philippe was involved but he was a pawn, a partner of convenience for no other reason than he owned a diamond mine, something which made it easier to hide the source of the diamonds. He had nothing to do with the murders, that was down to someone else. It was almost certainly someone he was involved with, but it wasn't him."

"Monsieur Lacoste, for all his power and influence, cannot escape all responsibility for what has happened," responded Le Grande, "And there is still the matter of the stolen diamonds. We will pick him up and talk to him. If he tells us everything and we can arrest all the people involved, we may be able to do a deal."

Carter nodded as Le Grande rose from his desk and went to the door of his office. He opened it and called a uniformed police officer over to him.

"Bring in Philippe Lacoste, we need to talk to him," he said.

The uniformed officer nodded before turning away and gesturing to two of his colleagues to accompany him. Le Grande turned back to face Carter and held out his hand.

"A bientot, Monsieur Jefferson. I will keep you informed."

Carter rose from his seat and took Le Grande's hand.

"Thank you, Inspecteur. A bientot."

While Carter was busy talking to Inspecteur Le Grande, a small inflatable dinghy, barely big enough to hold its two occupants, bumped gently into the bows of the Esprit de Jacques. Silently, Henri pulled himself up onto the deck of the boat, making sure that he could not be seen from the Capitainerie by the gendarme who had been sent to watch the boat. Gilles passed him a large bag and then followed him onto the boat. By the time he too was on deck, Henri had forced the plastic hatch above the forward stateroom. The superstructure of the boat hid him from the people on the quay as he dropped the bag onto the bed below and then slid himself quietly through the hole. Behind him, Gilles followed, though he found it more difficult to squeeze his larger frame through the small opening.

"I will check out the boat and find the best place to wait for him to come back," said Henri, once they were both inside the stateroom.

"I know this boat well," said Gilles, "The best place is in the master cabin at the back. And you can have a look in the engine room from there as well to see if it's a good place to put the bomb."

Cautiously, the two men climbed the stairs from the stateroom to the saloon. They knew that the bright sunlight would make it impossible for anyone outside to see them through the tinted glass. Nevertheless, they crept slowly to the back of the saloon, keeping their heads low, and then down the circular staircase into the lobby outside the master cabin at the stern of the boat.

Henri opened the small door in the lobby and looked through into a dark room; he could just make out the boat's engines by the light from the lobby. He bent down as he went through the door into the engine room. Inside, he switched on the light and surveyed the two huge Detroit diesel engines, each of which could deliver nearly a thousand horsepower to the boat's propellers.

Gilles did not to attempt to get through the door which was only four feet six inches high and less than two feet wide. Instead he waited in the lobby.

When Henri came out of the engine room, he looked at Gilles and said, "It is a good place. An explosion in there will send the boat to the bottom in seconds." He wiped his hands on a cloth he had found in the engine room and threw it back through the door. "When we are ready, when it is done and we are out at sea, I will fix a bomb under one of the engines. The explosion will rip the bottom out of the boat and it will go straight down, taking Jacques' body with it. It will look like an accident, as if the engine just blew up."

"OK," responded Gilles. "Now all we need is for Jacques to come back. Then we can put an end to this mess once and for all."

The two men went into the master cabin, being careful to leave the door to the lobby open so that they would hear Jacques returning. Then they sat on the bed and waited. They were ideally placed; the circular staircase leading from the cabin to the rear of the saloon would enable them to enter the saloon at the back and block off any possible escape by Jacques.

Fifteen minutes later, Jacques trudged across the gangway onto the Esprit. He was carrying several plastic shopping bags full of supplies he had bought in preparation for his departure from Port Grimaud and his heart was heavy. Yvonne was dead and now Eloise had deserted him. He didn't blame her for that; it was understandable in the circumstances but he missed her. He missed Yvonne too, but that was different. Yvonne was dead and there was no way back from that but Eloise wasn't dead, though she might as well be for all the difference it made. And now he had to leave Port

Grimaud, and everything he knew, before anything else bad happened to him.

Jacques unlocked the sliding door, opened it and took his bags of shopping into the saloon before closing the door behind him. When he reached the galley, he put the bags down and sat in the helmsman's chair. He leaned forward to put his arms on the wheel and then rested his head on his arms.

As Jacques sat there, pondering the events of the last few days, a noise coming from behind him dragged him back from his desperate thoughts. He turned his head to see what it was and saw Gilles coming up the last few steps from the master cabin.

"Gilles! What are you doing here?" he asked as he rose from the chair and went down the steps into the saloon, "And how did you get in? The door was locked."

As he waited for Gilles to answer, Jacques saw Henri coming up the steps behind Gilles. He recognised him immediately and a chill ran through his body as the horror of Yvonne's death came vividly and sickeningly into focus again. Right in front of him was the man responsible for her rape and death. Jacques looked round the saloon; his instinct was to run, but where to? Every fibre of his being screamed at him to get out of there; to get off the boat, somehow. But how? Gilles and Henri were blocking any escape through the saloon door and there was no other exit. He turned quickly, his heart beating faster and faster as he tried to think of a way in which he could escape from them. The sweat gathered in beads on his forehead and started to pour down his face as panic took hold of him. He ran back to the front of the boat and jumped down the steps leading to the forward cabins and the stateroom. He knew there was no way out there either but there was nowhere else to go. As he entered the stateroom, he saw the open hatch above the bed and a chance of escape. He was breathing rapidly now. He could hear Gilles and Henri coming down the steps after him. Leaping onto the bed, he reached for the sides of the hatch. Desperately, he tried to pull himself out of the room and out of danger and, as he pulled himself up through the hatch, a wave of relief came over him. He was safe! In a moment he would be off the Esprit and out of their clutches.

Then, as he was nearly through the hatch, he felt the iron grip of Gilles' hands round his ankles. He struggled, with all the strength he could summon, to pull his legs up after him but, slowly, he felt himself disappearing back down into the stateroom. He made a last huge effort and, for a second, thought that he had won the battle, but his arms gave way, they were no match for the weight of Gilles hanging onto his ankles, and he fell back through the hatch and onto the bed. Gilles let go of his ankles and Jacques turned to look at him. Henri stood beside Gilles, smiling. Jacques knew what Henri was capable of and it terrified him. Jacques shuffled along the bed. He pushed himself against the forward bulkhead and froze. Only his eyes moved as they flitted between Gilles and Henri and then settled on Henri who was holding a large knife and leaning against the door which led to the shower room in the corner. He wasn't looking at Jacques but Jacques could see he was still smiling, laughing at him. At that moment, they all heard the sound of someone else in the saloon above, and a voice calling.

"Jacques… Jacques, where are you? I need to talk to you."

Jacques recognised Eloise's voice and his heart sank. Henri's smile faded quickly as he put a finger to his lips and looked at Jacques through serious eyes.

As Eloise checked the master cabin and then returned to the saloon, Jacques hoped she would conclude that he was not there and leave. But then he heard her voice coming from the steps next to the galley.

"Jacques, are you down here?" said Eloise as she came down the steps and pushed the stateroom door open.

Gilles reached out and grabbed Eloise's arm. He pulled her roughly into the room and threw her onto the bed. She looked at Gilles, then at Henri and then at Jacques. Nervously, she wriggled herself up the bed until she was close beside Jacques, holding onto his arm for comfort. Her blue eyes looked into his; he could see her fear in them.

"Jacques, who are these people? And why are they here?" she asked, pushing herself harder into Jacques as if, by doing so, she would somehow be safe.

"They are the ones who killed Yvonne," said Jacques as he put his arm around her.

Gilles looked at Jacques. "It is time to leave," he said, "Go and start the engines and cast off. Then we can get under way."

Jacques cursed his stupidity. Why, oh why, had he not realised the urgency of his situation? Why had he not taken Philippe more seriously and left Port Grimaud immediately? He could have talked to his mother from the safety of another port. Now he was trapped, his father's warning repeating itself over and over again in his head.

"This is a big boat," he said, dismissing the incessant voice and concentrating on the bones of a plan. "I will need Eloise to help me."

"I don't think so. I'm sure you can manage if you try," said Gilles, moving menacingly towards Jacques and Eloise, "The girl stays here with Henri. Now get on with it! And don't forget to pull our dinghy up onto the deck."

Jacques realised that he had little choice other than to obey, at least for the time being, but he was reluctant to leave Eloise in the stateroom with Henri, a man he knew to be a rapist and a killer.

"If you touch her, I swear I will kill you!" he said with as much conviction as he was able to dredge from his fearful heart.

"Ah, oui. Now let me see. Where have I heard that before?" Henri smiled and tapped his chin with the knife before the cold hard look returned to his eyes.

"Don't mess me about, Jacques!" said Gilles sharply, "Get started. Now! I want this boat under way in two minutes. Understand?"

Not wanting to provoke Gilles unnecessarily, Jacques got off the bed to do as he had been instructed. First, he went to the forward deck and pulled the little dinghy up onto it. Then, he went to the helm station and started the Esprit's engines. Gilles stood beside him as he did. Eloise was alone in the stateroom with Henri. With the engines ticking over, Jacques looked at Gilles. "I need someone to cast off," he said.

"You do it," said Gilles. He was not about to show himself outside the saloon so that anyone who might be watching the boat could spot him and raise the alarm. "And don't forget who's with your girlfriend below. Just remember what happened to Yvonne."

Jacques glared at him. How could he forget what Henri had done to Yvonne? He would never be able to forget that; it would be etched on his mind for ever. But he wasn't going to let it happen to Eloise. He went out of the saloon onto the aft deck and walked across the gangway onto the quay.

As Jacques reached the quay and began to untie the Esprit's mooring warps, Philippe, who was being followed at a discreet distance by Conrad, passed the hotel on his way to the Capitainerie.

Slowly, Jacques untied the first of the Esprit's two mooring warps, all the while trying to think of a way to get himself and Eloise off the boat in one piece. But no matter how hard he tried, no ideas came into his head. Instead, his mind was filled with thoughts and fears about what Gilles and Henri might be planning to do.

Jacques threw the rope onto the boat and then went to the second warp and did the same with that one just as Philippe arrived at the Capitainerie from the Rue Grande. Jacques did not see Philippe but Philippe saw him and his pace quickened as he watched Jacques, slowly and reluctantly, walk back onto the Esprit.

As Philippe walked towards the Esprit, half raising his arm as if to hail Jacques, Conrad took his phone from his pocket and called Carter.

Once back on board the Esprit, Jacques raised the gangway and returned to the helm station where Gilles was waiting for him, watching his every move as he pressed the button to raise the anchor.

Jacques was about to push the throttles forward, and take the Esprit out of the harbour, when he thought he heard a shout from the quay. He wanted to investigate, but Gilles was standing behind him urging him to get the boat under way.

As Philippe got closer to the boat, he could see through the open sliding door and thought he recognised the person standing next to Jacques at the helm. When he was near enough to get a clear look through the door he knew he was right; it was Gilles! Thoughts of impending disaster ripped through him, filling him with alarm and he called out again but Jacques did not hear him.

With panic getting the better of him, Philippe started to run towards the Esprit as she slowly began to move away from the quay.

"Jacques!" he called out again, but to no avail.

He ran the last few yards towards the boat as fast as he could, thankful for all the hours he had spent in the gym keeping himself fit and in good physical condition. "*Jacques! Wait!*" he shouted at the top of his voice, but the words were lost in the sound of the Esprit's engines as Jacques pushed the throttle levers forward.

Philippe was still running as he reached the quayside and he took an instant decision. His son, and possibly his granddaughter, were on that boat and he had to try. The Esprit had moved about six feet away from the shore as Philippe leapt from the quay and reached for the end of the gangway sticking out over the stern of the boat. It was a desperate act, but somehow he just got to it and grabbed it tightly with both hands, his knuckles turning white from the ferocity of his grip. His body swung from side to side and his legs flailed about wildly as he struggled to keep hold. Jacques didn't see him as he concentrated on taking the big boat out of the harbour.

"Vite!" Gilles urged Jacques as he witnessed Philippe's success in bridging the gap between the quay and the boat. "Plus vite!"

Jacques wondered why Gilles was in such a hurry. He looked back and it was then that he saw Philippe hanging from the gangway. He didn't know what to do. He looked at Gilles who stared back at him.

"Keep going," instructed Gilles tersely, "Or I'll let Henri amuse himself with the girl!"

Jacques was torn between protecting Eloise and helping his father but he knew there was little he could do for Philippe. If he stopped the boat, Gilles would simply overpower him and take over so he kept the Esprit moving, and increased speed as they left the harbour and entered the bay.

When the Esprit began to pick up speed and her prow lifted out of the water, Jacques looked back and saw Philippe trying to get a foot round the side of the gangway so that he could work his way onto the boat, but it kept slipping off.

Within a minute, the Esprit was planing at full speed, moving towards the open sea. Philippe fought to hang on as the wind pulled at his clothes, but it was no use. He cried out Jacques' name one last time as, finally, he could hold on no longer and he dropped into the sea. Jacques heard the desperate cry and looked over his shoulder. He saw Philippe bouncing along behind the Esprit before coming to rest in the boat's frothy wake. Gilles pulled Jacques away from the helm roughly and pushed him towards the chart table. Not expecting the move, Jacques tripped and fell, hitting his head against the corner of the dining table and dazing himself.

With the boat still going at full speed, Gilles spun the wheel round to starboard. The Esprit lurched and heeled sharply to port as she tried to comply with Gilles' violent wishes. Below, in the stateroom, the force of the turn rolled Eloise off the bed onto the floor and threw Henri across the room.

Henri muttered under his breath as he recovered his composure and made his way to the saloon where Jacques was trying to get to his feet, a task made all the more difficult by the lurching motion of the boat.

"What's going on?" shouted Henri above the sound of the Esprit's engines which were still racing at full throttle.

"It's Philippe," shouted back Gilles. "He was hanging onto the gangway. He's in the sea now."

Henri stood close beside Gilles. They both stared intently through the front window as Gilles brought the boat round on a course aimed directly at Philippe who was floundering in the water. When Jacques saw that Gilles and Henri were engrossed in the act of running

Philippe down, he slipped quietly down the steps into the stateroom. He went over to Eloise and quickly lifted her to her feet, motioning to her to be quiet. Silently they crept back up the steps and ran past Gilles and Henri, towards the stern of the boat.

"Stop them!" shouted Gilles at Henri as he saw them go, but it was too late. Henri reached the aft deck just in time to see Jacques and Eloise jump off the transom into the sea.

Almost at the same time, Henri heard the sirens and spotted the police launch from Sainte Maxime heading towards them.

"Merde!" Henri hurried back to the saloon. "Gilles, look!" He pointed to the launch. "Forget Philippe and head out to sea. It is our only chance."

Gilles turned the wheel sharply again and the Esprit groaned under the strain as she turned away from Philippe and headed out to sea. The Esprit was fast for a boat of her size but she was no match for the police launch. It was soon alongside and a gendarme spoke to them through a megaphone.

"Mettez en panne! Mettez en panne!"

"Keep going," pleaded Henri in desperation, but Gilles knew it was no use. He knew they couldn't outrun the police launch and that before long a coastguard vessel would join in the chase and threaten them with its twin four-centimetre machine cannons. They might as well give up now. Reluctantly, he pulled back the throttles. The Esprit settled back into the water and Gilles turned off the engines.

By this time, a second police launch was on the scene and was picking up Jacques and Eloise from the sea.

Once in the police boat, Jacques remembered Philippe. "Monsieur Lacoste, he tried to help us," he told the gendarme sitting next to him. Jacques coughed to clear his throat of sea water. “He’s in the water too. You must find him.”

The gendarme spoke to the pilot of the launch and before long they had located Philippe. Jacques watched as they lifted him from the sea. His body seemed limp and lifeless.

“What’s wrong with him?” he asked, “Is he OK?”

One of the Gendarmes touched his fingers to Philippe’s neck. “Il est mort,” he said.

Jacques looked stunned and Eloise put her arm round his shoulders.

When the Esprit, piloted by a policeman and followed by the two police boats, arrived back at the Capitainerie, quite a crowd had gathered, drawn by the sound of the police sirens.

In amongst the crowd was Carter, who had hurried from Sainte Maxime when Conrad had called to tell him what was going on. He turned to Conrad and said, “We’ve got to find out what’s happened.” Then he saw the stretcher; the body it was bearing was completely covered with a blanket.

“Who’s that?” he asked one of the gendarmes carrying the stretcher.

“Je ne sais pas,” answered the gendarme, “Mais il est mort.”

Carter stepped forward and before they could stop him, he pulled back the blanket. Philippe’s blank eyes stared up at him and he quickly covered the body again as the gendarme he had spoken to gave him a withering look. He fell back into the crowd and quickly found Conrad.

“It’s Philippe,” he told him.

“I thought it must be,” said Conrad. “You should have seen him; it was something else, the way he ran and jumped and grabbed onto the gangway. You wouldn't have thought he was in his seventies."

Jacques and Eloise, wrapped in blankets and holding mugs of coffee, were still sitting in the police launch when one of the gendarmes touched Jacques on the arm and indicated for them to get out of the boat.

Carter watched as Jacques and Eloise, shepherded by the gendarme, left the launch. He turned to Conrad.

"Thank God, she's safe!" he said, relieved. He already had enough bad news to tell Nicole.

When Eloise saw Carter, she stopped and went up to him, leaving Jacques with the gendarme. As she spoke, she indicated Philippe's body with her hand.

"He never meant any harm, you know. It was just a money making opportunity that came along, one that he couldn't resist."

Carter nodded as Eloise returned to Jacques and they watched Philippe's body being loaded into an ambulance and driven off. The gendarme guided them towards a police car but before they could get into the car, Carter approached the gendarme and spoke to him.

"Where are you taking them?" he asked.

"To the Gendarmerie in Sainte Maxime," answered the gendarme.

"I need to speak to them," said Carter.

"You will have to talk to the Inspecteur about that."

"At the Gendarmerie?"

"Oui."

Jacques and Eloise were ushered into the back of the police car which then drove away and Carter turned back to look at the Esprit. He was sure he recognised one of the men now being escorted off the boat in handcuffs. The more he watched, the more certain he became that it was the one who had got away from them at the farmhouse.

"I don't know what's been going on out there," said Carter, "But I think I'd like to find out."

By the time Carter and Conrad arrived at the Gendarmerie, Jacques and Eloise had got out of their wet clothes and were sitting in an interview room wearing dressing gowns provided by the police. The room was small and windowless but, protected from the direct rays of the sun, it was cool. The only furniture in the room was a plain oblong table and four equally plain chairs, two at each side of the table. The walls were colour washed in a drab yellow colour and, on the floor were light brown carpet squares, most of which showed signs of having had coffee spilt on them. Sitting across the table from Jacques and Eloise were a gendarme and Inspecteur Le Grande.

"Has my mother been told that I'm here?" asked Jacques.

"She's on her way with some clothes for you," replied Le Grande, "And she's bringing something of her own for you too," he said to Eloise. Then he turned back to Jacques and said, "Carter Jefferson, I think you know him, he is asking to speak to you but first, I need to interview you about what has been happening."

Jacques nodded as Le Grande continued. "I know that Monsieur Jefferson works for a diamond traders' organisation in New York," he said. "And that he has been on the trail of some people who have been making fake diamonds. I have spoken to him about this case before, when he informed me about the events at the farmhouse where your sister was killed." Eloise relaxed visibly on hearing that Carter had spoken to the police. "I am not sure that he has told us all he knows about this case but I have checked him out with the authorities in New York and he appears to be who he says he is." He looked searchingly at the two of them. "You should have come to us and told us what was going on right at the beginning. Maybe then we could have helped." Le Grande eyed Jacques and Eloise closely. "I believe that you are both innocent in all of this but until I can establish beyond any doubt that you are, you must stay here. I will talk to you both again later."

Le Grande got up and left the room. When he had gone, Jacques looked at Eloise and put his arm around her. She leaned against him and put her head on his shoulder.

A few minutes later, the door of the interview room burst open and Claudine came in. "Jacques!" she cried, "What has happened? The police rang to tell me you were here and to bring some clothes for you and for Eloise but they wouldn't tell me anything else."

Jacques looked up at his mother and shook his head sadly as he spoke. "It was terrible. They were going to kill us. Monsieur Lacoste tried to help us... but he fell into the sea and was killed."

"I know. They told me Philippe was dead." Claudine's face blanked and she walked round behind Jacques and Eloise. She stared absently at a picture on the wall for several seconds and then closed her eyes for a few moments before turning to look at Jacques. "So who was it that did this? Was it the same people who killed Yvonne?"

"Yes, one of them," Jacques said. "But Gilles Renard too. *Gilles* is one of them."

"No!" said Claudine, a look of amazement on her face. "I have known Gilles for many years and although it is true that I do not like him much, I would never have suspected him of anything like this."

She reached over them and put the clothes she had brought onto the table. "I brought these for you," she said as she put her arms round the two of them and hugged them both. “I am so glad you’re both safe.”

The gendarme went to the door, opened it and called to one of his colleagues. A moment later a woman police officer arrived and took Eloise to another room to get dressed. Meanwhile Jacques dressed himself in the shirt and jeans his mother had brought for him. When he had finished, Claudine spoke to the gendarme.

“Can I take him home now?” she asked.

“I am sorry,” he answered, “but that will not be possible. The Inspecteur wishes to question him some more. You must leave now.”

Claudine protested briefly and then left the room, but not before she had given Jacques a kiss and a hug.

Chapter 19

The day after Philippe's gallant and desperate attempt to save the lives of his son and his granddaughter had resulted in his own death, Claudine telephoned Jacques. He had been released by the police the night before and had been keeping busy cleaning the Esprit. He did not welcome the interruption but Claudine left him in no doubt that she wanted to see him as soon as possible. When he asked why, all she would say was that she had something important to tell him. As he washed and pulled on a fresh tee-shirt, he tried to think what news she could possibly have that was so vital. Perhaps it was to do with Philippe's death. Maybe his father had left him something in his will. Philippe was a wealthy man but he had a legitimate family; surely they would be the main beneficiaries. He really wasn't very interested in whatever it was that she wanted to tell him so he dragged out his preparations and delayed the walk to his mother's apartment for as long as he could.

Eventually, as Jacques approached the apartment, unable to postpone his arrival any longer, he dragged his lethargic body up the stairs and opened the door.

"Jacques! You are here at last," Claudine said as she walked past him and closed the door. He smiled a weak smile as she turned to face him, her back to the door. "There is something I have to tell you. Something I have kept to myself for a very long time."

A serious look darkened Claudine's face and she took Jacques' hands in hers as she looked into his eyes.

"Jacques," she said, "what I have to tell you is this. Eloise is not related to you. She is not your niece, and you are not her uncle."

Jacques looked at his mother uncomprehendingly.

"What are you talking about?" he said, "You know that isn't true."

"What I know, Jacques, is that Philippe Lacoste was not your father."

Jacques looked at her unbelievingly. "But when I asked you, you said he was," he challenged, a note of anger creeping into his voice.

"I know." A frown appeared on Claudine's face and she let go of Jacques' hands. "I didn't tell you the truth. I'm sorry. I thought it best that you should believe, as he did, that Philippe was your father. But I didn't know about Eloise then. When I found out about Philippe being Eloise's grandfather, that changed everything. I wanted to tell you straight away but it was complicated. Now that Philippe is... well, now I can tell you the truth, at last."

"And what exactly is the truth, Maman?" Jacques was both disappointed that his mother had lied to him and angry because of the consequences of her deceit. He stared back at her as he continued. "Do you actually know who my father is?"

Claudine winced at Jacques' gibe. She took a deep breath and pressed on. "The truth, Jacques, is that your father was a man called Emile du Pont, a fisherman. He was a man of no consequence, not like Philippe, but he was a good man and he loved me very much. We broke up over something quite trivial and I took up with Philippe. But, by then... by then, I was already pregnant with you."

"You said 'was'. Is my father dead?"

"He was killed in an accident at sea, before you were born." Claudine took Jacques' hands in hers again and looked into his eyes. “Please tell me you don’t hate me because of this, Jacques,” she pleaded. “Please tell me this.”

“Of course I don’t hate you. And I’m sorry for what I said.”

Slowly Jacques’ mood changed as hope again took hold of him and lifted his spirits.

“Do you think Eloise will still want me when she knows the truth?”

“If she loves you half as much as I know you love her, then I am sure she will.”

Claudine was smiling now and she looked past Jacques as Eloise emerged from the bedroom.

“How could you ever doubt it?”

Jacques whipped round at the sound of Eloise’s voice behind him and saw her standing there, a slight smile lighting her face. He ran the few steps it took to reach her and took her in his arms, lifting her off her feet and wheeling her round. As he let her regain her feet, he smothered her with kisses and hugged her.

Still clutching on to Eloise with one arm round her shoulders, Jacques turned to face his mother and put his other arm around her, drawing her close to him. “Thank you for telling me. I know how hard it was for you,” he said in a soft voice and kissed her on the cheek.

Claudine smiled through the tears, tears of happiness, which now filled her eyes. “I owed you that,” she said. “I am so sorry about what you have been through. You too, Eloise, what we have all been through. Now I just want you both to be happy.”

“I know. And we will be,” said Jacques as he became pensive. “But this place holds too many bad memories for me. If Eloise is willing, if she will go with me,” he said as he removed his arms from around the two women, “I would like to get away from here. I would like to go somewhere new, somewhere where we will not be constantly reminded of what has happened." He took Eloise's hand in his and looked at her expectantly.

"Of course I'll go with you," she said, squeezing his hand, "But where are we going?"

"I don't know yet. Somewhere far away from here; somewhere where we can try to forget about all that has happened."

"Sounds exciting!" said Eloise, her enthusiasm obvious, "I can't wait. There are lots of places I'd like to see, places I've only ever dreamt of seeing one day."

Jacques saw the sad look on his mother's face and knew at once what she was thinking. "Why don't you come with us?" he asked.

Claudine smiled. "Oh no! I don't think so. You definitely do not want me tagging along with you and getting in the way."

"Madame Armand, nothing could be further from the truth," interposed Eloise, "We'd love you to come with us."

"No, absolutely not! You two need time to yourselves, time to heal, time to forget. The last thing you need is me hovering around. No, you two go, with my blessing." Claudine smiled affectionately at the couple before asking, "When do you think you will be ready to leave?"

"Everything is ready now," said Jacques, "I was preparing to leave because of Philippe's warning anyway and I don't see any point in waiting. Unless you think we should stay for Monsieur Lacoste's funeral?"

"No. Philippe was nothing to you, Jacques," Claudine looked at Eloise, "and I'm sure your mother will understand."

"She'll be here tomorrow morning," said Eloise. "I'll check if it's OK with her."

"If it is, then we'll leave tomorrow," said Jacques. "The police have said it's OK for me to go as long as I keep them informed about where I am; they'll need me back for the trial."

Claudine nodded. The police had told her that Jacques' testimony at the trial would be crucial in securing a conviction.

"And we'll come back for Yvonne's funeral too," added Jacques. "Just let me know when it's going to be."

"I will," said Claudine, her eyes filling up at the reminder of her daughter's death.

The police had told Claudine that the possible rape charge against Henri meant that they would not be able to release Yvonne's body until a detailed post mortem had been conducted and the defence lawyers had been given the opportunity to question the findings.

"I don't know yet when the police will allow it," continued Claudine. "They told me it could be weeks or even months. But I'll tell you as soon as I know."

With Jacques and Eloise's future decided, they enjoyed a farewell dinner with Claudine at her favourite restaurant. After they had finished their meal, they returned to Claudine's apartment, where they savoured a liqueur with their coffee before Jacques and Eloise left and returned to the Esprit.

When they reached the Capitainerie, they boarded the Esprit and had a final nightcap in the saloon. Then they went down the circular steps and into the master cabin. Slowly they both undressed and got into bed. Eloise snuggled up to Jacques and he held her close to him. They closed their eyes and fell asleep in each other's arms; they were much too tired for anything else. The events, and tensions, and stresses of all that had passed had exhausted them completely. Now that it was all over, they slept like babies.

The sun was shining through Carter's hotel window when he woke the following morning. He looked at his watch and saw that it was seven o'clock. He thought for a moment and then realised how little time he had. He leapt out of bed and went into the bathroom.

Half an hour later he was on the road to Nice and soon after that he had parked the car and was striding towards the entrance to Nice airport. Nicole was due in on the early flight from Leeds and he didn't want to be late for her. He checked the arrivals board and breathed a sigh of relief as he saw that the flight had only just landed.

When Nicole finally came through the door into the arrivals area, his face lit up. She looked beautiful in a knee length blue cotton dress with her hair resting neatly on her shoulders. They almost ran towards each other and hugged and kissed. When they separated, they looked into each other's eyes. Carter knew she must be going through hell and he wanted to help her. He wanted to make it all better for her but he knew he couldn't, only time could do that. They stared at each other for several moments before Carter spoke.

"It's great to see you," he said. "I just wish the circumstances were different."

"Yeah, me too!" said Nicole.

"Let's get going, shall we," he said as he picked up her bag and they headed for the exit.

"How's she doing?" asked Nicole as they came out of the airport building and walked along in the sunshine towards the car park.

"OK, I think," responded Carter, "It's been a horrible time for her one way and another but she's strong, like her mother. I think she's coping."

"And what about this boyfriend of hers, Jacques? What do you know about him?"

"Not that much actually. He's had a pretty rough ride too, and not just over the last week. But I think he's an OK guy. We'll go straight to the Capitainerie after we've dropped your bag off at the hotel so you can meet him and see for yourself."

Nicole nodded as Carter put her bag into the boot of his car.

As Carter and Nicole drove from the airport to Port Grimaud, on board the Esprit, Eloise and Jacques awoke from their deep sleep and got up. They had decided what they were going to do but there were some things they needed to deal with first, not least of which was to get Nicole's blessing.

By the time Carter and Nicole arrived at the Capitainerie, Jacques had tidied up the Esprit and Eloise had boiled the kettle and put some coffee in the cafetière. When she saw Carter and her mother at the end of the Rue Grande, she poured water from the kettle into the cafetière and went out to meet them. As she passed the steps to the master cabin, she called out to Jacques who was putting the finishing touches to his hair in readiness for meeting Nicole.

"They're here," she shouted down the staircase.

Eloise came out of the saloon and crossed the gangway onto the quayside. She waved to Carter and Nicole as they approached the Esprit and Nicole immediately ran over to her.

By the time Nicole and Eloise had finished greeting each other, Jacques had come out onto the rear deck and was watching from the stern of the Esprit. When Carter saw him, he gave him a wave and Jacques waved back.

Carter escorted Nicole and Eloise across the gangway and onto the boat. When they were all standing on the deck, Eloise began the introductions.

"Mum, this is Jacques," she said, a big smile on her face as she indicated Jacques to her mother, "And Jacques, this is my mother, Nicole."

Jacques and Nicole greeted each other with a kiss on both cheeks.

"You have a fine boat!" said Nicole smiling.

Jacques shrugged self-consciously and smiled back. "Eloise has made some coffee," he said, "Please, come into the saloon."

Nicole nodded and they all trooped into the saloon.

After an hour of polite conversation, during which Nicole warmed to Jacques and during which she confirmed that she had no objection to Eloise going away with him to an as yet unknown destination, they all came out of the saloon onto the rear deck. Carter, Nicole and Eloise crossed the gangway onto the quayside while Jacques remained on the Esprit. He leant on the guard rail at the stern of the boat as he watched them.

"I'll see you at the hotel," said Carter, feeling the need to leave the women alone to say their goodbyes.

"I won't be long," responded Nicole.

As Carter walked away towards the hotel, Eloise looked at her mother and a sad expression crossed her face. "Will you be OK without me for a while?" she asked.

Nicole nodded as she reassured her daughter. "Don't worry, sweetheart, I'll be fine. It's going to take time for us both to get over all that has happened but I think that maybe getting away for a while is a good way for you to start the process." Nicole looked up at Jacques. "And he seems like a good man. I'm sure he'll take good care of you."

Eloise smiled and sniffed. "Yeah, I'm sure he will. I love him very much. And I think he feels the same way about me." She paused for a few moments before continuing. "Are you sure it's OK for me not to come to Grandpa's funeral? We could wait and leave after that, if it would help to have me there."

"No, it's fine, honestly, Carter will be with me," responded Nicole, dismissing the idea with her hand.

"Seems like maybe you have found a good one too," said Eloise.

"I'm taking it one step at a time but, yeah, I think maybe I have. We'll see." They both smiled as they prepared to part and go their separate ways.

"Take care of yourself, Mum," said Eloise.

"I will. And you just make sure you stay in touch, OK?"

Eloise nodded and smiled as they hugged and kissed before she went back on board the Esprit. Standing on the deck, next to Jacques, she watched her mother walk towards the Rue Grande. Before she disappeared round the corner, Nicole turned and waved and they waved back to her.

Once Nicole had gone, Jacques climbed the steps to the fly bridge and started the engines. When he was ready he signalled to Eloise and she quickly ran onto the quayside, untied the mooring warps and threw them onto the boat before running back across the gangway. When she was on board the Esprit again, she raised the gangway and called to Jacques who pushed the throttle levers forward and the Esprit began to move away from the quay, across le Lac, and towards the gap in the breakwater.

When they were under way, Eloise climbed the steps to the fly bridge and stood next to Jacques. He put his arm round her waist, looked at her and gave her a peck on the cheek. The Esprit began to pick up speed, and with the wind in their hair, they smiled at each other before Eloise rested her head on Jacques' shoulder and sighed a happy sigh.

At the Capitainerie, Claudine emerged from where, unobserved, she had been watching Jacques and Eloise prepare to leave. She had decided not to accept the invitation to meet Nicole as she felt it would have been awkward, at best, given her past involvement with Philippe. She watched the boat pass through the gap in the breakwater and then she turned away and headed back home.

As the Esprit cleared Le Lac and headed out into the Bay of St. Tropez, Jacques pushed the throttles fully forward and the boat started to plane across the sea as she carried Jacques and Eloise away from their past and into their future.

A week later, Carter was back in Belize at his desk writing away furiously on his laptop completing his report to the FIDT. As he did so, Nicole came back into his mind. He stopped writing and leaned back in his chair, revisiting all that had happened.

Once again, he had successfully concluded his investigations and had solved the mystery of where the diamonds had come from. His connection with Nicole had complicated matters but it had also given him the chance to make contact with her. Seeing her again after so many years and then finding that his feelings for her were as strong as ever despite the passage of twenty-five years had been both challenging and enjoyable. From the time they had parted in Oxford, he had always hoped that one day he would find someone whom he cared about as much as he cared about her, but he never had and he had resigned himself to a life of bachelorhood. As he was letting his mind wander around these thoughts, he felt a touch on his shoulder.

"Penny for them," said Nicole as she stood behind him and put her hands on his shoulders.

Carter smiled and reached up to put one of his hands on hers. "Just thinking about all that has happened," he said as he looked up at her and smiled. "Especially the good things."

Nicole smiled back and kissed him on the brow before walking out through the French doors and onto the beach.

Carter watched her walk down the beach for a few moments before getting up from his desk and following her. When she got close to the sea, Nicole stopped and stared out towards the reef, deep in thought. Carter walked up beside her and put his arm round her waist and they both stared at the sea, revelling in its beauty.

After a few moments, Nicole suddenly grabbed Carter's arm and a smile crossed her face as she dragged him, unresisting, into the sea where they cavorted happily with each other, lost in the joy of just being together.

THE END